TO SAVE CIVILIZATION

"Douglas, I know your past. It was I who helped prepare the Table of Transits which the Ulama is using, using without understanding. Like all mongrels, they are consumers, not creators. I am a purebred; I was not satisfied with tables. I looked behind them and found—a Convolution!

"After you escaped, I had a contact check Gart's record. It did not fit the man who faced us in the dome, far less the soldier who has denied us Sherando through the summer. For the Ulama, Hudson's Bay was just another unused transit site to be watched. For me— it was the place where Douglas died. The Douglas Convolution. The memorial [ ] mathematician. I read your [ ] ognize a man who can help [ ] ization. We should be comrad[ ]

THE
DOUGLAS
CONVOLUTION

Edward Llewellyn

DAW BOOKS, INC.
DONALD A. WOLLHEIM, PUBLISHER
New York

FIRST PRINTING, OCTOBER 1979

1 2 3 4 5 6 7 8 9

 DAW TRADEMARK REGISTERED
U.S. PAT. OFF. MARCA
REGISTRADA. HECHO EN U.S.A.

PRINTED IN U.S.A.

1

Beginning

Ian Douglas (1945–1980) *American mathematician, developed the Douglas Convolution Integral (q.v.) Born Norfolk, Va., United States Marine Corps 1962–72, Sergeant, Navy Cross. BA (Columbia) 1975. Ph.D. (Harvard) 1979.*

Douglas demonstrated his mathematical talent by a short paper on Recursion Theory while still at school. At seventeen he enlisted in the Marine Corps where he served with distinction, was twice wounded, and awarded the Navy Cross for heroism in combat.

After graduating from Columbia he entered Harvard and the concept of his major work, the Convolution which bears his name, can be identified in his doctoral thesis: "The Conservation of t-Prime." His later publications are increasingly obscure, and the note in Acta Mathematica in which he defines his Convolution is almost incomprehensible without hindsight.

His ten years in the Marine Corps set him apart from his mathematical contemporaries, and the importance of his Convolution was not realized until many years after his death. Douglas himself was interested in some geophysical application which he never identified. Presumably it was to investigate this that he went alone to an inlet of Hudson's Bay in September 1980. His deserted camp and cap-

*sized canoe were found weeks later and it is be-
lieved that he drowned while making off-shore
observations.*

Dictionary of Mathematics,
Harvard University Press,
Cambridge, Mass.
(Terminal Edition, 2030 AD)

I did not drown in Hudson's Bay two hundred years ago.
The wave that swamped my canoe, swept me forward, and
stranded me here was a surge in time, not in water. The Encyclopedia presumes I died while investigating some "geophysical application" of my work. I did not die; I was
trapped. My Convolution suggested an interaction between
energy, mass, and time which would require the conservation
of the one at the expense of the others. I calculated when
such a conservation-conversion might occur, went to see if it
would, and got caught when it did.

The Encyclopedia calls me a mathematician and mentions
my ten years as a combat marine. Both facts are important.
Because I was a mathematician I blundered into a time-tran-
sit; otherwise I would have been dead for more than a century. Because I had been combat-trained I survived my
blunder; otherwise I would have been dead soon after arrival.
Now we are all in danger of death; that is why I am writing
this.

My biography, while generally accurate, is brief and the
twentieth century is distant, so I must tell you something of
my previous life if you are to understand my later actions. I
hope most of you remember enough history to put what I am
going to say into context.

I was a mathematician because I am the product of that
rare genetic combination which lets some people see non-ob-
vious relationships between abstractions. A talent not neces-
sarily related to any other virtue but too insistent to let itself
be ignored. I became a Marine because my father had been a
Marine and, unlike most boys of my era, I wanted to emulate
my father. There was a genetic factor in that also; an atavis-
tic component perhaps. A component my mother evidently
recognized, feared, and wished to direct, for after my father

was killed she handed me over to the Jesuits for my education. They were old-style Jesuits and gave me an education as superb as it was rigorous. At seventeen I escaped to the comparative comfort of a Marine boot camp.

My physique, my enthusiasm, and my schooling made me a prototype recruit. A bloody little war was warming up at the time, my promotion to Sergeant was rapid, and I became an expert in jungle warfare, specializing in deep penetration patrols—a trade in which bursts of violent action alternated with periods when one had little to do except watch and think. Protected from books and teachers, knowing all the mathematics a seventeen-year old mathematician can afford to learn before being blinded by knowledge, I had the opportunity to think for myself. And for the concept of my Convolution to germinate. I was not unique. I can quote a dozen major mathematicians who were good soldiers. War and mathematics have more in common than the intellectuals of my own era liked to remember.

I quit the Marines while that particular war was degenerating into a moral and military shambles. At twenty-seven I went to Columbia with the cynical outlook of a ten-year veteran and the clear vision of mathematical youth. A "mature student," distrusted by my teachers who classified all fighting men as psychopaths and my mathematical education as unorthodox. But by then my Convolution was so firmly rooted in my imagination that not even their sharp academic knives could cut it down. I went on to Harvard to learn the techniques I needed to prune and formalize. In my doctoral thesis, "The Conservation of t-Prime," I started to harvest the fruits.

As noted in my biography my publications were obscure; that obscurity was deliberate. I concealed the implications of my Convolution under a mass of partial differential equations so that later I could produce them to prove my priority and meanwhile be left undisturbed to exploit my new field. I now find that I hid them better than I had planned. The geophysical import, for example, was missed by my contemporaries and by almost all the mathematicians who came after me. That is why you have never heard of time transits. Why the idea still seems bizarre.

It seemed bizarre to me then. The phenomena suggested by my Integral were so fantastic that I was skeptical of my own reasoning. I wanted physical evidence. That was why, after leaving Harvard, I became a consultant mathematician to the Defense Research Agency at Fort Detrick. My contract gave me access to the Integrated Computer Complex, the only one in the world at that time with the capacity to solve my matrix. I needed the facility and so accepted the odium of working on that particular project, but I understood its beastliness better than my critics.

After three months I had enough evidence to demolish the hopes of the war-gamers, had I wished to do so. But with the remainder of my contract to run I continued to feed variables into the ICC, allowing the few people who knew what I was supposed to be doing to think that the output of my programs was still megadeaths per milligram.

They were not. They were the coordinates in time and space at which the conversion phenomena would occur—if they could occur at all. The solutions that emerged forecast that the only site I could reach within the next few years was a hundred meters off the shore of a remote inlet of Hudson's Bay. I went there alone in September 1980, a few days before the date and time I had calculated.

I was leaning over the side of my canoe, pouring powdered alumina onto the float I had anchored at the conversion site, when the roots of the equations became real and positive. I felt a twisting wrench, a timeless moment of isolation, a detachment from the physical universe. Then I was suddenly submerged in icy water, struggling to the surface, gasping for air. I fought for breath and knew the glory of success. I had shaken the pillars of the temple, and not by pouring gigawatts against a few atomic nuclei; I had shaken them by the power of my brain.

And pulled disaster down on myself. I had erred by about four hours in time. Worse still, I had underestimated the energy change in the conversion. The strain set up by the configuration of the solar system at that particular instant had released enough energy not only to transfer the few grams of alumina I had calculated. It had been sufficient to move ninety kilograms of man.

I struggled ashore exhausted, the cold numbing my mind and my body. It had been warm for a September afternoon in Hudson's Bay and I had stripped down to shirt and slacks to set up my survey equipment. I crawled out of a sea lashed by flurries of sleet and knew where I was but not when.

It was the same rocky beach with the black muskeg beyond. A havoc of gray clouds streamed low overhead. I stumbled across the rocks to a clump of stunted pine trees, and huddled under them against the biting wind. My instinct told me I must reach shelter soon or die of exposure, and I crouched wondering which way to go. My thoughts began to congeal as the cold overwhelmed my brain. I tried to savor my success before I died from it.

A helicopter came out of the swirling sleet, flying along the edge of the sea. I stumbled from my shelter, shouting and waving. It held its course and disappeared into another squall, but its crew must have seen me for as the squall drove past I saw it landing on the beach. I ran toward it, slipping on the wet stones, snow flurries closing about me. They cleared when I was a few meters from its tail and as I staggered forward the dome slid open and a man in a tan jumpsuit began to clamber out, presenting me with his broad backside. He was wearing a helmet, he had an automatic pistol on his thigh, and he was snarling at somebody in the cockpit, "You dumb bitch! There's nobody here."

I stood behind him, swaying, trying to speak, strangled by my immense relief. I was saved. Gasping for breath I looked past him and saw the face of a girl, her hands tight on the controls. Her eyes went wide and she shouted, "Sir—behind you!"

The man swung around. I held out my empty hands. "Please—"

The fear on his face allowed no logic; he grabbed his gun. A gun in the hand of a terrified man is death. I flung myself at him and sent it sliding away among the rocks. I fell—half-raised myself—trying to calm his panic, to make him understand that I was unarmed, that I was freezing. But he turned, leaving me on my knees, and began to clamber into the helicopter, reaching out to the girl for help, shouting, "Up—take it up!"

The warmth of the cabin was my whole desire. I could not let him leave me. I launched myself after him, clutched him as the machine started to rise. The girl cried, "Let me go, sir! Let go! I can't—"

He twisted wildly. I lost my grip, caught the edge of the

door, and his booted heel took me in the face. My hands slid. I clamped onto his legs. He gave a hoarse shout and a spasmodic jerk. The helicopter tilted, shuddered as the tips of the rotor slashed the rocks. Then we fell free, locked together, while the machine pinwheeled away up the beach.

I tried to hold him, to explain, but he went mad with fear and I caught his frenzy. Within instants we were both seeking death grips. He was a strong man of about my own height and managed to break away. Kneeling, he made the mistake of reaching for his knife, and I was on him. He ducked his head as I dived for his throat and his helmet smashed my mouth, but my attack sent him sprawling face down on the edge of the sea. Blinded by my own blood I threw myself across his head, forcing his face into the water and the pebbles. The desperate twistings of his nose and chin hollowed out a little pool. In it he slowly drowned.

I lay on him for minutes after he was dead, until cold and growing agony drove me to my feet. My lower jaw sagged down onto my chest, my nose was blocked, something was swelling in my throat. The helicopter had crashed into a clump of pine trees farther along the beach; the pilot was hanging in her harness, half out of the smashed dome, broken and limp.

By now I was reduced to the drives imprinted on me years before, imperatives which had saved me in the past. I turned over the man I had killed. His name-tag said "Capt. Jan Gart." I undid his belt, unzipped his coveralls. His thermawear was warm and dry. Shivering violently I stripped him. He lay on the edge of the sea, the snow drifting against his naked body. I tore off my own soaked clothes and struggled into his. The coveralls hung loose so I snapped on his gun-belt to hold them tight. I put on his helmet so that the chin strap would support my broken jaw.

If I had been able to think I would not have hoped to live. But I had reverted to the wounded animal, an animal trained to struggle while it could move. Out of the past my dead Survival Instructor goaded me: "Use the aircraft. It's protection." I sucked air past the growing lump in my throat and staggered through the falling snow toward the wreck.

I arrived half-conscious and found it lodged beyond my reach. I tried to climb the slippery tree trunks, thinking dimly of shelter and perhaps a radio. I collapsed into the snow collecting around the roots. It was growing dark. I could hardly breathe. I was going to die.

I recovered consciousness with a bright light in my eyes and somebody shouting, "Here's the Captain. He's alive." I tried to speak, choked, and fought for breath.

"He's obstructed. Extend his head." "Get him into the ship." There was pain as I was lifted. Then an unfocused face above me, an aluminum deckhead beyond. They were doing something to my neck. I could breath again, but I could not speak. A voice, "Easy Gart. There's a tube in your throat." In the background, urgently, "Sir—we're icing. Have to lift off." Then the jerking sway of a big helicopter rising. I felt a needle in my arm.

My next coherent memories are of lying in a warm bed, unable to speak because of a tracheotomy tube, unable to see clearly past my swollen eyelids, unable to open my mouth because of wired teeth. My frostbitten hands were bandaged, my right arm was tied down by an intravenous infusion. I could only lie helpless, listen to the snatches of conversation around my bedside, and attempt to construct a picture of where I was and what had happened.

His name had been Gart—Captain Jan Gart. His pilot had been killed in the crash that activated his impact beacon and brought the rescue team up from the Lake Simcoe Post. In the darkness, the wind, the drifting snow, they had landed only long enough to find me, dressed in his uniform, and to extract the body of his pilot and some kit from the wreck. The rescue ship had started to ice and they assumed that was why the cutter had crashed. Aircraft weren't equipped to operate under those conditions any more. It was a desolation of ice and muskeg up there. The wreckage of the cutter would lie under the snow until the next spring—or forever. They had no idea of what this Captain Gart had been doing. Who knew what the hell the Patrol did anyway? They spoke about me with distaste.

I had killed some kind of a cop: that was the first message to reach me. I immediately abandoned attempts to communicate and relapsed into apparent semiconsciousness. Their accents were strange, but the import was clear. All I then knew about your society was that the first man I had met had reached for his gun with murder on his face. I had killed him. A man who goes for his gun deserves what he gets. Gart was responsible for his own death—and the death of his pilot. But his colleagues, whoever they were, would not see it that way. In any society the police try to revenge their dead; in a police state they usually succeed. And that was the kind of state I assumed yours to be.

I was wrong of course, but I only discovered that later. None of his colleagues did appear. Three uniformed officers held a brief enquiry around my bed, listened to me croak "Icing," and went away. I sensed dislike but not suspicion.

The Anglic they spoke, the clothes they wore, the furnishings of my room, were so familiar that I assumed my transit prediction of two hundred years had been too long. Only when I found that I was indeed in September 2170 did I realize how static civilization had become. You are frozen into the artifacts of the early twenty-first century. I was so imbued with the restless change that had distorted my own era that I had thought it the normal pattern instead of the wild anomaly which it had really been.

It took me longer to discover I was in neither Canada nor the United States, but in something called "Sector Ten"; that "US" now meant United Settlements, a world federation of twenty-seven Sectors and seventy million people. In 2030 out of the six billion women alive only four million were fertile. You are their fifth generation descendents. The mothers of all the rest had used Impermease and unknowingly sterilized their unborn daughters.

I deduced this and more from the televiewer my nurse put in my room to amuse me during the few hours she let me stay awake. It presented a well-ordered, hard-working, and unimaginative society. I know now this is generally true; at the time I thought it a propaganda facade. Half-doped, I endured five days of simpleminded dramas, saccharine music, and agricultural advice. On the sixth day the surgeon took the tube from my throat and allowed me to use the washroom. By then I had identified the capsules of Paxin which were forcing me to relax and I started flushing them down the john. My nurse never seemed to imagine any patient not doing exactly as she ordered.

Freed from tubes and tranquilizers I was able to search Gart's kit. His identity card and log book told me that he had been a captain in some force called the "Guard," serving with a unit called the "Patrol." Thereafter I spent most of my time in bed, apathetically watching the televiewer, feigning tranquility, and planning escape. So far nobody had questioned my identity, and my image in the washroom mirror told me why. My scarred and swollen cheeks, my purple eyelids, my flattened nose, my wired jaws, made my reflection easy to reconcile with the face that stared sullenly out of the photograph on Gart's ID. My wired teeth forced me to mumble, my frostbitten hands saved me from having to write. Nobody who came to my room during those first ten days seemed to have known Gart nor wanted to know me.

I began to hope. It is the dogtag which marks the man. They had read "Capt. Jan Gart" on my coveralls. They had expected to find a Captain Gart. We see what we expect to see; that is the essence of camouflage. One has to be sensitized by suspicion to see more than the obvious, and Paxin makes most of your people unsuspicious. They accept face values and are accustomed to faces of all shades and shapes. Variety is the norm; mixtures of cultural and racial residuae the usual pattern. They would find uniformity unusual; they expect diversity. And so the color of my skin, my accent, my mumblings of an occasional archaic word did not bring comment.

My injuries were my disguise; they were also my bonds. I could hardly move, even had I known where to run. Time is one-way. There is no retreat to the past. To survive I had to bluff, heal fast enough to avoid arousing medical interest, and learn what I could from a hospital bed.

I still knew little when, on my tenth day in the hospital, I heard steps outside my room. Three people. One of them was my surgeon, a woman with cold decisive hands and a voice that sent my guts into spasm. "Captain Gart's in here, Director. He's sedated. Do you want me to wake him?"

"Let's look at him first." A man, speaking with authority. Director of what? I closed my eyes as the door opened.

"So that's Gart!" The same cultivated accent. A lady. "He's not what I pictured."

"Only met him once. That was enough. His crash seems to have improved his looks." A laugh. "Doctor, I want to talk to Captain Gart. Is he rational?"

"Certainly. He's only tranquilized. But he's still suffering from postconcussive retrograde amnesia."

"She means," cut in the lady, "that he won't be able to remember how he killed his pilot."

"I mean," said my surgeon, "that he has some memory loss. Also a fractured mandible. That, Rajuna, is a lower jaw! It is immobilized by wires around his incisors and canines. His front teeth! So he cannot articulate properly. You may find him difficult to understand, but he should understand you. Grip his shoulder firmly when you wish to wake him and allow him time to stabilize. Good day, Shapur. Good day, Rajuna." The door closed and I felt myself being inspected. I dared not open my eyes.

His name was Shapur. He was director of something sufficiently important for the surgeon to escort him to my room. The woman—she must be Rajuna—was saying, "Are we going to have to use this thug?"

"I hope not. But he's the only Patrol Officer in the Sector."

"Patrol! The dregs of the Guard!"

"Maybe. But they'll shoot to order. And fly over the wilderness. If we have to contact those barbarians—"

"I don't think they are barbarians." I heard her move to the foot of my bed. "Was he trying to contact them when he crashed?"

"Up there? No, he was on a job for the Ulama. Watching some pickup point for pilgrims."

"Watching for pilgrims? What waste! A smashed cutter and a dead pilot." The bitch was blaming me. "He's not much use without a pilot."

"The Order's sending a replacement. Reluctantly. Gart's got a bad record already. But the Prioress promised to transfer the best available. The Ulama has another pickup point to be watched next spring. I want Gart back in action before then. We'll need a team ready to shoot if Sila tries a putsch." I felt a hand squeezing my shoulder. "Wake up, Gart! It's Shapur—Director of Security."

The top cop! Slowly I opened my eyes, pretending confusion, groping for time. His face was staring down into mine. He did not look like a cop. It was an aquiline face, deep eyes, the hint of an epicanthic fold, straight mouth, narrow lips, a close-trimmed black beard. The face of a proud man in his prime with his rank so clear that, driven by an old discipline, I struggled to sit up.

He pressed me back. "Relax. And listen. Can you understand what I'm saying?"

"Yes, sir," I mumbled.

"This is Rajuna, the new Director of Special Systems."

She was studying me. Slim and tall, her blue jumpsuit set off the bronze of her skin, the brown of her eyes, the sheen of her black hair. Her beauty was classic and arrogant, her lips curved into the slight smile of amused disdain. She responded to Shapur's introduction with a nod that combined courtesy and contempt. She, like Shapur, wore a small pistol at her waist.

"You made the surveillance?"

I nodded.

"And—as usual—nobody there?"

For one moment I was free to choose, to astound him with the truth. I struggled to speak, looked from the man to the woman, saw the contempt in their eyes, and was incoherent from my weak anger and my wired teeth.

He took my stammer as agreement, and made my decision for me. "Blame the Ulama for such futilities. I saw the report that went to Guard HQ—you're all clear as far as Malta's concerned. You only mumbled about icing. That was wise. Stay quiet. And listen carefully. Your surgeon says you'll be strong enough to travel in four days. I want you out of here. Understand?"

I nodded.

"Out of circulation. Away from the Guard too. There's an old Patrol base at a place called Ive, near the frontier. I'm having it reactivated. You'll be alone there. Oh, I'll arrange for a pair of girls so you'll have some amusement later!"

Rajuna laughed as I muttered, "Thank you, sir."

"A replacement pilot's on her way from Naxos. She'll pick up a fresh combat cutter, come here to collect you, and take you to Ive. You'll convalesce there. No outside contacts."

"Who'll unwire his teeth?" asked Rajuna from the foot of my bed.

"Your pilot can call the doctor from the nearest Guard depot. But don't start drinking with him. Is that clear?"

"Yes, sir."

"When you're fit, initiate a patrol along the Ive section. There hasn't been one for decades. Operationally, do your job. Cooperate with the Guard. I don't want complaints from

Marshal Mitra. But don't get killed hunting bandits. I may need you. If I call—come fast and ready to shoot. Understand?"

"Yes, sir."

"Your new pilot will have detailed orders. Let her handle things until you've recovered."

I mumbled something about doing my best, and they left me.

I lay sweating, regretting my lost chance to confess, and wallowing under information overload. I had been swamped by a torrent of unknown names. I grabbed onto the few facts. Some religious organization called the "Ulama" had known that something might happen on that inlet of Hudson's Bay. Nobody had really expected it would. Ostensibly Gart had been there to pick up any pilgrim who appeared. His real job was hit man for Shapur. I had inherited the role and would have to act the part. From our brief and deadly contact, from Shapur's contempt, I knew Gart. A type I detest but can imitate. There is a streak of Gart in most men.

In four days a woman from Naxos, the Greek island where Theseus dumped Ariadne, would arrive to collect me. I would have to let myself be collected. Shapur was sending Gart to some isolated spot called Ive. Near a frontier. And presumably beyond the frontier was the wilderness, the place only the Patrol flew over. My refuge when I was fit to run.

Four days later I was hardly fit to walk across the room. My nurse had told me to get ready for discharge and left me to suck my breakfast through a straw. I had shaved and struggled into Gart's uniform, and was sitting exhausted on my bed when Diana appeared.

In that first moment I did not see Diana. I saw only the heavy automatic pistol holstered on her thigh. Here was my jailer or my executioner. Whichever she was I was too weak to resist. I stared at her.

"Are you Captain Gart?" Her voice was even, her accent precise. Her blonde hair was tight about her head, her body firm under tan coveralls. But it was her gray eyes that held me; they had the hue and hardness of agate.

I nodded.

"I'm your new pilot, sir." She stood in a position of relaxed readiness, the habitual posture of certain dangerous men I have known, but which I had never before seen in a woman.

"What's your name?" It was the only sensible remark I could find.

"Diana."

She was Diana. Slim, taut, curved like a hunting bow; as finely balanced and as deadly. She bore the brand of the professional. I had caught only a glimpse of Gart's pilot in that open-mouthed moment when she had seen me over his shoulder. That girl had shouted a warning. This Diana would not have shouted. She would have spoken softly—or she would have fired without speaking.

From that morning until now Diana has served with me. God knows what she really thought of me then. At first I tried to wear the mask of Gart; it hid me for a while but cracked in the crunch. I was not "dregs of the Guard" but a sometime sergeant in a proud corps. Perhaps the report I have told her to prepare will let me see myself through her eyes. For among her many skills is the ability to write a clear concise Anglic, an ability which by now you know I lack. Her phraseology tends to be terse and formalized, but this reflects her training rather than her thinking. She has all the normal human drives, but either suspended or channeled to support a sense of purpose more resolute than I would have conceived possible.

It has been Diana, in fact, who has written most of my previous reports, transforming my rough notes into accurate ordered statements. Like all of us she has changed with our changing situation, but I hope she can still write as objectively as she could. The rest of you are supplying all the emotion I can stomach.

I have told her that you will need to know the facts if you are to be convinced by the logic of events, and I have left it to her to decide what is relevant. As she finishes each section she will give it to me. If I have any useful comments I will add them, but I will wait until the whole is complete before I let Diana, or any of you, read the entire story.

II

September 2170

He has told me to write this report on how we got where we are, so that you will be convinced by the "logic of events." I don't know what he means by that phrase and neither, I suspect, does he, but I take it that I am to include all I judge relevant.

I am not what I was, but I will review events as I saw them then. In September 2170 I was recalled to Naxos, briefed, and posted to a Patrol team in Sector Ten. Karen, the Pilot, had been killed in a crash and Captain Gart, the officer, was in a hospital at Lake Simcoe. My orders were to take him to Ive for his convalescence, and then to reestablish a patrol along that section of the frontier.

I found him sitting on his bed. His nose was flattened, his face bruised, and his teeth wired. He was physically weak and emotionally unstable. He stared at me when I entered his room and stood trembling while I adjusted his coveralls, shortened his gunbelt, and tightened the straps of his helmet. When dressed I had to urge him to walk with me to the hospital lobby while an orderly took his kit to our cutter. At the desk he gestured with his swollen hands so I signed his discharge papers, collected his medical reports and medication, and cleared a path for him through the clustering civilians. He followed me out onto the hospital square and then stood looking about him.

"That's our cutter, over there."

He started toward some civilian aircraft, so I went ahead to ours. When he arrived he gripped the rim of the dome, stood panting, and then began to climb into the pilot's seat. I eased him over to the officer's and closed the dome. He had a panic reaction, scrabbling at the catch, so I snapped on his

18

safety harness, started the turbines, and waited for his order. When he began to fumble with his harness release I took off.

He sat rigid, staring downward, first at the hospital and then, as I flew south, at the countryside. He seemed so apprehensive that I myself began to look for something unusual, but the pattern below was typical of a developed Sector. I had never served in Ten before but it appeared more advanced than most. The railroads were double-tracked, the roads mostly hard-surfaced with trucks and Ground Effect Vehicles moving along them, the farms well cultivated, and villages numerous. By the time we reached Lake Ontario I assumed he was suffering from a post-traumatic anxiety reaction.

When we crossed the falls he stared at the metal recovery operations along the south bank of the river and muttered, "Christ—Buffalo!" It surprised me to find that he was a Christian. As we started over the Alleghenies he asked, "Ive, this place we're going, where is it?"

I showed him Ive on the navigator chart. He whispered, "Virginia!" (the prechaos name of the area), and then sank back into his seat and closed his eyes. He roused himself when the mountains that marked the frontier appeared ahead and asked, "Those—are those the Blue Ridge?"

I told him they were.

I did not understand his next question, partly because of his wired teeth and his unusual accent, partly because the words seemed nonsensical. He repeated it. "Beyond them?"

He was serious, so I said, "Wilderness. Across the continent to the frontier of the Eleventh Sector—the Pacific Sector."

He had a sudden attack of vertigo and put his face in his hands. We flew into cloud and by the time he recovered were five hundred meters above Ive. I waited for his order but he sat staring at the base below.

Its only novelty was the red brick from which it was built. Otherwise it was typical of the star-shaped fortresses of the Consolidation Period, and like all those in Sector Ten it had ceased to serve its original function. The fire-fields between the bastions were overgrown; decrepit warehouses stood along the rusted spur of the narrow-gauge railroad, and a cart-track straggled up to the gates which now stood permanently open.

I had checked on Ive's condition and history when I had got our orders. It had once been shelter for the farmers against barbarians from the mountains and a base for the Patrol teams which had gone out against them. But the barbarians along the frontiers of Sector Ten had long since chosen to join civilization, the occasional outbreaks of banditry were handled by the Guard, and Ive had been relegated to minimal maintenance. This, as judged from five hundred meters, meant that it was being allowed to decay, but it appeared peaceful, so I asked, "Shall I land, sir?"

He hesitated, then nodded. I angled down, skidded in low across the fortifications, checked, held, and dropped the last ten meters in a true vertical to touch without a trace of impact. Extra flair is traditional in the first landing at a new base, even if an old man limping toward us across the grassgrown courtyard was the only person to appreciate my skill.

Captain Gart did not. He sat with his eyes closed, his knuckles white on the handgrips. I hit his harness quick-release. "We've landed, sir. Your helmet's tipped!"

The flash of anger when he opened his eyes was his first appropriate response that day. I helped him alight and he stood leaning against the dome while the old man introduced himself as the Compradore.

"Things aren't too tidy, sir. But it's a lot to look after, and they haven't given me no help. I've hired a couple of maids for you, sir. Only local girls—but they're keen. They've fixed up your quarters pretty good. The tall one's Kate, sir. The other's Sue."

Two young women had come to the door of what must once have been the Seneschal's house. They giggled when Captain Gart looked toward them but stopped when they saw his face.

I cut into the Compradore's excuses. "The Captain's been wounded. He should be in bed."

We flanked him as he swayed up the pathway to the front door, the Compradore describing how he had once been a Sergeant in the Guard and wounded himself. Between us we supported him into the house and through to a bedroom. I made Kate and Sue help me get him undressed and into bed, then I sent them to prepare a meat broth. I spooned it into him, gave him his medication, and watched him until he fell asleep.

When I had eaten my own meal I went out to service the cutter. It was dusk by the time I returned to the house. Kate and Sue were chattering in the kitchen and I hushed them for the Captain was still asleep. The relaxants had removed the tensions from his devastated face but the disfigurements remained. The civilian doctors at Simcoe had simply cobbled him together.

His record suggested that his incompetence had already killed one Pilot. At present he was damaged and frightened. There must be a good reason for the Order to have allotted him a Pilot of my caliber, but it was not obvious.

Five days later, when Doctor Hassan flew over from the Guard base at Rimon, it was still not obvious. I watched the doctor carry out an adequate physical examination, and left him trying to extract a medical history. Later, in the parlor, I asked for a prognosis.

Doctor Hassan was a small man with a black beard and the quick eyes of one who avoids Paxin. He took a cup of coffee from Sue, patted her rump, and studied the X-rays.

"His jaw's healing well. The scars will fade. There's not much I can do about his nose. He may want it fixed later. Hair-line fracture at the base of the skull. Don't look alarmed! They never give trouble. And don't mention it to your Captain or he'll be afraid to shake his head." He laughed, tossed the X-rays onto the table, and stared at me. "So you're Diana. Rated of the First Class, eh? Never met a Pilot with that rating before."

"There are few with it."

"Then why are you wasting your talents in America? Things have been quiet here for years. Is that druj business going to turn into something?"

He was referring to the druj raids during August, the first in Sector Ten since the beginning of the century. They had come suddenly out of the wilderness, butchering farm families with typical abominations. "I go where the Order sends me. I don't know why I've been sent to America."

He lit a cheroot and called for more coffee. "I served with the Patrol on the Yalu. Officers were a bunch of bastards. But the Pilots were superb. Lots of action there. Naxos sent us the best. But they never sent us a girl rated First Class."

The decisions of the Order were not Doctor Hassan's concern. "How long before Captain Gart's fit for duty?"

"He'll heal fast. Should be able to unwire his jaw in about

six weeks." He put down his cup. "Something else about his health worrying you?"

"I left you to talk to him."

"He's not much at intercourse while he can't open his mouth. Eh, Sue?" He chuckled at his own joke. "If you mean his memory—amnesia's common after head injuries."

"A retrograde amnesia covering a few hours. He's forgotten much more. Concussion can't affect the protein complexes. Only organic damage does that. But he has hardly any motor or perceptual defects."

Doctor Hassan stared at the tip of his cheroot. "They teach you girls a lot of things at that Academy on Naxos, don't they?"

"Many useful skills."

"But not neurology!" He laughed. "And you were on that damned island—how long?"

"Five years. I graduated at nineteen." I resent personal questions but he was my official physician and so could ask them.

"Tell me about your life before you went there."

"I'm the daughter of a sea captain. I grew up aboard ship. As a young girl—" I blocked as I hit amnesia and saw the point he was making. "I know there are memory areas I can't access now. The Academy had to free channels so we could store new knowledge. I accepted that when I volunteered. But when I'm debriefed those channels reopen."

"So the gaps don't trouble you. But your Captain's worried about his. Afraid he'll be thrown out of the Service if Malta hears. He's trying to relearn without attracting attention."

"But concussion—"

"Diana, accept my professional opinion! Head injuries to people who've been through the Academies can produce unusual effects. Some less pleasant than your Captain's amnesia." The doctor walked over to the fireplace. "I've tried to convince him that the gaps'll fill in with time. You can help him more than me."

"How?"

"Encourage him to ask questions about things he's forgotten. Tide him over until his memory returns. Get him out to practice familiar skills. Above all—reassure him. At present you're scaring the hell out of him."

"In your professional opinion, are the probabilities of his regaining full effectiveness high enough to justify my efforts?"

"You cold-blooded little—" His fingers drummed on the mantelpiece. "No, that's not fair. Most Patrol officers have plenty worth forgetting. Why your Order teams you girls with such brutes I don't know! Charioteers to thugs! But Jan seems different from most. Maybe some bad patterns shaken out by that crack on the head. He could become worthy of even a Pilot with your exalted rating." He studied me. "Diana, ever heard of dominant genetic clumping?"

"No. Why?"

"Because you're a good example. Freyer identified your pattern before the chaos. A high-survival clump of sex-linked traits which travel together and surface every few generations. Rare—but intriguing."

"How do I show it?"

"Gray eyes, blond hair, narrow hips but adequate pelvis, small breasts, lithe figure, short reaction-times, intellectual ability."

"Those check." I considered the list. "And my senses are unusually acute. Especially smell."

"Are they now?" remarked Doctor Hassan, drawing on his cheroot and exhaling the smoke into the parlor. "And there's another trait I almost forgot. The disposition of a wolverine!" He laughed at me and left.

I followed his advice. I explained to Captain Gart the possible side effects of head injuries on graduates of the Service Academies. I told him to question me directly rather than waste time with the circumlocutions he had started to use. I assured him that while we formed a team he could trust me absolutely. "Pilots always honor the Code, even if some officers do not."

He became less suspicious although he still chose to question Kate and Sue rather than myself. They were as anxious as I for him to recover his health; he was of little use to any of us while his jaws were wired. Sue, the younger and less patient, was continually complaining that all the conditions of her employment were not being fulfilled.

Kate was more sensible. She was an excellent cook and a hard worker, as the daughters of farmers are taught to be, but she also had a native intelligence seldom found in young

women of her class. She told me she had been classified for
training as a tech, but she wanted to marry a farmer and
homestead in one of the underdeveloped European Sectors.
Not for several years, she emphasized, because there were experiences any wise girl should seek before marriage.

It was in search of such experiences that she had come to
work at Ive. "A Patrol officer! Everybody knows what Patrol
officers are!" She looked at me across the kitchen table, her
brown eyes large. She was a handsome young woman. "But
the Captain, he wants a teacher more than a partner. Asks
me about things I learned in school."

"Kate, answer his questions. His accident affected his
memory."

"I answer the ones I can. He likes me to keep talking.
Doesn't talk much himself. But how he reads! Nobody reads
like the Captain."

No officer certainly. He spent his convalescence inside the
Encyclopedia, his logs, military manuals, and old school
books. He studied "The News" every Sunday when it arrived
and searched through that mass of underedited facts for the
rest of the week. He read more in one day than I had seen
any other officer read in a complete tour of duty.

He was a healthy man who, before his crash, must have
been in better physical condition than most officers. At the
end of a month his only real disability was his wired jaw, although he developed a gamut of psychosomatic complaints to
avoid meeting outsiders or the demands of Sue. Psychologi-
cally he also grew stronger; he changed from frightened and
silent to irritable and sullen. As soon as he was fit to fly I
took him out for retraining as Doctor Hassan had suggested.
He proved to be an excellent marksman with an automatic
rifle, but was barely adequate with a combat pistol. As a flyer
he was abysmal.

In this he was no different from his fellow officers, but although I explained that few of them could even fly a combat
cutter let alone pilot one, he insisted I teach him. I did my
best. I would climb to two thousand meters. He would take
over, balance precariously until he made some clumsy movement, follow with an even clumsier correction, and we would
fall out of the sky.

I would let the cutter tumble to a few hundred meters
above the ground before resuming control. The cockpit would

start reeking with his sweat, but time and again he would order me back up for another attempt. On one occasion he managed to invert us completely, and after I had retrieved him he stabbed his hand toward a silver cutter which, having seen our extraordinary maneuver, had quickly changed course to give us a wide berth. "Those civilians can fly. Why can't I?"

"Civilian cutters have semiautomatic controls. Their performance is degraded, but they're easy to handle."

"What's so special about this damned machine?"

"It's a high-performance system with an accelerated response. Very short time-constants. Stability is traded off for sensitivity. To control a combat cutter one must solve ten differential equations simultaneously. That task is beyond even a computer. Only a Pilot can fly a combat cutter tuned for optimum performance." He was staring at me so I translated my explanation into simpler terms. "You're sitting in a compound pendulum hung from an eccentric airscrew. You have to sense twelve changing variables and fuse ten separate control movements into a smooth whole. You are not able to do it. Few men can. They lack the required genetic pattern."

"Genetic pattern? What the hell?"

"All successful combat Pilots are female. Certain women are born with low sensory thresholds. A sex-linked pattern of perception. The pattern needed by a Pilot."

"Why the devil—?"

"Because a Pilot's senses have to extend out into her machine." I enjoy describing my art, but seldom have an interested audience. "The controls are served with direct feedback. I can feel every shiver of the lift surfaces, every air eddy over the elevators, every flex in the airframe. I can sense the thrust of the turbines, the grip of the rotors. And the instruments are in the predicter mode. They give me feed-forward as well as present status."

"Christ!"

"A Pilot needs such intimate interactions if she is to unite with the cutter so the combination can give peak performance."

"You kind of couple with the thing?"

"Exactly." I was pleased he understood, and I climbed back toward two thousand meters. "Optimum coupling for informational impedance matching."

"Every flight a mating flight?"

That was the first time I had heard him attempt humor. I took my hands off the controls. "Now try to sense what I have described!"

We had a hectic fifty seconds and I did not take over from him until the skids were brushing the treetops.

"Goddam machine!" he muttered. "Engineered to boost the Pilot mystique!" He did not object when I turned toward Ive, but presently asked, "Those degraded civilian cutters—how can I borrow one?"

"Borrow a civilian cutter!" I had found I could usually divert him from some eccentricity by a show of surprise. "I don't know! And I don't advise you to try!"

He took my advice, as he accepted almost all my suggestions during those weeks of his convalescence. He was so amenable that I judged his command potential poor. I now know that his amnesia was more extensive than I then realized, and only his determination and good fortune allowed him to cope with his fragmented memory. If Malta had had an adequate medical report on his condition he would have been invalided out of the Guard immediately. But by the time he did admit that large parts of his memory had been obliterated by his accident his abilities had been so clearly demonstrated that his retirement was never suggested.

Diana has an eidetic memory, total recall, and a minicorder which she runs whenever she thinks something is about to happen. So I cannot dispute her facts so far. I can question her selection and interpretation.

III

October 2170

On the twenty-first of October I took Captain Gart to Rimon to have his jaw unwired. It was a trip he had tried to avoid by attempting to remove the wires himself with a pair of side cutters. After gashing his lip he agreed to let Doctor Hassan do it, explaining his nervousness by saying, "Don't want to meet anybody who knew me before the crash."

That was unlikely; he had only arrived in Sector Ten in late August and had gone north immediately. But he was hypersensitive about his damaged face, and he slumped silently beside me as we flew southeast, fidgeting with the bandage he had wound round his mouth to hold an unnecessary dressing over his cut lip.

Rimon was as somnolent as were all Guard bases in Sector Ten at that time. It was early afternoon and from the air it appeared as deserted as Ive. Ships, trucks, and gevs were drawn up in parade lines, none showing any sign of recent usage. Only the medship, parked near the entrance to the sick bay, had a crew. I landed alongside.

Captain Gart climbed slowly to the ground, hitching the bandage up over his mouth. I reported to the tower, cut the turbines, and was getting down myself when Doctor Hassan came out of the sick bay, buckling his helmet and shouting to his crew. When he saw us he called, "Sorry, Jan. You'll have to wait. There's a farm on fire, near Mantio. District Officer radioed. Asked me to come over. Some fool farmer may have burned himself along with his barn."

"Wait here?" Captain Gart looked uncertainly around him as the medship lifted off. He fiddled with his bandage and muttered, "Maybe we should go along. Might be able to help," and had clambered back aboard before I could answer.

27

Our takeoff was delayed because the tower operator was busy on another channel and by the time I got clearance the medship was far to the west. I picked up the course and we had only gone a few kilometers when a General Alarm sounded on the radio. The District Officer had arrived above the burning farm, reported bodies in the farmyard, and then shouted he was under automatic fire. Moments later his crash-beacon had come on.

"Christ!" said Captain Gart. "A raid!" He stared after the distant medship. "Doctor Hassan—is he armed?"

"Only pistols. Shall I shift to overdrive?"

"Overdrive?" he echoed uncertainly.

"Full ahead?" I snapped.

"For God's sake—yes! Go. And fast!"

The sudden harmonic of authority in his voice made me glance at his face. He had pulled the bandage from his mouth, lost his expression of subdued alarm, and was reaching to take the rifles from their racks. Although we were now bucking toward full speed his movements were easy and proficient. He checked the guns, warmed them with quick bursts through the ports, positioned the spare magazines, thumbed the safeties, and relaxed back into his seat. For the first time since we had been together I felt he knew what he was about.

We were approaching the frontier when the farm came up ahead, marked by a column of black smoke rising high into the still air. I saw a crashed cutter in one corner of the home pasture, then a burning tractor with a blackened body tied to it. The only aircraft in sight was the medship which had circled and was now hovering. The medic flyer was calling Rimon. "By the Bull—it's a shambles! Can't see anyone alive. The bandits must have bolted. We're doing down to the DO."

I was about to acknowledge the interception when my hand was slapped from the switch. The Captain tried to yell through his teeth, "Stay up! Stay high, you young fool!" Then he cursed as the medship began to drop toward the crashed cutter.

I had started to follow it down when he grabbed my arm. "Hold! Hold three hundred! Watch that junction." He slid open his gun port. "Hedge and wood."

I kept my course and height as we passed over the burned buildings, the mutilated bodies, and the gutted cattle in the farmyard. Then I followed his gesture and banked slowly, watching the hedge-wood junction. For what, I did not know until I saw the muzzle-flash. I jumped the cutter vertical on total turbines an instant before tracer arced through the air-space we had just left. "An auton!" I said, cutting the throttle before the rotor blades disintegrated.

The Captain's burst had gone wide. The auton's second burst caught the medship as it landed. The gunners had been waiting to position us both for a perfect knockdown, close enough for the shells to penetrate our armor, yet high enough for us to be killed by the crash if we survived the shot. But they had waited too long before realizing we were not being drawn into their trap. I saw it clearly. I had learned of such strategies. Yet if Captain Gart had not stopped me I would have followed the medship into the ambush.

Doctor Hassan had jumped from his heeled ship and turned to drag a crewman out after him. The Captain was calling on his communicator. "Owen—there's a dip in the field, about fifty meters from you, in line with the barn. It's your only cover."

The doctor waved. One medic staggered to his feet clutching his stomach. Another clambered from the ship. I danced the cutter, moving it in a random pattern to prevent the auton predicting, while Captain Gart gave bursts of covering fire. "They're there!" he muttered. "Both medics hit."

I glanced below. The three had reached the dip and dragged themselves to the rim. Automatic fire from a barn to the east and a wall to the west was now sweeping low over the field, forcing them to hug the earth. They had only their side arms. In minutes, while the auton held us aloft, they would be rushed from both sides.

We were too high to help. If we dropped low enough to give effective support the auton would knock us down. We must dive through the auton zone, land in the depression, and use our rifles to hold off attacks until relief arrived. Our chances of getting there were not good; an auton is deadly tracking a metal target at short range. But we had to make the attempt. I checked my surge of sadness and waited for his order to dive.

Instead he called Rimon, stared at the scene below, and then said, "Up two hundred."

I hesitated, trapped between instinct and impulse.

His voice bit like a spur. "Up girl! Up! Across that wood-lot."

We swept above the small wood where the auton was hidden.

"Down—fast—far edge of wood. Drop me—there!"

I touched. He jumped from the cutter. "Get back up. Three to five and jank. Keep moving. Contact base. I'm going to zap those gunners. Listen on com. I'll leave my mike open." He slapped the side of the dome. "Get topside!"

His jargon was archaic but his meaning was clear. I soared above the field, trying simultaneously to dance the cutter, give covering fire, and inform base. From Captain Gart I heard only heavy breathing. The thought of a Patrol Officer crawling through wet undergrowth had never before occurred to me. Neither had it occurred to the gunners. They were not watching their rear.

There was one shot—a second—and the auton stopped firing. "Waxed 'em. Waxed both of 'em!" gagging sound as though he was trying to stop himself from vomiting into his teeth. "No others here. I'm taking over the gun."

I dropped low. "There's about twenty around the edge of the field." Then I saw one clearly. It looked like a man. It was a druj.

Slugs began to bounce off my belly armor. The Captain's voice came low and brutal. "Up—up you silly bitch! Before they smash your tail!"

I rose and called, "Rush starting." Then I stabilized to give aimed fire as the raiders broke cover.

They were druj! The first I had ever seen; worse than I had ever imagined. They looked like humans and fought like disciplined devils. Their assault and enveloping teams attached with fire and movement. I dropped the leaders of the wedge but they were closing on the medics when an auton salvo swept over their heads. They hesitated, the second burst went among them, and they realized they were under fire from their own gun. A third burst and they lost formation, breaking back to cover.

"Watch 'em—but hang high!" Captain Gart had raced across the field to throw himself prone beside Doctor Hassan.

"They're moving along the hedges, heading for the wilderness. Can I track?"

"No! Hold station."

I hovered, catching glimpses of the survivors, hoping for a target, but they used ground well and I could snap off only one burst before they disappeared. An armored gev came roaring across the countryside and I signalled the last druj position. It slewed round, raced to the edge of the forest, and as it could not get between the trees it fired a few rounds at them before lurching over to the farm.

Two Guard gunships and a second medship arrived. If the auton had still been in action it would have knocked them down in turn and stopped the gev. Captain Gart called, "Diana, come on in." I landed as the medship took off with the wounded and he and Doctor Hassan were starting toward the smoldering farm. When I followed he waved me back. I recharged magazines while I waited.

Presently the two men returned, walking slowly across the field. The Captain took off his helmet and leaned against the side of our cutter. The doctor went straight to his medship and salvaged a silver flask. He took a long pull and passed it to Captain Gart. "Here, Jan."

The Captain sucked a mouthful through his teeth and offered the flask to me. I drew back. He muttered, "You didn't see the kids!" and took another mouthful.

A truck convoy arrived, and some silver cutters landed. This was the first druj raid in our area and the farm began to swarm with Guardsmen, Wardens, and curious civilians. They were building a pyre for the District Officer. The druj had not had time to mutilate his body as they had mutilated those of the farmer's family. One of the dead druj was wearing a necklace of freshly harvested childrens' fingers. "I shot that creature," said Doctor Hassan, drinking again.

Captain Gart went to look at it and a medic in mask and gloves came running up. "Better not touch it, sir. May be diseased!" We watched him sealing the corpse in a plastic bag.

"What are you going to do with it?"

"Thermite the filth, sir. Well away from here."

"Doesn't look diseased to me. Dirty. Undernourished. But not diseased."

"There's a virus theory of druj, as for everything that goes wrong!" The doctor took another pull from his flask. "But they won't learn much incinerating 'em without autopsy. My profession—bunch of old women!"

I had to speak up. "The druj are the Agents of Evil: the
Children of Ahriman!"

"That's the Order's line, eh Diana?" The doctor laughed.
"If you can't find a virus to blame—blame the Devil! Or
God!" He sniffed the smoke from the funeral pyre. "Loaded
with hallucinogens. Let's get the hell out of here. We've done
our bit. Can Boadicea give me a lift home?" He slapped me
across the seat of my coveralls.

"Careful, Owen!" called Captain Gart, as my hand half-
rose before I could block the reflex. "She's on automatic and
she's short-fused!"

"No sweat. She won't stun her surgeon. See?" He spanked
me a second time to prove his point as I swung up into the
cockpit. Then he clambered into the rear of the dome.

As I took off I saw the horror in the farmyard and mo-
mentarily let the cutter slew. Captain Gart grabbed the silver
flask and thrust it at me. "Take a slug, girl!"

I jerked my head back, nauseated by the stench of ethanol.
"It is unlawful!"

"She's conditioned against hard booze." Doctor Hassan
recovered his flask. "Jan—thank God you broke through your
conditioning—sorry—education. Or we'd all be dead." He
hunched forward, breathing fumes into the cockpit. "How
come?"

"How come what?" Captain Gart shifted in his seat.

"How come you did a dropoff like that? I was with the Patrol before. Those pandours never moved their asses!"

"Outflanking that gun? It's in the manuals. A standard
drill."

"In the manuals! Balls! You thought for yourself."

"It was obvious."

"Not to the Patrol officers I knew it wouldn't have been
obvious. What—"

Captain Gart was becoming embarrassed and I broke in to
divert the doctor. "Doctor Hassan, for a surgeon you use a
pistol well."

"First time I've ever killed anybody. On purpose that is.
It's legal. A military surgeon can carry arms to protect his
patients against a savage enemy. Even the old conventions allowed that. And the druj are sure savage. Though today it
was my patient protecting me." He gripped the Captain's

shoulder. "Jan, I'll unwire you. Soon as we reach base. I'm still sober enough for that."

We landed at Rimon and were surrounded by an admiring crowd. The medship had brought back news of our exploit. I followed the two officers into the sick bay to help in removing the wires, ready to do the simple surgery myself if necessary.

But Doctor Hassan was deft. Afterward the Captain leaned over a basin, rinsing his mouth and spitting out bloody water. The doctor wiped his hands. "Come over to the mess, Jan. Some of them'll know you saved their necks. The Patrol's popular for once."

Captain Gart hesitated, then shook his head. "Not tonight, Owen." He stood, opening and closing his mouth, feeling his jaw. "Now I can eat and talk—I want to eat and talk with Diana. God, it's good to be able to spit! Anything special I should do?"

"My own program. A hot bath. A good meal. Bottle of Burgundy. And then bed—a bed with a pretty girl in it. Better still—two pretty girls." And the doctor went off whistling.

After we had landed at Ive Captain Gart started toward the house. He stopped when I climbed to the engine nacelle. "Diana—leave that damn thing alone. Come and have dinner."

"We were on overdrive. I must check the turbines while they're hot." When he began to argue I added, "Sue and Kate have been waiting over a month for you to perform according to contract."

He stared at me, cursed, and stamped into the house. Later, I had to warm up my own meal, for both Kate and Sue were busy. When I went to bed I heard their giggles as I passed his door.

He came into my room at three, and I woke to find him silhouetted in the light from the full moon. I sat up instantly, alert for the kind of indecency I had learned to expect from drunken Patrol officers. But he stood quietly by my bed, looking down at me, and presently he asked, "We're partners now, aren't we? Shared guilt of blood and all that?"

I nodded.

"Friends and comrades? Guard each other's flanks?" He smelt of ethanol and the girls. But his voice was pleasant, now that he could articulate, although his accent was strange.

Edward Llewellyn

I nodded again.

He walked to the window and stared toward the mountains. "Somewhere—there's a brain behind those devils."

"There is physical embodiment of Evil somewhere in the wilderness."

"Evil? Okay—Evil! I've never seen anything like that farm! And I've seen—" He stopped.

"I had never met the druj before today. They are not like the bandits I have fought. Their—ceremonies! Those show what they are. And today they baited a trap."

He continued to stare toward the black shadow of the mountains. "No escape," he said softly. "No escape out there. God! Thrown back into this bloody business." He turned to face me. "Di, you're stuck with me. For better: for worse!"

"We're a Combat Team. Today we were good. We can become the best in the world. The best there is."

"Enough to fire any girl's ambition? Partners! We share too much, Diana. Tastes I'd almost forgotten. Disgusting at first. Tastes of war. Tastes of love. God help us—we get to enjoy 'em!"

"Those tastes—they're the hormones." My tongue went to my lips at the memory. "One tastes the circulating hormones. They flood the body before action."

He laughed, left the window, and stood above me. "May I touch you, Diana?"

I do not like to be touched when I am not on leave, and usually I do not allow it. But that night I nodded. His renewed self-confidence had to be protected.

All he did was to take my chin and tip up my face. He looked into my eyes for a long time. At last he kissed my forehead and went back to his room.

IV

Winter 2170

The druj had appeared suddenly upon an almost undefended frontier, and during the next eight weeks they spread havoc out of all proportion to their numbers. Whoever controlled them picked his targets well. A party would attack some isolated farm, murder the occupants with extreme cruelty, slaughter the cattle, and be back into the woods before the Guard arrived.

We assumed they armed themselves from the many prechaos weapon dumps still hidden in the wilderness, but they did not produce another auton so we were able to fly along the margin, intercepting them as they came out of the forest and harrying them as they withdrew. We were the only Patrol team in the Shenandoah area and our success increased with our experience, largely because Captain Gart studied their patterns of attack and identified their most likely targets. We caught some raiding parties in open farmland and were able to vector the Guard onto many others. Toward the end of the year, as the weather worsened, they began to move South and by January our part of the frontier was again quiet.

The Sector Council was calling the druj the insane descendants of renegades who had retreated into the wilderness and were now filtering back toward civilization. In our reports I emphasized that it was only in the Shenandoah Valley that we found the remains of druj encampments. Captain Gart was cynical about the care I took in preparing the reports for Sector HQ; he did not understand that any task a Pilot undertakes must be done well. I converted his scribbled notes and my own recordings into detailed dispatches so that Marshal Mitra's staff could use them if they wished. I made them

concise, accurate, and elegant* because each report is a
creation in its own right and should be as perfect as possible
in terms of its purpose. Their preparation gave me pleasure; a
pleasure I could not expect Captain Gart to appreciate for
like most officers his language skills were limited and his
spelling was often obsolete.

Intelligence sent us what information they had; there was
little of value. "These satellite pictures show clusters of barbarian villages, but far to the southwest. And most of them
seem abandoned."

"Pictures from the weather satellite? That went out of action ten years ago! Haven't they got anything up to date?"

"Crew reports of transcontinental jets. They've been told to
watch for movements. All reports negative."

"And all from ten thousand meters! Nobody knows what
the hell's going on out there!" He waved his hand westward.

"Probably nothing they could see. Ahriman is generating
these creatures—"

He walked away, as he always did when I mentioned the
spiritual origin of our physical conflict. He was a materialist.
I too am a materialist in the sense that I recognize Evil can
act on the physical world only through physical means; the
Light and the Darkness fight through men and women, not
through magic. The miraculous reflects physical realities at
present unknown. The Light is not capricious. It established
the laws which allowed Time of Infinite Duration to bring
our universe into being, and It does not break Its own laws.

He was impatient with my faith, but we did agree that the
druj must be destroyed by force. We began a methodical
search of the wilderness within our range. We flew over
forests and mountains swept by rain, sleet, and snow. We
landed on old roads, fallen bridges, deserted plazas. We ex-
plored decaying buildings. We skimmed up rivers.

We failed to find any trace of recent occupation or passage, but these remains of prechaos civilization made him

---

* *I was taught to rate a report by its "Fog Index" (FI)**. Diana
started her report with an FI of 5.6 which was admirable. In the above
passage she has risen to over 10 as her verbosity increases.*

**$FI = 0.4(x/y + 100z/x)$ where: x = number of words
                                      y = number of sentences
                                      z = number of polysyllabics*

depressed and angry. "The bastards!" he exploded one January afternoon as we stood among the ruins of a village in the Shenandoah mountains. "They wrecked everything!"

"These people died out through their own folly. They did not heed the Teacher's warning against Mogro.* Their daughters were born sterile."

"The barbarians—the bandits—where did they come from?'"

"Survivors who became savages. They kidnapped women from the Settlements."

"Kidnapped? I've read some Settlements gave away fertile girls."

"Apostate Settlements! They traded women like cattle!" I found myself shaking. "There—across the valley—Sherando —the most evil—!"

"Cool it, Diana! That place was blasted seventy years ago. It's no problem. Our problem's the druj They practice every atrocity except rape. Why? They're all males."

"Because they're devils, and so without sex. Druj is old Persian for devil. They're not born—they germinate! They're the children of Evil!"

"Diana, on some things you're plain crazy! The druj, they're manic. But somebody rational is in control."

"Ahriman—the Lord of the Lie!"

"Oh, for God's sake!" He stood brooding, the snow drifting around us. "Whoever it is, we've got to kick him back to Hell."

On that we were agreed, and he began to grudge every hour we spent at Ive, every day we were not ranging over the wilderness. His zeal coincided with an invasion of the base by contractors and workmen, for the Guard had been asked to make Ive operational and the Guard sees safety in numberless details. The engineers restored the fortifications, installed a command center, a remote-access computer terminal, micro-linkages, and garrison support facilities. The Quartermaster shipped us the stores, ammunition, and assorted paraphernalia to outfit a fortress manned by a company.

The garrison never reached that strength. Ive was almost

* "Mogro" was the trade name of the insecticide; "Bacan" the cancer prophylactic; "Noncon" the contraceptive. All were Impermease, the miracle drug which stopped cell division. In insect pupa, in cancer cells, in the ovaries of a female fetus!

thirty kilometers from the frontier and the Guard needed men to cope with druj raids farther south. During the renovations we had a platoon under a sergeant, but before the work was completed this was reduced to a squad under a corporal. Captain Gart avoided everybody and kept away from the fortress by initiating patrols of three or four days. We would pick a safe campsite such as the Pinnacle, stay there for the night, and get under way at dawn. This allowed us to extend our range westward and use all the short hours of winter daylight.

We also established what he called "emergency dumps" of fuel, food, and ammunition. These seemed redundant, for Search and Rescue was the most efficient of the Guard's operations and its SR ships the only ones that would fly over the wilderness. But I accepted them, as I accepted many of his unorthodox ideas, because I had never before served with such a dedicated* officer; one who preferred the hardships of the winter wilderness to the comforts of base.

He was an exemplary companion. He did a share of the chores and never made an indecent move, even when he had been away from Kate and Sue for almost a week. We spent our days together in the cutter and our nights in a small tent hitched to it; our intimacy made me realize the extent of his amnesia. It was simplest for me to assume that I had to reeducate him in almost everything.

But what he had lost in information he had gained in flexibility. His amnesia forced him to originality and showed me the rigidity of my own thinking. Because Pilots may have to face unpredictable situations we are limited by fewer intellectual constraints than most people. He seemed to have lost all his and the effect on me was to loosen mine, for as his trust in me grew he began to talk.

I have served with officers who never stopped talking and officers who spoke only in grunts. In general I prefer the latter, for Patrol Officer monologs are usually obscene, boastful, or maudlin. They talk only about themselves. Captain Gart would talk about everything except himself, and he would draw me into conversation so that I found myself discussing with him topics which were not my concern.

---

* *Dedicated to avoiding everybody, keeping away from Ive, and preparing the escape hatch for what I still thought was inevitable—the day when my cover was blown.*

One evening while I was undressing and he had crawled into his sleeping bag, he said, "Owen phoned just before we left. He's going on leave. Place called Parnesia. Know it?" He glanced at me and then looked quickly away He was meticulous in respecting my modesty.*

"On the Mediterranean. Sector Eight. I went there once."

"Have I been there?"

"You certainly have!" I searched through the document case and found his pay account. "Here—eighteen months ago. You were in Parnesia two weeks and you spent a year's pay."

He tried to look at the account without looking at me, and scowled at the figures. He was cavalier about money, there was little use for it at Ive, and I kept all our accounts. "Must have been quite a party. Pity I can't remember. Diana, you don't seem to approve?"

"Parnesia's excessive. Even for a Sybariticum in a free-enterprise Sector."

"Free-enterprise Sector? What do you mean?"

"Sector Eight is uncurbed capitalism. The least-regulated in the world. It also has more brothels than all the other Sectors put together. Parnesia's a favorite for Patrol Officers on leave. And you know their tastes!"

He flushed. "Reclue me on Sector economics "

"Most have mixed internal economies; like here in Ten. Government handles large operations. Private enterprise the smaller ones. Agriculture's private. That seems the mix most people prefer."

"But there are other kinds?"

"Almost every economic system ever imagined has been tried somewhere or another. Only the ones that work well enough to satisfy the narod last. I suppose you've never been to Six?"

"I don't think so. Why?"

"It's doctrinaire Marxist. No private ownership at all. Also no brothels or bars. I go there for the skiing. Lots of good skiiers."

"And lots of police!"

"Police? What's good skiing got to do with police?"

"To keep the healthy narod in line."

* *Diana gave me every opportunity to respect it!*

"The only Sector with a large police force is Parnesia. The wardens are enough to handle the drunks in most Sectors. They're not very energetic any place. In Six the job's a sinecure. People who don't like Marxism simply move to a Sector they do like. Surely you remember that basic? Anybody can move anywhere at any time. If you want to sell out the Sector, government has to buy. A Sector that tries to push people around too much would soon find itself bankrupt and depopulated."

"Yes—of course." He lay on his back, frowning up at the roof of the tent. "And the Sector economies interlock. No Sector manufactures a complete anything or grows everything it needs."

"That's another basic. In the United Settlements no Sector can be independent of the others."

"And nobody can fiddle the piaster! A contented commonality!" He laughed. "It's unnatural. Simple-minded Utopian economics. It can't work! But it does. Why?"

"Because it's common sense."

"That's never sufficient reason for anything human. The narod are contented all right. Because of that Paxin stuff? No—it's not as simple as that. Before this druj business started, most of 'em seemed positively happy "

"Why shouldn't they be? They have everything reasonable human beings could need. If they want more they can get it by working for a higher classification. Any narod with brains and ambition can make autarch. If they want to fight they can join the Guard."

"So everybody's happy except misfits like you and I, Diana?"

"I did not join the Order to be happy. And I don't think that was your reason for transferring to the Patrol. As for most autarchs—I doubt they are happy. They are rotten with nepotism and cursed with ambition."

Captain Gart grunted. "It's all so inefficient. But it works." He lay brooding as I drifted toward sleep, then jerked me back by his sudden exclamation. "Wealth! Any system'll work if you're rich!"

"But most people aren't rich."

"I mean our civilization's so damned rich. We're seventy millions. We've inherited the wealth of twelve billions. Metals for example. Veralloy lasts for almost ever, so things don't wear out. You told me our cutter was built more than forty years ago. And even for the others—we don't have to mine an ounce of ore—a gram of ore," he corrected himself. "Scrap from the old cities'll keep us going for a thousand years. Same with power stations, fuel, guns, every damned thing. The Affluence built like mad and stored like crazy. Cocooned to last. That's how they kept their overheated economies going. Better than wasting stuff in a war, I guess. But we've inherited it all. Ratio's two thousand to one."

"In those terms—yes, we're rich," I said slowly. I had never thought of it in those terms.

"So we'll never have to build another nuclear power station. But some things we may have to build. And when we do—will we remember how?"

I sat up, startled by his vehemence. And by the concept behind it. "What do you mean?"

"Well—for example, the met satellites we inherited have worn out, one by one." He ignored my bare breasts in his excitement. "Will we ever put anything into orbit again? I'll tell you this. There isn't a mathematician in the world today who can handle topological transformations." He dropped back onto his pillow.

It was absurd for a Patrol Officer to criticize the competence of the mathematicians, but I continued to sit, considering what he had said. None of it was my responsibility. There were people trained to deal with such problems. But who were the people concerned? The frequent failures in recently built equipment was a fact I had observed too often. Our cutter was forty years old because I had used my seniority to insist that I got a combat cutter built in the 2130's, the last decade when they built to absolute specifications. Did they build combat cutters any more? Did they know how?

By the time I realized I did not have an answer to his question it did not matter. Captain Gart was asleep. I lay awake for another ten minutes, worrying about something that was nothing to do with me.

V

February 2171

Ive had been restored to operational status by the third week in February and the Corporal's squad was withdrawn. We had the fortress to ourselves, and we began to spend our nights there, which pleased the girls and gave me time to maintain our equipment properly.

We continued our patrols during the day and returned one evening to find a signal from the Director of Security waiting for Captain Gart. He read it with obvious alarm. "Diana, this is from that autarch I told you about. The one who visited me in hospital. He wants me to call him back. Do I have to?"

"A Director of Security can ask the Patrol for support."

"Ask? Or order?"

"It's usually the same. Most Patrol officers have records they don't want reviewed."

"And I guess I've got one like that?"

"You have!" I was no longer astonished by the extent of his memory defect, although forgetting Parnesia and much else in his past was probably due to psychological defense rather than neurological damage. "Your record now is much better than it was."

"'But I'd be smart to do what this Shapur wants?" When I nodded he stood crumpling the signal in his hand. "Dregs of the Guard! The rest—they despise us."

"Not you. Not any more. But the Guard will distrust the Patrol as long as it gets involved in local politics. That's anathema to the Marshals."

"I've got no choice." He cursed. "Politicians make us shovel their shit. Then the Guard says we stink!"

His metaphor was crude but apt. Most Patrol officers welcome political involvement for they usually profit. Pilots cooperate for the practice, provided the act itself is within the Code. But I did not mention the limitations on what I could do, for the Captain was already confused and the ethics are complex situational. "Shall I get Shapur on the circuit?"

He nodded. "And monitor what he says." We were in our new command room surrounded by extension phones, but Captain Gart was still unsure about how to access the civilian communication system. I tapped out the return call code and heard the voice of Shapur; an accent which marked him as an autarch by birth as well as achievement.

"Gart, here's another job for those damned Ecclesiarchs. Copy the details."

"Go ahead, sir." He made scribbling motions at me.

"Place called Sherando—"

"Hold it!" He covered his mouthpiece. "Diana—what's wrong?"

"Later!" I was annoyed that he had seen my reaction.

He shrugged. "Sorry, sir. Sherando you said? The old Settlement?"

"That's it. Somewhere in the Shenandoah Valley. February twenty-eighth. The Ulama want it watched all morning. As a precaution. They're not expecting anybody, but they say it's a rendezvous for returning pilgrims. God knows why they picked Sherando. Or why a pilgrim can't walk back to civilization on his own feet. But I've got to humor those fanatics."

The Captain was rubbing his forehead. "Sorry to ask this, sir. But that crash—affected my memory. What happens if a pilgrim does turn up?"

"Evacuate him to Ive. Then call me. But don't call unless you've got somebody. And Gart, I've heard about your amnesia. It's improved your performance. But cut down the heroics. You're acquiring a reputation. That makes you more useful. But I'd have no use for a dead hero."

"Sir, the druj—"

"Marshal Mitra says you're doing a good job. But I've got my own jobs for you. So don't get killed doing his."

"Sir, the Guard—"

"I know you enjoy blood-sports Gart. But if you overindulge I can have you grounded. Remember that!" A click as Shapur hung up.

"Arrogant bastard! Does he think we hunt druj for fun? And there haven't been any to hunt for six weeks! Diana, don't look so shocked. You know we both get a kick—" He stared at me, then stepped over. "What's wrong?"

"Sherando! The apostate Settlement!"

"Oh, that! I thought it was the suggestion that we might enjoy our work. Got a guilty conscience about Sherando, too?"

"Of course not!" Very few things can make me angry when I am on duty but being patronized by a brain-damaged Patrol Officer was one of them.

He put his arm around my shoulders which was a worse insult, but one I accepted because he meant it kindly. "Sherando's only a pile of ruins. We've flown past it often enough. Nothing there. And no druj around—yet."

"It's a nidus of Evil."

"Christ! It was sterilized seventy years ago." He frowned. "Ecclesiarch? Am I supposed to know what an Ecclesiarch is?"

"An Ecclesiarch is a religious leader. No, you might not. You're a Christian. And Christians are notorious for religious ignorance!"

"Me? A Christian? Why do you call me that?"

"Because you're always invoking the name of your Savior."

"Oh, for God's sake!" He walked to the wall, studied the map, then swung on me. "The Ulama? It's a bunch of Ecclesiarchs?"

"Yes."

He waited. When I did not expand he grumbled, "They're preachers?"

"Some call them that."

"Why's Shapur surprised they'd use Sherando as a pilgrim pickup?"

"Have you read its history?"

"Some kind of religious row." He shrugged. "They closed it down."

"It was the most powerful Settlement in America, probably in the world. It survived the chaos by trading women. It bought off its enemies with fertile girls!"

He laughed, and I nearly knocked him out. He saw my hands turn and stepped back. "Cool it, Di!"

"Sherando refused to aid the other Settlements when they were weak and struggling. After they were strong and united it was declared apostate. It was cursed. It is still cursed."

"They smashed it."

"The Order took revenge for the women Sherando sold. The Order will never allow such infamy. We are strong enough—"

"So your Order got revenge. But did it get the women?"

"I don't know." I had become too tense for rational discussion. "I'll fetch you the record. That should give the details."

He was playing with the computer terminal when I came back with "Sector Ten: Origin and Development." He tried to push it aside, but after I had pointed out to him that if he was going to get mixed up in Sector politics he had better know something about the Sector he took it off to his room.

He brought it down to breakfast the next morning and dropped it on the table. "Hard to pick up once put down. Neat censorship!"

"What do you mean? The truth's all there."

"In exquisite detail. Who the hell would struggle through this unless someone like you was on his tail?" He ruffled the leaves. "A thousand-page battle between text and footnotes. With time out for tables, graphs, maps, statistics, and irrelevant information. But no index! A real work of scholarship. Took me half the night to extract the Sherando story. Never done it without your nagging." He poured himself coffee and lit one of the cheroots he had started to smoke. "That's smart censorship. Hide the facts in the data."

I left the table and opened the window. Cheroots before breakfast! "But you did find the truth about Sherando?"

"Most of it." He came and stood beside me, looking across the courtyard toward the winter mountains. "Those Elders! Did you know they had pull in Washington and Richmond before the chaos started?"

I shook my head. To me those were only the dim names of vanished cities.

"The Elders had political pals all over. My guess is that they were dealing in fertile girls from way back. With the right people. Sherando was the only Settlement to get police protection while there were still police. They had warehouses of weapons for after the police faded. By the end of the chaos they controlled the Valley. Do you realize why they wouldn't help the other Settlements?"

"Because they were evil!"

"Because they were smart. They had it made. Well dug in.

Huge supplies. Plenty of fertile land. And a surplus of fertile
women. They planned to wait until the other Settlements
went under. Then they'd have inherited the eastern sea-
board."

"They were heretics. Schismatics!"

"They had allies. On other continents too. They claimed to
be orthodox. It was losing that made them heretics."

"They lost because they were evil. Only a few Settlements
went heretic."

"The Guard closed 'em. Their leaders bolted to Sherando.
It was—"

"A nidus of evil. The truth crushed Sherando. The Order
destroyed it. The Order is the Sword of Truth!"

"Now, maybe. In those days it was a bunch of female fanatics on Naxos. The Guard, a gang of successful merce-
naries based on Malta. The Patrol—the offspring of their
union. No wonder we're tainted!"

There was much truth in what he was saying. I sighed and
turned from the window. "The Patrol was not always as it is.
Our team is as good as any that ever was. And the Guard has
courage."

"But few brains." He walked back to the table and picked
up the book. "For example, there's a clue here about the druj
they haven't noticed." He thumbed through the pages; he was
right about the difficulty of finding anything in that packed
thicket of small print. "See—first reported druj raid. In the
Shenandoah Valley. Just after the Elders rode west."

"Sherando was famous for its breed of horses."

"You miss the point. When your Order started to attack in
strength the cadre took off. Then the druj appeared. Everybody was too busy fighting druj and evacuating survivors to
go after the Elders."

He was suggesting that Ahriman had sent his devils to
cover the retreat of his sermants. I read further in the report.
"What is also interesting," I said presently, "is that the druj
disappeared within a few months."

"Doesn't that support my hypothesis?"

I hadn't heard any hypothesis. "Druj have appeared at various times, in other parts of the world, since then."

"I don't think so, Di." He shook his head slowly. "I've read
the reports of those so-called druj raids. They're all within
the range of human brutality. A broad enough range. But

druj cruelty's unique." He walked back to the window and stared again at the mountains. "I think they've appeared only twice. Both times in the Shenandoah Valley. Once after the Elders evacuated. And now!"

He canceled the patrol for that day and returned to the computer terminal. I found him attempting to solve a set of partial differential equations by numerical methods, inserting trial constants and cursing the results. He mumbled about optimizing our search patterns in terms of time and fuel. I told him there were stored programs for such tasks and that the model he was using was unsuitable. I offered to show him the appropriate algorithm but he told me to go and screw my servos.

Instead I spent the day rechecking the cutter's hydraulics and later, when I looked in at the terminal, he was scrawling "Recurrent Error—Two" on a printout. He scowled when he saw me in the doorway, and snarled that I needed a bath.

I was in one when he walked into my bathroom, waved his cheroot at the steam, and sat down on the john. For once he ignored my nudity and looked at me. "Diana, what did your Prioress tell you about my job? Before she shipped you out?"

"That you were in the hospital after a crash that had killed your Pilot. That I was to replace her."

"What else did she say? Go on, girl! I can read you now. You always tell the truth, but you rarely tell all of it!"

He called me "girl" when he was unsure of himself. I gave him what he had asked for. "The Prioress said that normally the Order would have refused to assign a replacement Pilot of any rating to an officer with your record. Certainly not a Pilot of the First Class."

He blasphemed. "And to what do I owe that honor?"

"The omens suggested you are a nexus in the reticulum."

"A what?"

"A center of likely action," I explained.

"From omens? Does your Prioress post you Pilots according to what she finds in the guts of goats?"

"The omens are conditional probability forecasts based on Bayesian statistics."

"The read-out of some sacred computer's replaced the liver of some holy cow, eh?"

"The omens aid the Synod in its decisions. The omens

identified you. They seem to have been accurate. You've certainly been at the center of action."

He chewed his cheroot. "That's all you know?"

"About your duties and the reason for my posting? Yes."

"What about your duties? What instructions did she give you?"

"Only the General Exhortation: To defend the Light against the Darkness, Truth against the Lie, Good against Evil."

"Did they really condition that bull into you?"

"Faith is not a conditioned response. The Truth shines by its own Light. My faith comes from logic. Not from brainwashing or emotion!"

"Christ!" He stared at me. "A Jesuit with tits"*

We flew reconnaissance over Sherando the next day. Desolated seventy years before it sat barren and brooding by a man-made lake, circled by great earthen ramparts on which only coarse grass and hardy weeds now grew. The surrounding fields which had once been among the most fertile lands in the valley were still treeless; the forest came only to their edge.

"They sowed it with salt!" muttered Captain Gart, peering down.

"Not salt. Powdered permac."

"Modern and more effective. God—what a maze!"

The Settlement was a warren of roofless houses. The plaza was bare, its sterile surface swept by the winds of seventy winters, dead leaves blown from the forest piled against its walls. Opposite the main gates, a large building had been mined by the sappers and lay in ruins. In the southeast corner, near the ramparts, stood a concrete platform with two veralloy posts rising from it.

The place sent up a miasma of evil which made my skin prickle, but which he did not seem to notice. We circled and took pictures. The light snow on the surrounding fields was unmarked by tracks; even the deer did not approach Sherando.

We returned at dawn on the twenty-eighth of February,

---

* *I am sorry that Diana chooses to report my tasteless remark. But, except for her sex, she would have been an ideal postulant in the Society of Jesus during its more rigorous days.*

and this time he made me touch down on the rampart over-looking the lake. It was a cold and lifeless sunrise. We sat in the cutter watching for some unexpected pilgrim to come trudging out of the forest. Captain Gart began to fill the cabin with the stench of his cheroots, so that I was finally forced to get out and walk along the rampart, struggling with the depression which hung like a cloud over the ruins.

Presently he joined me and was almost jovial. "Cheer up, Di! There's nothing hiding down there." He studied the buildings behind us while I watched the edge of the forest. The dangers were spiritual and those he could not sense.

Suddenly he touched my arm. "Recognize those things?"

I looked unwillingly. He was pointing to the concrete platform below us in the corner of the plaza. "Maybe—some kind of an altar?"

"An altar!" He laughed. "And those metal things stuck into it?"

"Religious symbols, perhaps. These people were heretics."

"Religious symbols! That's an idea. Like a cross?"

"Could be. I don't know."

"You may be close, Di." He gripped my arm. "On the right—a gallows! I've seen men hanged from things like that."

I was startled. "How could you? There have been no executions for generations. Capital punishment was abolished—"

"On the left—a whipping post! Look, the manacles are still there."

"It's of veralloy, so it will last—"

"Never seen one used. Not a post built for the job!" He stood staring down at the plaza. "Now I know why they had surplus girls to trade."

"How?"

"Hanged the men who objected."

I looked at the post and recognized he was right about its purpose. "I've seen whipping posts in museums. Before the chaos—they were common."

"In America? Like hell they were! The bastards." He was studying the walls in the corner of the plaza. "See those holes? This corner was filled with stands. This is where they put on public entertainments. And got their kicks!" He scowled. "A man kicks when he's hanged!"

"So does a woman. There's a famous line in Homer. When Ulysses hanged the maids."*

"Homer? For God's sake!" He stood gazing toward the lake, as though a pilgrim might suddenly appear walking on the water. We spent a morning of cold watching. Nothing happened. There were flurries of snow. Gray clouds rolled along the crests of the Blue Ridge mountains. Beyond the barren fields the bare branches of the forest waved and moaned. The lake rippled, deep and dead. Not even reeds grew around its margins. There was only mud between the black water and the brown grass.

At noon he sighed. "That's it. We'll wait another couple of hours—in case some hadji is late!" He strolled up and down the ramparts, ate the sandwiches I made, drank more coffee, smoked more cheroots, and when the ghost of the sun was dropping toward the Shenandoah Mountains he said, "I'm going to walk round that lake."

I did not want to be left alone on the ramparts, so I followed him across the fields and down to the frozen shore. He walked slowly, studying the ground. The mud was black and smooth, quite different from the red earth of the Valley, and was unmarked by birds or animals. Nothing drank from the waters of Sherando. His mood was as black as the mud, and I stayed well behind him. About halfway around the lake he stopped to kick at a frozen mound, then suddenly bent to crumble some of it between his fingers. "Manure!" he said as I joined him. "A horse!"

I sniffed the dried stuff. "At least a year old. Probably two."

He began casting around, then called, "Diana, what do you make of that?"

I knelt to examine a spoor in the frozen mud. "A hoofmark."

"Anything else?"

"An old mark. Probably the same horse that dropped the manure. Sherando was noted for its horses. There are still some running wild in the Valley."

"Are wild horses shod?"

---

* *"They kicked their heels awhile, but not for long."* Diana insisted on showing me the quotation that evening as an example of male brutality. Her Order taugh its Pilots nothing without a purpose, not even Homer!

I looked more carefully. Now that he had pointed them out I saw marks in the spoor that could be nails. "No," I said, standing up. The implication was absurd. "So this one could not have been."

He moved toward the lake and found another mark, but did not call me to inspect it. "That horse came from the lake. But as long ago as two years?"

"The spoor's above the water-level. It's well-weathered. So it could be two years."

He stared at the lake. Then he said, "Let's get to hell back to Ive."

I was glad to go.

VI

Vernal Equinox

Spring was coming but the druj had not yet returned when Shapur phoned a second time. We had started a patrol southward down the valley to pick up any sign of their approach when his call came through on the Guard net.

"Gart, I've got an escort job for you. Come now. About forty-five kilometers southeast of Ive. Here's the reference."

Captain Gart punched the position into the navigator while I changed course. "A prechaos villa," Shapur continued. "Farm a kilometer away. You'll see my cutter parked behind the house. Land near and come in."

"Escort what, sir?"

"I'll explain when you get here. And come fast!" Shapur broke contact.

I was checking the index. "That villa belongs to the Director of Special Services."

"Rajuna!"

"You've met her?"

"Once. In the hospital. She came with Shapur."

"She's a talented woman."

"She's a prize bitch!" He studied the rich farmlands below for a few minutes, then asked, "What's her last name?"

"She no longer has one. And don't ask her what it was. She'd take it as an insult."

"Good God!" He digested this. "What's wrong with asking her name?"

"Autarchs, like Ecclesiarchs and Pilots, get a new name, a single name, when they take their oath. The oath is supposed to break all family ties. But these days many autarchs make family compacts. Rajuna's father, for example, was once gov-

52

ernor of this Sector. She became an autarch by her own ability. But she'll be hypersensitive to any hint of nepotism."

"So she's beautiful, bright, and blue-blooded!" He laughed. "Diana, what's your family name?"

"I don't remember. Memory returns with debriefing. But I know I'm the daughter of a sea captain, a Master Mariner. I come from a seafaring—"

"So you've often told me! Another aristo! Who called you Diana?"

"It's my initiation name." I banked hard. "There's Shapur's cutter, the one wearing a Director's colors. Parked by the orchard." I circled the lovely old house standing among lawns and gardens.

"Plush!" murmured Captain Gart. "So that's how the autarchs live!"

"The ostentatious ones, like Rajuna."

"You know a lot about her?"

"She's six years older, but at twelve she was upper tenth top percentile. As I was later. Few children in the whole world classify so high, and they tell us about our predecessors."

He laughed. "And briefing doesn't block that memory. Your Order—"

I interrupted. "Shall I land, sir?"

He nodded, so I skidded low over the trees, checked, hung, dropped and touched silently to show any watching autarch how a combat cutter could perform when flown by a Pilot of the First Class.

"Grand-standing again!" grumbled Captain Gart as we walked toward the house where an agitated steward, obviously timid, was waiting to show us into the library.

It was a long room with three walls of glass and one of books. A pair of autarchs were at the far end; Shapur talking on the telephone and Rajuna staring out toward the farm. Both glanced at us as we were announced.

Captain Gart saluted. Shapur nodded and went on talking. Rajuna gave a correct bow with the hint of the voltairian smile some autarchs affect. She was wearing a tight green gown, intricate with gold embroidery. Her black hair was elaborately dressed, jewels flashed from her fingers, her ears, and her autarch pistol. She epitomized the elegance, the ability, and the atavism of her class. Her perfume was one that few men would notice but to which most would respond. She studied the Captain; I smelled him starting to sweat.

Neither of the autarchs acknowledged me. Shapur snapped, "Mansur—get them going!" hung up the telephone, and walked toward us. He was of about the Captain's age and height, but slimmer, and moved with grace and strength. His jumpsuit was gray and his pistol filagreed. "Gart, you remember the Director of Special Systems?"

"Yes, sir." The Captain gave an uncertain bow toward Rajuna.

"She wants some important stores moved. Loaded in a gev—parked in that farm. A crew's standing by. Ten Wardens are coming from Maylan as escorts. You're to strengthen them."

"You mean—overfly the gev, sir?"

"Overfly? No—no. I want you in it. And your girl." He glanced at me, an indirect acknowledgment. I am usually invisible to autarchs and I ignore them.

"Sir, you must be expecting—"

"Not expecting. But an attempted hijack is possible. You are a precaution. Your orders are simple. If anybody tries to stop the gev—shoot!"

"But not to kill," added Rajuna.

"Ma'am, in a crunch, it's hard—"

"Ma'am!" She laughed. "How delightfully archaic! Captain, my name's Rajuna."

"He is archaic," said Shapur. "Like his trade."

"Sorry, my lady—Rajuna—" He lifted his hand to his face. "Brains got scrambled in that crash. Don't always say the right thing."

"Your brains may be scrambled but your behavior's improved!" snapped Shapur. "If you're attacked, kill as many as you like. I know Raji—we'll have to cooperate with Sila afterward. But he's dangerous. Some dead friends might discourage him."

"The gev, sir, where's it to go?"

"You'll be radioed after you're on your way."

"The cargo, sir?"

"Not your concern."

"It is if it's liable to explode!"

Rajuna laughed. "Captain, it's only explosive in the political sense." She had been enjoying the rising tension between the two men but had seen it might get out of hand. "Perhaps you should go and check the gev. It will be dark in an hour and the escort will be arriving soon."

"Yes, Gart—go and look over the damned thing." Shapur turned his back on us. "Raji—I have to talk with you before I leave. As soon as the gev's under way, come to Maylan. I'll need every Director's vote I can get if the Council—" He saw her glance at Captain Gart and snapped, "Go on, man! Go and check that machine!"

The Captain saluted and I followed him out of the library. We walked in silence until we reached the muddy lane leading to the farm, when he stopped, took off his helmet, and wiped his forehead. "Diana, I don't like this! The arrogant aristo! That bitch of a woman! We get jumped by some rival gang of politicos. I kill a few autarchs. Shapur'll let me be crucified if it suits him."

"No, sir. You're acting under his direct orders. They were clear. They are legal. And I have them on minidisc. Even if Shapur loses—we're covered."

"My God, Diana—you've been recording?"

"Of course. On such occasions I record everything for my report."

He looked relieved and replaced his helmet. We trudged up the lane and splashed across the farmyard. The gev was parked in a large open-ended barn. There was no sign of a crew. He stood staring at it. "Am I supposed to know about these things?"

"Their tactical use."

"I mean, can I drive one?"

"Some officers can. But not all."

"I suppose you can?"

"No. I've not been trained to handle gevs. The Order doesn't use them."

"Nice to find something you can't do." He looked at it for a few moments. "Crew's probably asleep." He let out a roar that would certainly have awakened them if they were. Nobody appeared. He cursed and clambered up into the cab. "Christ!"

"What?" I vaulted up beside him.

"That!" He was pointing to the name plate on the dash, the usual array of letters and numbers. He read aloud, "USMC—LVS—SKN27."

"A manufacturer's reference."

"Like hell! United States Marine Corps—Landing Vehicle Supplies." He looked around. "So this is what the corps built up to! Over a hundred and fifty years old."

"It's mostly veralloy. Should last a thousand. If properly maintained. Which this one is not." I tested the radio. "Inoperative." I looked more carefully. "Made inoperative."

"God, where's that damned crew?" He jumped down and went to search the buildings while I checked through the gev. There was a small galley behind the cab, and a two-bunk cubicle aft. Both were empty. The cargo hatches were battened down and locked. I met him in the yard as he came bursting from the farmhouse.

"Nobody there. The bastards have bolted. After faulting the radio. Better tell Shapur." He pounded down the lane toward the villa.

We were less than halfway when Shapur's cutter rose above the trees of the orchard and streaked northeast toward Maylan. By the time we reached the gardens Rajuna was walking back toward the house. She stopped when she saw us. "Are the Wardens here?"

"Wardens? No! But the crew's gone. After wrecking the radio."

Her voltairian smile faded. "So the coup's on! And before we expected. Sila's threatened the crew. Probably the Wardens also. He knows the cargo. He'll come to seize it."

"Ma'am—Rajuna—stay with us. You'll be safe in our cutter."

"I'll be safe in my own house, Captain. That's where Sila will expect me to stay." Her fingers clenched. "But I'll be damned if I'll sit and let that fool take over." She turned toward the farm. "It's the gev he wants. We must move it."

"I can't drive a gev. Neither can Diana."

"Can't she?" Rajuna looked directly at me for the first time. "Well, I can. Come on!" She started across the lawn and when her high heels sank into the turf she kicked off her shoes. A few steps later and she unzipped the side of her gown so she could run.

"Christ—a real snafu!" Captain Gart gave me a push. "Stay with her, Di. I'll fetch the guns."

We reached the gev as a ship appeared to the north. "Sila!" Rajuna snapped. She hitched her gown to her waist, swung up into the cab, and slid into the driver's seat. Her slim figure was due in part to a tight green girdle.

Captain Gart arrived loaded with ammunition and rifles. He tossed mine to me and climbed aboard as Rajuna started the turbines. He took the port turret and I the starboard so that we were both standing a little above and behind her, our heads out of the open hatches. She opened the throttles and the gev lifted onto its air-cushion, flinging a storm of dust and straw up into the barn. Then she checked her gauges and eased the vehicle out into the yard.

The ship had landed in a pasture by the farmhouse. Armed men were jumping from it. An autarch called and waved when the gev appeared. Rajuna fed power to the turbines and we surged across the yard and out onto the road.

The autarch fired a warning shot. Captain Gart replied with a burst over his head. The group scattered, going for cover. A slug bounced off the cab's armor.

"That's it!" called the captain, slamming down his hatch and crouching at his gun-port. "Go for their legs, Di!"

I tried to, but was only able to get a few shots away as we slewed past the ship. Then we were clear, accelerating down the narrow road, followed by random firing. Captain Gart opened his hatch and looked astern. "They're boarding their ship," he said to Rajuna. "What now?"

She did not answer but swung off the road, shattered a gate, and sent the gev dipping and skidding across open plowland, through two hedges, and out onto a lane. Then she stopped.

"What now?" repeated Captain Gart.

"I—I'm not sure. If Sila knew the pax was here, he probably knows where I planned to take it."

A silver cutter came low over the fields, saw us, and climbed to hang above the lane. "A spotter!" said the Captain, changing magazines. He put a line of tracer toward it. Then he shouted at Rajuna. "Keep moving. Any damn way you like. But don't sit on your ass waiting to be slammed!"

She started south down the lane. A second silver cutter came from the east and put a burst across our bows. It banked and made another pass, this time kicking up spurts of dirt around the gev. "If he tries again—zap him!" growled the Captain, starting to sight as the cutter began a third approach. "Straight and level! Fuckin' amateur!"

"And no armor!" I added, taking aim myself. As a target he was too easy to kill. Both of us must have felt the same, for both our bursts caught his tail. He went fluttering down beyond a clump of trees.

"Oh God!" gasped Rajuna.

"His rotors were parachuting," I reassured her. "He'll crawl out!"

Two more silver cutters arrived and joined the spotter, all staying at a safe range. The ship came up astern, made a detour as it passed us, and then dropped behind a low rise ahead. The lane dipped down. Captain Gart grabbed Rajuna's shoulder. "Right—girl—right! Go cross-country. Down there they'll block us. Right, I say!"

She glanced up, saw his face, and swung the gev. We went over the ditch, through the hedge, and across a green field of winter wheat. The three cutters closed, firing spasmodically, then dropped back at the threat of my tracer. The Captain was checking map and compass. "Steer two—one—five." When Rajuna hesitated. "Two fifteen degrees. Goddammit— southwest by south!"

"Two fifteen," said Rajuna calmly. "But why?"

"That ship's waiting till we're blocked. Then he'll take us. So head for the river."

"The river?"

"The James, girl, the James. About three thousand meters. Banks may give us cover. And for God's sake—keep this thing moving!"

Rajuna's hands tightened on the controls as she rammed the turbines to full ahead. The gev took up the motion of a badly trimmed tanker in a heavy seaway. The next time Captain Gart shouted, he picked his words with more care. "Slow now! River's ahead. Left—left—" He was conning from his open turret. "There's a way down. Take it easy!"

We lurched and dipped, slithered and straightened, then we were sliding through Johnson grass and mud. "Hard right!" called the Captain. "Good. Head upstream. Steady as she goes. Jeez! What a ride!"

The river was broad and shallow. We moved slowly over gravel, rocks and rushing water. The cutters made another attack but were the rankest of amateurs and only one burst hit our armor. I knocked the tail off the cutter that came closest and that finished their sortie.

A railroad bridge appeared ahead. The ship was sitting on it. Captain Gart grabbed the binoculars and cursed. "Rajuna—dead slow!"

She brought the gev almost to a halt in the middle of the stream. Our loss of way encouraged a cutter to try another pass. This time I fired to kill.

"Crew's strung out across the bridge. On the near rail. They're handing something out from a box. Charges!" He slammed the binoculars into their holder. "Blasting charges! They'll blast us if we try to run that bridge."

"But he wants the cargo. The pax—"

"That'll be okay. They'll just blast the cab. Sila's set to hunt us. And bomb us from the air."

"No—no! Not even Sila would do that!" She was still so conditioned by absurd autarch proprieties that she could not imagine a fellow autarch breaking them.

"Rajuna," said the Captain, speaking slowly to calm her while he searched the south bank of the river, "When men taste blood they act like greater fools and bigger bastards than you can imagine. Your friend Sila's got explosives in that ship. He's ready to use them. I'll not trust my neck to his sense of right conduct." He gripped her shoulder. "Over there! That pile of rocks. A way up. Try it." She hesitated and he exploded. "Try it, girl—try it! Or surrender—and let me fuck off home!"

The gev surged across the river under her anger. It went at the bank with a rush, like a Percheron trying to jump a gate. It smashed down reeds and bushes, lurched and reared as it took the slope, hung teetering on the lip. Then its bows slammed down onto the top of the levee and it spun to face upriver.

"Attagirl!" yelled Captain Gart. "Keep going. Along the bank. Fast—fast!" In language and behavior he was becoming more archaic with every round that bounced off our armor. He threw himself across the cab, cramming himself beside me on the starboard side. "Di—keep your gunport. I'll take the turret. Enfalade the cabron!"

Rajuna accelerated along the top of the levee toward the end of the bridge. Some of the men on it started to run. "Slow—dead slow. Now—stop! Stop on the tracks!"

The gev sat down. The whole length of the bridge was under our automatics. We swept it from end to end. The run-

ners were dropping, disappearing, jumping into the water.
The ship was shivering as our slugs shook it. Then it exploded. We crouched behind our armor as the debris rained
down.

"Take her ahead now. Easy! Easy!" Captain Gart was
stroking Rajuna's hair, gentling her. "No hurry." A cutter
came at us out of the dusk. "Diana—give that flyboy some
tracer. Rajuna, right. Down the bank. Slow and easy. That's
the ticket." He took his hand from her hair and straightened,
looking ahead from his turret. "Hard left! Upstream. Steady.
Good girl!" He patted her shoulder as he sometimes patted
mine after I had completed a maneuver well. "Keep moving."

The roar of the turbines came back from the banks and we
left a spume of mud and spray. The farmland on each side
changed to woods. "We're getting close to the wilderness,"
said Rajuna in a voice near shock.

"We're going into it. Safest place for the night. Your pals
won't come after us there." The hills began to rise black on
each side of the James and in the last of the twilight we
found an island with trailing sandbars. "Heave-to!" said the
Captain.

The gev put down with a sigh. Rajuna cut the turbines and
we sat for a moment in the sudden silence. "I'm going to
piss," said Captain Gart and climbed from the cab onto the
deck. There was the sound of him doing it. I wondered
whether his crudeness was natural or intentional.

Probably intentional. Rajuna was starting to shake and he
was trying to treat shock with shock. I began to recharge
magazines. Presently she whispered, "How many—how many
did we kill?"

"Not enough," called the Captain before I could give my
best estimate. He clambered back into the cab. "They were
about to blow us apart. Remember that before you go soft."
He slumped into the co-driver's seat. "Any way of getting a
signal to the Director?"

"Shapur may not be Director now!" She put her face in
her hands.

The sight of a woman with her face in her hands triggers
something primitive in Captain Gart. Several times when I
had been relaxing my facial muscles I had found myself
being comforted. He put his arm round Rajuna, squeezing
her. "Shapur'll be okay. I know a survivor when I see one.

And if it's Paxin you've got under those hatches—you've still got it. You'll be able to make a deal."

I suggested I scout the nearest farm and phone.

"Like hell! We're all staying here. Behind armor." He decided he had given Rajuna her quota of comfort, removed his arm from her shoulders, took off his helmet, and loosened his coveralls. "God—I wish I had a smoke!"

I thanked God he had not. A cheroot would have made the cab intolerable. The smell of Rajuna's perfume and the Captain's sweat was already too much. I said, "I'll check the vessel," and went on deck.

The gev was lying steady, the water creaming round her, far enough from the shore to prevent the approach of any enemy, druj or human. I went aft, listened to the wind and the waves, and lined up the silhouettes of two hills so a change in bearing would warn me if we started to drag an anchor during the night.

That was absurd! We weren't anchored. We were squatting on the bottom. But the deck, the darkness, the rushing water, reminded me of the nights when, as a young girl, my father had allowed me to take my turn at anchor watch. I blocked the errant memory and continued my patrol. By the time I got back to the cab Rajuna had her head on Captain Gart's shoulder and he was stroking her hair.

"There's a sleeping cubicle aft," I suggested. "Rajuna, why don't you lie down? Sir, show her. You know where it is."

She spoke to me directly for the first time. "Thank you, Diana. But I'll take my turn at staying awake."

"Leave that to us. You must sleep. You're our only driver. And tomorrow you may have to drive with the same skill as you drove today." I turned to the Captain. "I'd prefer the first watch, sir. Why don't you help her aft. The catwalk's narrow. The light's on in the cubicle and the hatch is open."

Neither argued. Captain Gart handed her out of the cab and guided her through the darkness as they edged aft. I saw him help her through the hatch into the cubicle. Her gown was again hitched up around her waist. Her tight girdle had been loosened. Her slim legs and smooth thighs reflected the light from the hatch. Captain Gart followed her down the ladder and dropped the cover behind him.

I stood in the darkness of the foredeck, waiting for night vision to develop. When the outlines of the banks had become clear I started to make rounds. I went aft along the cat-walk past the cargo hatches and when I reached the stern I could see well enough to scan the river downstream. It was too swift and rocky for anything but another gev to approach.

I turned to go for'rd, and saw the small port which neither Rajuna nor Captain Gart could have noticed, for she had taken off her gown and he was helping her ease out of her girdle. I continued toward the bows.

On my next circuit they were both naked. After a fight Captain Gart was always hungry and Sue and Kate had told me how much pleasure he could give a woman when he put his mind to it. Rajuna was enjoying both his skill and his desire. Interest held me for several minutes.

It was an intellectual interest; an attempt to reconcile an absurd, undignified, and uncomfortable process with the delight which I could see it was giving. A delight I had enjoyed in the past and would again in the future. But to a Pilot on active service such behavior seems as unnatural as a hunger to breed instead of eat must be to a seasonal species outside its mating season. One knows how orgasm acts, but the sensation is as hard to recall as for an individual with cerebral blindness to remember color from her memories and a knowledge of physics.

But my last briefing was eight months back, and Captain Gart was more male than any man I had known. In retrospect I can see his effect on me from the increasing wordiness of my reports and my use of his archaic slang. That night, watching the Captain and Rajuna couple and recouple, I found thoughts about debriefing and leave starting to rise from my subconscious. I broke away and continued my patrol.

On my third circuit they were asleep in each other's arms. I let them sleep until dawn and then woke them with hot coffee. She thanked me, but Captain Gart, dragging on his clothes, complained because I had not called him to take his trick on deck. I bit back a remark to the effect that he had performed his tricks on the bunk. Sarcasm is not my forte when on active service, and my tendency toward it was another sign that my briefing was wearing thin.

We went down the river through the morning mist and came out of the wilderness as the sun was rising. As soon as we reached the first farm Captain Gart told Rajuna to pull the gev over to the bank and began issuing orders.

"Raji—move this thing out to midstream and wait there. If you hear shots or if I call on the com, shove off up river. Diana, have your rifle ready. You girls stay in the cab and keep closed-down till I get back."

"And while we girls are sitting in the middle of the James," asked Rajuna, "what will you be doing?"

"Contacting Shapur. If I can't I'll call Marshall Mitra and ask for a ship to lift us out. The Guard owes me that much."

"Then you'll need Shapur's access number. I hope he's still accessible!" She scribbled on a card and we watched him scramble up the bank and start across the fields toward the farmhouse. Then she moved the gev out onto a sand-spit, cut the turbines, and remarked, "Jan may be an overbearing bravo, but he doesn't seem the blackguard his record suggests. May I ask your opinion?"

"Only if you want the truth."

"I do. What kind of a man is he?"

"As a fighter, the most able officer with which I have ever served. I don't understand why his previous record was so bad. It is now excellent."

"Since you took him in hand!" She eyed me. "And as a man?"

"Like all men, but less selfish than most; less lazy and more sincere. Before authority, he either flinches or blusters—as you saw yesterday. When alarmed he tends to bully—as you saw just now! As a male? You know better than I!'"

She laughed. "But you respect him?"

"More than any man I have ever met. On duty or on leave."

"And you Pilots, you always speak the truth?"

"As we see it. If we speak at all."

"You must be uncomfortable people to have around!"

"Few who demand the truth really want to hear it."

"On Naxos, that's what they teach you? To fly, to shoot, to speak the truth?"

"And much else that is vital."

"It's vital to speak the truth?"

"Of course! Nobody challenges a perfect shot. Nobody

questions the word of a Pilot. So we are never challenged and always believed."

"And you give the rest of us shivers!" Rajuna shivered herself. "That's why we try to ignore you. Are you insulted?"

"No. We are what we are. People dislike being protected. They resent it when they know, and scorn it when they don't. You're on the Council, Rajuna, so you will understand."

"Yes, perhaps!" She fiddled with the control column. "When you're on leave do you tell people you're a Pilot?"

"On leave I am not bound by the same code. But I usually speak the truth; it becomes a habit. I try to avoid being asked. If a man learns I'm a Pilot he's liable to be repelled or fascinated. Usually for the wrong reasons."

"Would you meet Jan on leave?"

"No. He can't ski." I turned to look at her. "Rajuna, last night must be a single episode."

"You mean—" She bit her lip. "Did you imagine I'd take a Patrol Captain as a partner?"

"Captain Gart is an unusual man. He shows a superficial crudeness. Beneath, there is some kindness and real intellect. Devious and untrained. But far above the norm for his trade."

"He's also an accomplished lover!"

"So Sue and Kate tell me. They're his present partners."

"Why should you care if I take him? You're not estrous now, and you've just told me you won't see him when you are."

"Because there is danger ahead. You know that?"

"Of course I do! That's why I wouldn't move over for Sila. That's why I'm sitting in the middle of this damned river with a torn gown while that thug of yours goes blundering through farmyards. But what has danger got to do with my enjoying Jan?"

"He is the only first-rate soldier on this frontier. To become involved with you would ruin him."

"Ruin him? I could help him!"

"Your help would ruin him as a part of my combat team." She stared at me. "Diana—"

At that moment Captain Gart arrived on the bank, shouting and waving. He had left his communicator behind during his hurried dressing, and we had to wait for him to board to hear his news. "All over. Shapur's at Maylan. He's the new Lieutenant-Governor." He slid into the seat beside Rajuna. "Sila's dead. Killed when his ship crashed!" He laughed. She shivered.

We returned the way we had come, with a farmer yelling as we crossed his wheat field. "I'll see he gets damages," said Rajuna as she parked the gev in the barn. A squad of sheepish Wardens were waiting to act as guard. We climbed down and walked toward her villa. "Come to the house, Jan. Get cleaned up. Have some breakfast."

He hesitated, caught my eye, and checked his impulse. "We'd better drop out of the picture. "But—" He stepped forward.

"Jan!" She took a pace toward him, frowned, laid her hand on his arm. "You and I—it would not be—"

He put his arms around her, pulled her to him, kissed her on the mouth. She responded before she freed herself. Then she stood back and I smelled the sweat from both of them. "Perhaps—I am very grateful. Shapur is in your debt. In yours also, Diana."

They stared at each other. Rajuna commenced a formal bow, then turned suddenly and walked quickly away through the orchard.

VII

May 2171

During the winter we had planted sensors at strategic points in the wilderness, and these bore fruit in the spring. Three days after our rescue of Rajuna and her Paxin we detected the first druj moving up the Valley. They had been coming north with the sun, raiding sporadically and keeping the Guard busy, but when they reached our segment they stayed beyond the mountains.

By April we estimated there were more than a thousand concentrated near the western end of the Rockfish Gap. Captain Gart thought that their Master was preparing to send them through in strength. He alerted the Guard who increased their gev and gunship patrols but otherwise paid little attention to his warnings. Apart from druj raids the Guard was faced with a flare-up of old-fashioned banditry.

Our primary duty as a Patrol team was to monitor movements near the frontier. Captain Gart expanded our responsibility. When he saw how little effect our reports were having he started to warn the narod. We flew to every farm within forty kilometers of the Gap and advised the farmers to get ready to defend themselves. The foothills would soon be swarming with druj.

We had gained a local reputation from our successes in the fall, and the farmers accepted his warning but not his advice. Good land was available in safer Sectors. Rather than expose their families to death by torture they began to sell out and go. The government of Sector Ten was forced to buy, and this caused consternation in Maylan. Mansur, the new Director of Security, a squat man who reminded the Captain of a toad in tinted glasses, arrived at Ive to complain that we were starting a panic and upsetting the Sector economy.

66

Since shooting Sila and sleeping with Rajuna the Captain had lost his awe of autarchs and become contemptuous of Wardens. He took Mansur into our command center and showed him the concentrations of druj marked up on the displays. "They're slipping through the Gap already. Within a week hell's going to break lose."

Mansur left looking worried and promising to do all he could to persuade Marshal Mitra that a threat was building up. A Guard HQ Company was moved to Ive. Two days later the druj hit.

They hit along our whole segment in a drum-fire of raids. The Guard brought in every ship and gev available and, because Ive was operational, command was effective. By May the area was again clear and the druj were withdrawing across the Valley. The Guard would not cross the frontier except in hot pursuit, so we, as Patrol, were the only unit free to harry them. By this time we knew the trails they were using and, guided by our sensors, we were able to intercept many of their exhausted packs. Their Master continued to pull the survivors back in the Shenandoah Mountains, leaving only scouts around Sherando. One of them almost caught us when the Captain landed to check a cluster of planted sensors. I had to lift him out with slugs zipping past, and he chose to ride back to Ive on the skids.

A ship wearing the colors of the Governor was parked in the square and I saw Rajuna standing beside it as I came in to land. I touched gently and jumped down to check the Captain, for I had used overdrive for a fast lift-off. He unclipped his harness and then, as she walked toward us, he grabbed a strut and bent over, vomiting.

"Jan! Jan! Are you hurt?"

For the moment he was unable to speak so I answered for him. "Captain Gart usually throws up after a jump on the skids."

He straightened and wiped his mouth with the back of his filthy hand. "Diana treats it like an oil-change!" He winced and grabbed his side. "I'm okay. Bruised a rib, maybe. Welcome to Ive!" He smiled.

A smile on the Captain's damaged face was an alarming expression, but Rajuna smiled back. "Thank God! I thought you'd been wounded."

"That was last week!" He winced again. "Got another escort job?"

"No. But I've got an invitation from the Governor."

"The Governor?"

"Shapur's Governor now. You didn't know?"

"Too busy druj-hunting."

She grimaced. "I hope the need for that will soon be over. With Shapur Governor—" She broke off, then said, "He invited you to his first levee. When you didn't answer I came to discover why. He knows you're busy, but you'd be wise to come."

"A levee? Good God! When?"

"Today. His ship's here for you. I've told your servants to get your uniform ready."

"My uniform? Oh, of course." He hesitated, confused. "Better get cleaned up. Diana, please entertain the lady Rajuna while I'm changing." He started toward the house.

"The lady Rajuna!" She stared after him. "His etiquette's antiquated!"

"Or avant-garde." I invited her into the parlor. She probably guessed I had intercepted Shapur's letter, but however suspect her motives in coming to Ive I had to act the host. I poured her wine and she went to examine the Captain's expanding collection of books and microfiche. After a few minutes she remarked, "Jan's tastes are catholic."

"He claims to be some kind of a Christian."

"That is not quite what I meant!" She turned toward me, smiling. "But he does not share your religion?"

"He is a soldier. That is enough." Rajuna, like most autarchs, was probably an atheist. "I hope you remember my warning."

Her smile snapped off. "I remember your insolence! And I ask you to remember who I am."

"You are Rajuna, Director of Special Services. You have used your inheritance well."

"You impudent—" She stepped toward me, her hand falling to her pistol.

"I meant your genetic inheritance. I was not suggesting nepotism."

"You brainwashed brat! What right have you to warn me of anything?"

"Rajuna, we share the top percentile. We are of different

ages and we have followed different paths. But I can speak to you as an equal."

"You speak to me as a zombie! You dare to threaten me?"

"Not threaten—warn. If you seduce Captain Gart you will be harming our mission."

"Your mission! Hunting poor madmen for sport! You're worse than any druj."

"Rajuna, whether the druj are madmen or devils incarnate, they are the tools of Ahriman."

"Ahriman indeed! That primitive nonsense! Why am I standing here listening to insulting bombast from a dehumanized girl?"

"Because we saved your Paxin and Shapur's life. Because you may need us again. So remember, I do not care who runs this Sector. Nor how many autarchs shoot each other in your selfish squabbles. We will help you only if by helping you we are also defending civilization."

"You will help only— You talk as though you're in command."

"Captain Gart is always in command. But control shifts with information. Whoever has the information must make the decision."

"And that is you?"

"Only on occasion."

"How interesting! And does your Captain realize that you take over when you judge it necessary."

"Implicitly, yes. Explicitly, no. And he wouldn't believe you if you told him. He is flexible in some things, rigid in others. He patronizes or pities me as a poor conditioned girl. But he has his share of male hypocrisy. He is ready to use my skills for his own advantage."

"When, in fact, you are using him?"

I shrugged. "We both serve the Light. And although he will not admit it, he too believes in Good and Evil."

"What a mass of contradictions you are! I'm beginning to understand why your Synod arranges for blackguards to be posted to the Patrol. Murderous fools whom they think you Pilots can manage."

"Captain Gart is no blackguard!"

"Diana! My poor Diana! We share more than the same percentile. You are as proud as I am. And quite as jealous."

"That is absurd! Pilots on duty cannot feel jealousy."

"Well—you're feeling something, so you're still human."
She laughed, then frowned. "It's disgraceful that your Order
is still allowed to turn idealistic young girls into murderous
Amazons!"

"Perhaps. But today you saw something of the risks we
take. Both of us have been wounded in the last month. The
druj are real and their acts are evil. There are women and
children alive who, but for us, would have been tormented to
death."

"I don't question your courage or your competence. It is
the use to which they are being put that I detest. For the moment it may be necessary. But more important than hunting
druj is to end the need to hunt them. That, Diana, is my aim
on the Council."

"Then there is no conflict between us. Why did you come
here?"

"Not to seduce your Captain, as you seem to suspect.
Seduce—what a delightfully old-fashioned ring that word has!
Diana, you are starting to talk like him."

"Then why did you come?"

"To help him." She walked to the window. "In the gev you
called Jan extraordinary. He is. Do you realize how few able
men there are in the Sector?"

"I have yet to meet one."

"Jan has a native ability. He is uncouth, blustering, educated only for his task." She glanced toward the bookshelves.
"Though he seems more literate than I had realized." She
turned toward me, "In short, my dear, he deserves a better
future than flying over the wilderness shooting at maniacs."

"Or of being Shapur's gunman. Rajuna, don't infect him
with your ambition. That is a disease of autarchs. Whether he
knows it or not Captain Gart is in the service of the Light.
And the Light needs champions now that Ahriman has ap-
pealed to arms."

Rajuna slowly shook her head. "Your absurd religion!
When I said help him, I mean help him. I am a Member of
the Council."

"You are more than that. You are probably the most gifted
autarch in this Sector. Help him to do his duty and you will
have my gratitude and hold me in your future debt. Harm
him—and you will answer to me!"

She held her hand, ignoring the insult. Then I saw her eyes widen. Captain Gart was standing in the doorway.

Apart from his face he is a fine figure of a man, and he wears a uniform well. That afternoon he wore it better than usual, for Kate had put an elastic support around his chest to ease his cracked rib, and so prevented him from dropping into his usual round-shouldered slouch. Also the girls had made sure that his turn-out at the Governor's levee would do us all credit. His epaulets gleamed, his buckles shone, his buttons were buffed, his leathers had a high polish. I had never seen him in such splendor.

Kate and Sue had dressed him up to impress the Governor. They had certainly not considered what effect his appearance might have on Rajuna; autarchs of her rank do not consort with Captains in the Patrol. But her expression and a whiff of her sudden sweat told me her mind and her glands were responding to something more intriguing than a Patrol Captain. Whatever may have been her intentions when she arrived, her physiology was in control when she left.

I tried to warn him, but he waved me away and walked with her to the ship. Kate and Sue stood chattering excitedly as we watched it rise and head east toward Maylan. I went to my room, troubled by Rajuna's remarks, her reactions, and my own emotions.

The girls stayed up late that night, picturing the glories of the Governor's levee, and waiting eagerly for Captain Gart to describe them on his return. He did not return for three days, and when he did the traces of Rajuna's perfume told us he had spent the nights with her. There was a stormy scene, with Sue describing him in extreme terms, the Captain defending himself in embarrassed confusion, and Kate weeping quietly in the background. It culminated in my having to fly Sue back to her father's farm in the middle of the night.

He came to me in the morning, still protesting his ignorance. "What the hell's eating Kate? What got into Sue? What have I done that's so dreadful?"

"Only behaved like most Patrol Officers would if given the chance! But Sue's a decent girl and won't stand for it. Kate's kinder. I've persuaded her that your actions were partly due to your brain damage."

"My brain damage!" He towered over me. "Diana—I'll damage you if you don't tell me what all this is about."

I moved to the far side of the table, more to protect him than myself. "You've been away from home for three nights fornicating with another woman. Of course Sue and Kate are outraged. They're not Parnesian prostitutes!"

"Fornicating! I haven't—"

"Don't lie! You stink of Rajuna. Even Sue could smell her on you."

"So what? So I slept with Rajuna—"

"If you only slept with her there's little harm!"

"Diana—you insolent bitch! All right, I screwed her, if that sounds better. I screwed her on the gev. You pushed us together. You played the pimp. What's so different if I screw her in more comfort than a two-foot bunk?"

"A what bunk?"

"A two-foot—you know what I mean!"

"The difference? On the gev you were a soldier under arms, dominated by primitive male drives. Society makes allowances. A man ready to kill is a man ready to rape! A soldier under arms is released from many constraints. Sue and Kate would have been sad if they'd known. They couldn't have complained. But when you walk out of your own home, leaving them so proud of you, to fornicate with another woman, they have every right to be outraged! As I am! I realize your memory's fractured and your inherent sexual morals nonexistent. But I never imagined your external morals had been abolished with your memory. In fact, I don't think they were. Not even you, unaided, could be so foolish, ignorant, and selfish!"

"Diana, I don't know what you're talking about!"

"Oh yes you do! Rajuna decided she'd amuse herself. She tempted you, and you fell! Now you're trying your usual excuse when you're ashamed of something you've done. Bluster your way out! Plead amnesia when you're sodden with guilt!"

"Rajuna tempt me? I had to shove hard to get her into bed!"

"Don't boast of that in front of Kate. Or I'll be flying her home too!"

He became pathetic. "Diana, why did you push Rajuna and me together?"

"Because you were both as tense as flexed shocks. You both needed relief, and a few hours sound sleep. She might have had to drive for our lives the next day. But to start an affair! Autarch women have the morals of polecats!"

"Diana—you're a vicious little prig!" He stalked off. Presently he stalked back. "Rajuna's going to help us. After all she's the Director of Special Services."

"She hands out Paxin and other aids to keeping the narod placid! She was also the partner of the new Governor. To be replaced by a Patrol Captain! That's an insult Shapur won't forgive!"

"Bull! Those autarchs don't run each other's lives. Also—I met Marshal Mitra at Rajuna's villa. He congratulated me on our success."

"The Marshal's an overworked old soldier with an incompetent staff who thinks he's at last got a good Patrol Combat Team."

"I don't want to spend the rest of my life flying over the wilderness alongside a frigid female with the fangs of a cobra!"

I was appalled at the way I was overreacting. I certainly needed rebriefing. Why hadn't Naxos recalled me months ago? Before I could stop myself I had said, "So you were after more than fornication? That makes your behavior even more despicable! Ambition! What kind of a career can Rajuna be planning for a blackguard with a scarred face, a sordid past, and a scrambled memory?"

That finished the conversation. It finished all conversation between us on non-operational subjects for the rest of the month. And there were few operations to discuss. The druj had disappeared. Rajuna, as a Director was able to allot the Captain a civilian cutter, a machine that even he could fly safely, so that he could go and pleasure her without involving me. I had never known a Patrol Officer to have a silver cutter at his disposal before. His final act of vulgarity was to wear civilian clothes when he flew it.

I concentrated on getting our equipment into first-class condition, ready for the day when Rajuna tossed him out. By the beginning of June the overhaul was complete and I was in the command center updating displays when the Captain's civilian cutter came lurching over the walls to land with a thud on the square. Those cutters might be built to stand the kind of treatment he was giving his, but it made my stomach cramp to hear the shocks bottom on the landing gear.

My stomach cramped again a few minutes later when he

came into the room. He was wearing a colored dashi which would have looked silly on a young autarch and was disgusting on a Patrol Officer approaching forty. He ignored me and went to study the relief map of the Valley which covered one wall. After several minutes of silence he called, "Diana, come here!"

I walked over as slowly as discipline would allow and stood beside him, staring at the display. Finally he spoke first, "Haven't you finished overhauling that damned machine yet?"

I had been working fourteen hours a day for the past week while he had been fornicating with Rajuna, but all I said was that I planned to have the cutter operational the next morning.

"Make sure it is! We've got another surveillance job. And this time those sanctimonious rishi on the Ulama say there'll be somebody there." He had acquired Rajuna's cynical impiety along with her smell. "Did you hear, girl? They say there'll be somebody to pick up."

"I heard that. You didn't say who or where." He was bursting to tell me.

"Where? See this lake in the Shenandoah Mountains? Lake Byrd?"

"Yes. We've flown over it. When you were still flying west in a combat cutter, and not east badly disguised as a civilian."

He swore, but was too eager to astound me to make my remark an issue. "Do you know whom we're going to pick up?"

"It's a druj-free area, so some pilgrim presumably."

"Some pilgrim! I'll say." He looked down at me. "A member of the Ulama. An Ecclesiarch!" He saw my reaction and lost some of his hostility. "An Ecclesiarch named Kahn."

"An Ecclesiarch!" I breathed.

"A genuine certified holy man. That seems to thaw you."

"It is a great honor. To aid an Ecclesiarch returning from a pilgrimage."

"They've sure snowed you, Di!" He stared at the map. "Ever met an Ecclesiarch?"

"No. There are Pilots who fly ships for the Ulama. They are specially selected and my profile does not suggest I am suited for such a responsibility. I did hear one preach. He was inspiring. He explained things—"

"Perhaps Kahn will be able to explain some things to me

too!" He laughed. "Diana, set me straight. What religion is an Ecclesiarch?"

"Panreligious. The Light shines on them and through them. They interpret the words of the Teacher in terms of all valid creeds. To you, for example, he will be able to show how the Teacher brought the Gospel of Christ into harmony with the present age."

His face shadowed. Deep within him were still the foundations of an old faith. He gripped my shoulder with something of our previous comradeship. "Di—I hope you won't be disappointed with this Kahn."

"It would be impossible for me to be disappointed by an Ecclesiarch. Even if he does not speak to me I will get strength from the aura of grace which surrounds him. The accumulated mana of his long life."

"Long life?"

"Ecclesiarchs are reputed to live for a hundred and fifty years. That may be only a pious belief, though of course they live ascetic and therefore healthy lives. They are blessed."

He patted me gently. "I'll break his sacred neck if he doesn't spread some of his mana over you!" He returned to the map. "As soon as you've put the cutter back together we'll fly a recce over Lake Byrd. Get some pictures."

Diana's bias is obvious. There is no point in my rebutting all her irrelevancies, but there are some things I must explain.

I had realized that the Ulama knew about time transits when I discovered they had been responsible for my own welcome. Their knowledge was limited and what they knew they kept secret. There was no mention of any such phenomenon in the literature, and I had been able to make a thorough search from the Ive terminal. The area of scholarship in which your age excels is the meanest—cataloging. You cross-index without reading in the best tradition of library science.

The Ulama's "pilgrims" were obviously people who had made the time transit, but although Gart's logs showed he had waited at a number of places there was no record that any "pilgrim" had actually arrived. My own arrival had certainly been unex-

*pected. The rendezvous at Lake Byrd with this Ec-
clesiarch Kahn seemed unique; they had given his
name and rank. One of their own was coming so
presumably the Ulama knew when he had left. Ecclesiastical longevity probably owed more to my
Convolution Integral than to the grace of God.*

*I say the Ulama didn't know much because their
ETA for Kahn was wrong by two days. It had been
wrong for the transit at Sherando by two years. I
had been able to calculate corrections for the
coefficients in my Convolution Integral from the
data on my own transit and so made the equations
immensely easier to solve. But the Ulama must still
be using a table of times and places based on my
uncorrected Convolution and crunched out by some
giant number-crusher in the Age of Affluence. The
Ulama's use of mathematics reminded me of the
Church's tables for finding Easter. Some premedie-
val astrologer-astronomer had calculated wrongly
and his mistakes had been made sacrosanct as
Golden Numbers.*

*Both for the literature search and for solving my
equations I had to use the computer terminal. At
first I had gone to some pains to disguise the fact
that I was a mathematician, but my caution was su-
perfluous. Whenever she saw me at the terminal Diana would come and inspect what I was doing and
then tell me how to do it better. Because she has
learned to manipulate symbols after the manner of
an engineer she thinks she understands mathematics. I now realize that Diana was incapable of
recognizing what I was. The concept of a Patrol
Officer knowing more than she did was beyond her
imagination.*

*She also refers to my "superficial crudeness," and
as if to prove her point she quotes my crudest remarks verbatim. In fact when I had to live and
fight like a combat soldier I reverted easily enough
to thinking and talking like one. Descartes, who in-
cidentally was also educated by Jesuits, would have
led his storming party into Prague shouting the ar-
got of the camp; when teaching mathematics to a*

Queen he would have spoken the elegant French of the Court. Laplace was born a peasant, died a marquis, and was always a snob. Gauss, the true Prince of Mathematicians, was the son of a bricklayer and talked like one. Mathematicians have only one thing in common: those transcendent moments of contact with absolute truth. Otherwise they are as foolish, as brutal, as bloody-minded as other men. Not all of us are marked with the Harvard imprimatur; the Marine Corps stamped its pattern on me more deeply than did the Yard. That is one reason why I was unpopular with my colleagues.

I mentioned earlier that I was educated by old-style Jesuits. By seventeen, when I escaped to the Corps, I had had an excellent introduction to mathematics together with a thorough grounding in selected philosophers. And I had learned enough about comparative religion and various heresies to recognize the sources of Diana's cult.

Its founder, the man you call the "Teacher," started with Zoroastrianism and added elements from every subsequent revelation to produce a mishmash with something for everybody. During the Affluence the world must have been swarming with gurus peddling synthetic religions, but only the Teacher had foreseen the danger of Impermease, warned his followers against it, and established Settlements to isolate them from it. So his religion survived along with your great-great-grandmother's. Today the Order follows his Gospel as the creed best suited to its own purpose, the Ulama uses it to perpetuate its power, and the autarchs interpret it to support their privileges.

Diana believes it. She has been saturated with its dogma mixed with the mysticism of her Order. For five years on Naxos gigabits of information were pumped into her, and her emotions were armored by a Code and a Doctrine. She has an answer for everything and an ability to do almost anything. She was born with a superb body and an excellent brain. The Synod trained and moulded a gifted girl to produce their paragon—Diana.

VIII

June 2171

For all his cynicism he understood the importance of our task. We reconnoitered Lake Byrd and took photographs. I studied the old maps while he played with the computer terminal, which kept him at Ive and away from Rajuna.

Three days before Kahn was due we reexamined the pictures. He pointed to a clump of willows toward the southern end of the lake. "Could you slide in under those? At night, without floods?"

"The moon will be full. In three days moonset will be about five. So around four the moon will be low enough both to silhouette those trees and flash the surface of the lake."

"You'll be able to taxi under 'em?"

"If the night is clear. And if I have to. But it would be safer to plant a transponder among them as a beacon. And safer still to land in daylight."

He grunted and returned to his matrix algebra, an interest as unexpected as his arrival in my room at two in the morning. "Kit up! We're leaving."

I rolled out of bed and began to dress, not arguing, but reminding him that according to his orders standby was not for another two days. "The Ulama—"

"To hell with the Ulama! We go now. It's a full moon and a clear night."

The night was clear except over Lake Byrd which was covered by a low mist, and there was no wind to give the ripples which identify a water surface. An altimeter is only accurate to three meters, so I had to let down cautiously, catching the echo by ear. Fortunately the mist thinned moments before I touched, the moon gave flashes of white fire as the wavelets spread from the skids, and I could hold them just brushing as

I eased across the surface of the lake and slid up onto the bank under the overhanging branches of the willows.

We both sat silent after I had parked to let the tension drain out of us. My underwear was soaked; he stank. Presently I said, "Few Pilots would have been able to make that landing."

"You're a clever little girl! How long is this damned fog going to last?"

"Until about an hour after dawn. Certainly not until the day after tomorrow. That's when Kahn is due."

He ignored me, took his rifle, and clambered from the cutter. I immobilized the turbines and followed. He was standing in the shadow of the willows, staring out into the mist. From the photographs I knew we were facing about a thousand meters of marshy meadow with the forest beyond. To our right the trees came to within three hundred meters of the lake. The old map showed that somewhere among them was a road paved with permac and so probably still clear of undergrowth. Kahn, I guessed, would be arriving down that road.

The dawn, brightening behind us, turned the mist to a white blanket. The scents of the early morning were delightful and he did not ruin them by lighting a cheroot. His impatience grew as time passed and nothing happened. He kept glancing at his watch. Finally, when the hidden sun was up, he muttered, "I think Kahn's going to arrive about halfway along this edge of the lake. If the damned fog hangs on we may miss him. Come with me." And he began to walk slowly through the reeds fringing the margin of the water.

We trudged through the mud for twelve hundred and seventy-three paces. Then he stopped and gripped my arm. "Diana—stay here and listen out. I'm going farther, about three hundred yards."

"Three hundred what?"

"Three hundred paces." He gave a gesture of irritation. "Call me on the com if you see or hear anything."

I could hear all kinds of things. The fish were jumping. The morning birds were singing. They reminded me of how the birds of morning used to join and then replace the nightingales during our night vigils in the groves of Naxos. And I began to feel the same sense of wonder, of growing awe; the prelude to a great occasion. I felt the current of Time bearing moments of decision down upon me. The mountains, the lake, the forest, all were numinous. Their magic seeped into me, strengthening me for some great challenge. I stood alone in the white mist, praying with a fierce joy, as I felt the spiritual and the physical preparing to mingle.

The sun began to clear away the mist and the harmony of fragrance from the forest swelled up with its growing warmth. Then came a clashing discord, a taint, a stench. The fetor of druj. I called on the com and got no answer.

They were in the forest, coming closer. As I started to sprint along the edge of the lake I heard a splash and the Captain's shout. I broke through the mist to find him helping a black-bearded man in worn coveralls out of the water. Kahn, the Ecclesiarch, had arrived.

Urgency did not allow ceremony. "Sir—your Grace—there are druj among the trees." I pointed. "Directly to the west!"

"For Christ's sake!" Captain Gart swung around, lifting his rifle, calling over his shoulder, "Kahn—this is Diana. My Pilot."

I caught his hand. "The cutter—quickly—come!"

He must have been on pilgrimage for many months. His beard was long and ragged: his face ascetic, dark, lean from fasting. His brown eyes, deep, burned with a sacred fire. He freed his hand from mine, unslung his rifle, snapped on a dry magazine, and thumbed his safety. "Druj—I feared it!"

"Let's move!" Captain Gart started to run toward the cutter. Kahn followed. I guarded the rear. But we had only gone a few hundred meters along the shore of the lake when the mist finally rolled away and the druj came out of the forest.

They charged straight at us, bounding over the coarse grass and low bushes. Had it not been for my warning they would have overwhelmed us there and then. One got to within five meters of Kahn before I shot it through the chest. More came running, crouched down, from among the trees. A light machine gun opened up and we dived for the only available cover, a log on the edge of the lake. From behind it we were able to stop the second wave.

We were trapped. The LMG held us pinned. More druj were sliding out of the woods, darting behind hummocks and bushes. If we tried to run for the cutter we would be dead within ten paces. I shouted to the men, "Across the lake— now—while you can! I'll cover!"

"Pipe down, Diana!" snarled Captain Gart.

He was beyond reason. I turned to Kahn, prone beside me. "Go, your Grace, go! You must not die here. It is our time for the Bridge. Not yours!"

He stared at me, reloaded, did not speak, and made no move.

"Across the lake!" I implored. "While the mist hides you. While we hold them. Back to the Settlements. There is your duty. Ours is here!"

"I don't know——" He was shaking his head.

I was swept by an unique fury. "Kahn—don't shame us by your death. Finish your task!"

"My task—"

"It is to aid you that I was born into the world. For that I must leave it. Don't betray us. Go, your Grace, go!"

"What the hell are they up to?" Captain Gart was peering around his end of the log.

"Working in close," said Kahn. "They wish to capture us alive."

"Balls! They don't take prisoners. Watch it! Here they come again." The druj broke cover in a screaming assault. By the time we had cut them down Kahn had disappeared into the mist low over the water.

"The bishop's bolted!" gasped Captain Gart.

"We must cover him while we live," I said.

That was for longer than I had expected. The druj did not attempt another frontal assault but, as the mist cleared, they moved their LMG to lay furrows in the lake behind us, fencing us with fire while they prepared their attack. I was content. We had given Kahn the best start possible. I ran over my resume and waited for the end.

It came suddenly. The sun was up and the mist gone when three druj who had crept to the edge of the reeds charged together, lobbing grenades. We dropped the druj but the grenades exploded beside us. "Tear gas!" gasped the Captain. I glimpsed him, groping blindly for his knife, about to cut his throat.* Then I was rolling in the water, my own knife knocked away, three druj clawing at me, unable to see through my tears.

They tied our hands and hauled us up from the lake. They hit us when we tried to struggle but, half-blind and choking,

---

* No! Cut hers! Diana's crazy religion forbids suicide.

we were helpless. They dragged us through the reeds and west across the meadow. By then I was starting to see again and was walking to save from being dragged. Jan was limping and cursing; otherwise we were only bruised.

Their stench was the worst. They were animals but without an animal's instinct toward its own kind of cleanliness. Only their weapons were clean. They themselves were filthy, naked, their hair matted, their thighs smeared with dried feces, their skin scratched from thorns and scarred with old wounds. They had become what man once was. They were animal-man with modern weapons. And their weapons were their only care.

They left their wounded to die; they let their dead lie where they lay. They barked to each other in a monosyllabic Anglic. They ignored Jan when he shouted at them. They hit him when he tried to fight but only hard enough to subdue. There was no understanding in their eyes. They showed no anger, no emotion of any kind, now that the fury of battle was over.

Ahead of us, out from under the trees, a horseman rode. The druj quivered and hurried us on. The horseman checked and stood, waiting. A heavyset man on the largest horse I had ever seen. A chestnut mare, a beautiful animal, standing steady, while her rider lifted a communicator to his mouth.

"I have him! This is Axe—by the lake. Hurt his foot, otherwise undamaged. He has his woman with him. I'll bring 'em both in. Yes, Padron, they'll be fit to talk. He lowered his communicator as we were thrown on our bellies at the hooves of his horse.

His expression showed that he was a creature of the Lie. Malevolent triumph, cruel amusement, undisguised hatred. Clean shaved, short red hair, brown eyes. Under middle-age; ancient in evil. The druj, pushing me to obeisance, feared him.

"Stand 'em up! Lemme see 'em!" His voice was the rip of a saw through bone.

We were jerked to our feet. My hair was caught, my head pulled back. I was forced to stare up into the horseman's face. He had the profile of a hatchet. He was called Axe. His veralloy helmet was of curious design. He wore a camouflaged cuirass of the same metal. He had a pistol holstered at his belt and a carbine in the boot behind his saddle.

Jan was sagging between two druj, trying to keep his left foot off the ground. The horseman chuckled. "Somehow I imagined someone more handsome! So your Grace has bruised his heel? And Padron is waiting to talk with you. You'll have to ride." He shouted toward the trees and two druj emerged leading a pack-mule. "Mount him on that. No—the other way! Face him to the tail!" He watched as Jan was roped astride the animal, sitting backwards, then turned his attention to me. "By the Bull's balls—a blonde! Tell me, bitch, are you fertile?"

I stood silent. He reached down and hit me across the shoulders with his riding crop. The druj held me so I could not flinch. He hit me again. "You'll squeal like a cut cat when I take you. But the boss first. A run will warm you up." He pushed out his spurred boot. "Tie her to that!"

My wrists were lashed to his stirrup-iron. He wheeled the mare so I was dragged by my arms until I managed to haul myself up and stumble along beside his horse. He led the way through a strip of woodland until we reached the old road and turned along it. The permac surface was barren and unbroken except where the poisoned ground beneath had heaved. Great oaks had grown up to its edge, their branches interlaced above us, so we went down a tunnel through the forest.

I tried to observe and reason, but at intervals Axe leaned down and hit me. Each blow broke up my chain of coherent thought, and with each impact I felt the mare's flank quiver. After a while I realize that my silence was annoying Axe and he hit me more often, so I began to cry out for I do not enjoy being hit by a riding crop. I lost my footing and was dragged. I regained my feet, stumbled on for about a kilometer, fell again, and did not have sufficient strength left to save myself.

"For Christ's sake—you'll kill her!" shouted Jan.

"For Christ's sake!" mimicked Axe. But he reined in, reached down, twisted his hand in my hair, and lifted me so I could stand. He rammed my mouth against the toe of his boot, laughed, and put the mare into a slow walk.

I could no longer maintain even that pace. After a few hundred meters I fell again. Axe halted, cursed, and shouted to the druj to cast me loose from his stirrup. I could not prevent myself from asking for water before collapsing. He hesitated, then unhooked the canteen from his saddle and tossed it to a druj who held it for me to drink. After a few moments of rest they pulled me to my feet, put a rope around my neck, and led me stumbling behind the mare.

I lost count of the steps, but after several kilometers Axe had Jan taken from the mule to limp along beside him. He did not halter Jan as he had haltered me.

We rounded a bend and ahead was a crossroads with packs of druj squatting between the trees and a group of horsemen waiting at the intersection. They were dressed and mounted much like Axe, but even in my exhaustion I knew from his bearing the one who must be Padron.

He was astride a magnificent black stallion. He sat his horse like a conquerer. He had blue eyes and fair hair. He was a purebred and beautiful. His easy smile as we approached made the skin at the back of my neck crawl as it does when one moves near to power.

"Padron— I got him. Here he is!" Axe put his boot between Jan's shoulders and shoved him forward.

"Here is who?" asked Padron in a soft voice which made the druj tremble and the horsemen shift in their saddles.

"Kahn—I got Kahn!"

"So this is Kahn?" The smile broadened and became more terrible. "Then why does he wear Gart, Captain Jan Gart, on his chest?"

"What?" Axe leaned forward to look. Jan's ripped coveralls had fallen back so his name tag was clear. Axe read it, cursed, and lashed him across the back.

Jan said, "You bastard! I'll get you for that!"

Padron waved Axe back and asked, "Where is Kahn?"

"Who the hell's Kahn?" Jan stared up at Padron. "How the shit can I tell you where he is if I don't know who he is?"

Padron laughed. "Kahn's the man you came to pick up. Where is he?"

"Him? He took off when the shooting started. Across the lake. Hope he's drowned!"

"Unlikely." Padron turned to Axe. "Kahn's heading for the valley. He has several hours start but a long way to go. You should be able to run him down." He looked at me, standing in my halter. "And who did you think this girl was?"

"Kahn's whore."

"You fool! She's Gart's Pilot. They've got a cutter parked somewhere."

"I didn't see any cutter. Just these two."

"I imagine they landed last night. Bring her here." He studied my face, then asked gently, "Where is your cutter?"

I said nothing.

"Closer—that's better." He leaned down, caught my hair, jerked me over to his horse, and turned up my face. Then he drew his knife.

"Chief—she's mine! Don't cut her yet!" shouted Axe.

Padron held the tip near my right eye, watching me flinch. "You've more immediate problems, Axe," he said, and gestured with his knife.

Jan went berserk. "No—the cutter's in the willows. South end of the lake. You'll find it anyway. And it won't fly."

Padron let me go. "So Kahn cannot escape in it?"

"She's immobilized the motors. Always does when she parks. I don't know how. Anyway, nobody can fly it but her. Kahn'll kill himself if he tries."

Padron nodded. "Axe—check the cutter. Don't damage it. And don't waste time over it. Stay with your pack." He wheeled his stallion, calling to the other horsemen. "We've a day's hunting ahead. Spread well out. Whoever brings Kahn down can have this girl for a few hours. She'll provide more amusement than a deballed druj." He saw my expression. "They won't kill you!" Then he reined his horse over to study me more closely. "What do you want?"

"To have this halter removed. It is unlawful. I did not surrender."

"By the Bull's balls—the girl knows her rights!" Padron leaned down from his saddle, and lifted the noose from my neck. He dropped it at my feet, looked into my face, then turned to Jan. "Gart? I've heard that name on your radio. You knocked out our auton last year!"

"Only doing my job. Thought I was fighting bare-assed gooks."

"And what do you think now?"

"Dunno." Jan took a sidelong glance at the horsemen. "Dragoons?"

"Dragoons!" Padron called to one of his lieutenants, a tall black. "Ras, how do you like that title?"

"Appropriate," said Ras softly. "Padron, we must talk to this pair."

"We will. After we've caught Kahn. I'll send 'em back to camp." He had Jan put astride the mule, but this time facing its head. Then he raised his crop in a sardonic salute and trotted away down the road.

Without a horseman to drive them the druj moved more slowly. They treated me as they treated the pack animals, hitting me when I lagged but letting me drink when we forded a stream. They lifted Jan from his mule so he could drink too. As he put his head down beside mine he whispered, "Diana, I'm going to act the thug. May make that bastard Padron despise me and get careless."

"I understand, Jan. The Light—" Then the druj jerked us apart.

After some six kilometers the permac ended, and we turned onto a trail through the forest. We climbed a hill, rested at the crest, went down into a valley, crossed a creek, and took the road on the far bank. A little after noon we passed through an area of squalor and scattered offal typical of a druj encampment. A few druj were squatting by crude shelters hidden under the trees; they looked up at us with incurious eyes and then returned to cleaning their weapons or staring blankly at the ground. Their stench enveloped us. After another five hundred and twenty paces the creek widened to form a large pond and we came to a second camp.

This, the camp of the horsemen, was the opposite of the kraal of their slaves. There were three large transportable domes and a number of small ones, all hidden under the trees. Four loaded gevs were parked on the road, the auxiliaries of one running to give electric power to the camp. There were radio antennae above the central dome. Pathways had been cut between the domes and the spoil piled back; from the withered leaves on the drying branches I judged the encampment about a week old.

I could see no horsemen. There were a number of druj at work, cleaner but just as incurious as their unwashed fellows. The horses and mules tied among the trees were well-fed and well-groomed. The camp was an ordered place.

Our guards tethered us near the main dome, giving us enough scope to lie down but keeping us too far apart to talk. They hit us when we shouted to each other. They watered and fed us when they fed the pack animals, throwing us strips of the same jerky they were chewing on themselves. Jan spat the stuff out but I ate mine and then stretched myself on the ground to sleep. I would need all my fortitude when Padron returned. I prayed for Kahn's safety and gave thanks that the indignity of the halter had been removed. There would be other indignities but those were a part of what one faced when one chose to fight the Lie. The halter had been a symbol of shame which even the enemy could only use when it was deserved.

I closed my eyes and concentrated my thoughts. I was to take my place in a long procession; I would be among those women who had died agonizing and detestable deaths for their beliefs. I meditated on La Poucelle de France and her fortitude during that night in her cell at Rouen waiting the morning when they would take her out and burn her alive. Her memory gave me strength.

IX

Artemis

I was awakened by the jingle of harness; a column led by Padron was riding into camp. His expression showed that Kahn had not been taken; his glance as he dismounted marked me as a surrogate victim.

Flanked by his lieutenants he strode into the dome. A druj hitched his stallion's head to a nearby tree, loosened the girths, and began to water him. Other horsemen were dismounting, shouting to their druj, but I concentrated on the stallion. He was jet-black, magnificently male, the finest horse I had ever seen. After he had drunk he looked around, noticed me, and we scented each other. The contact occupied my mind and subdued the sadness which, in a Pilot, replaces fear. The stallion was a good horse, fiery but not vicious. An unwitting servant of the enemy, as innocent of Evil as, I now realized, were the druj themselves.

Axe, among the most guilty, came to the door of the dome bringing with him five creatures in white chitons. For a moment I took them to be enslaved women and was swept by my Order's hatred for such abominations. But as they led us into the dome I saw they were only doctored druj altered into the semblance of girls, as mindless as their cruder companions.

The dome was the pavilion of a chieftain. Padron, washed, shaved, his dusty leathers repolished, was sitting behind a long table. Ras, a classical nilote, was on his right. On his left was a yellow man who reminded me of an old samurai painting. As I was pushed to stand in front of them I realized I was facing three purebreds. They are now so rare that I had never before seen three together.

Jan was cursing the castrates, telling them to mind his

ankle. Padron had him pushed to a chair and waved him to silence. For the moment he was not interested in Jan. He was interested in me. And not as a prisoner, an enemy, a source of information. He was not even interested in me as a woman. I was an intelligent victim, whose suffering might divert him from his own.

He studied my body. His blue eyes flicked up to my face. "So you are a Pilot of the Order! What class?"

He was probing for a pretext. I said nothing. Silence would give him a quick excuse.

"I have heard," he said softly, "that Pilots cannot feel pain."

That is untrue. We learn how to cope with pain, but we do not welcome it. I commenced controlled breathing.

"Let's test the truth of that story!" Padron reached for his riding crop and ordered the castrates, "Strip her. Put her across the table."

Jan exploded. His wrists were bound but it took five castrates to subdue him. As they dragged him down he shouted, "Lay off her! She's on automatic! She don't know nothing!"

Padron laughed. Jan's agony would add zest to my pain, "Why should you care if I whip her?"

"She's my Pilot. Damn you, Padron! Would you want to watch your horse flogged?"

"A good try, Gart. But a false analogy. These Pilots are a peculiar breed." He saw that the druj, finding they could not get my coveralls over my bound wrists were about to cut the fabric. "Don't rip her clothes!"

They untied my hands and pulled my coveralls from my shoulders, down to my waist, over my hips, down my legs. My underwear, clean on for combat that morning, was now filthy and I was glad to be rid of it. I did not struggle. It was useless to fight and would only have increased the amusement of the horsemen crowding the dome.

"An authentic blonde!" said Ras, leaning forward.

"And beautiful," said the yellow man. "Padron, do not damage her. In case it is I who ride down Kahn tomorrow."

"Saz—I'll leave her useable." Padron gestured. "Across the table!"

The castrates pushed me forward, forcing me to bend. Ras, reaching out, caught my left wrist, Saz my right. They dragged on my arms, pulling my stomach up against the edge of the table, pressing my breasts down onto the wood. Ras patted the back of my hand, as though comforting a child.

"You bunch of gutless sads!" shouted Jan in an attempt to divert them to himself. "You know what you shiteaters are? Hell's Angels on horseback!"

Hell's Angels on horseback. An appropriate phrase. I felt Saz's grip tighten on my wrist. Padron, moving to stand behind me, snapped, "Gag that clown!"

Then he hit me. He hit me three times. I jerked by reflex but stayed silent. Ras and Saz gently stroked my forearms. Then he hit me again, a number of times. I gasped, because the force of his blows drove the air from my lungs. He became impatient.

"Turn her over!" I was on my back, looking up at the ring of faces, crowding in to watch. Padron's blue eyes were glowing above me; small windows into Hell. From the floor came choking sounds as Jan fought with his gag.

The fiend was shaking Padron, but he strove to keep his words light. "I fear this is crude. There are more advanced techniques, Gart, as I expect you know. But the whip works well enough with most women. Let's see if it will work on a Pilot." He hit me hard.

All my muscular reflexes, except those of my larynx, responded. He let my shudderings die away, then lifted his crop for another stroke.

"Your black stallion," I gasped, "What's his name?"

"Satan." He stood with his whip poised. "Why?"

"He's the finest horse I've ever seen."

"The finest you ever will see. Sumac out of Syrian Goddess. He's—" Padron saw in my eyes the gleam of my small success. "You tricky bitch!" He brought the crop down with all his strength.

My reflexes included a scream. I writhed on the table, fighting for muscle control. His lips relaxed from snarl to smile. "She feels!"

"Padron!" Jan had bitten through his gag and spoke as I had never heard him speak before. "Padron—" His voice lashed across the dome and jerked Padron around. "Hit her again—and you and I are cinched. Enemies—through death and after!" A challenge as deadly as the tip of a poised knife. A challenge that transcended bound hands and local advantage.

A challenge few could make and Padron did not ignore. The immanent eternal had, for an instant, touched Jan's mind, letting him show himself as an Avenger. And also the obverse, inherent in the challenge, as a potential ally. The possibility of either forced a pause. Padron looked down at Jan.

"So—we're not yet enemies?" The challenge hung. "But what about her?" He tapped my belly with his crop. "Now she's started to sing—let's hear her song! Tell us, bitch, what is the purpose of your Order?"

I licked my lips. The savor was the same as before combat. Padron raised his whip. Jan, reverting, shouted, "Tell him! That's an order! Tell him about yours. You're always soundin' off about your Order. It's no secret!"

"The purpose of my Order?" I looked up into Padron's blue eyes, glad that Jan had released me to face the Devil down. "To defend the Light against the Powers of Darkness. To harry the Shadows back to Hell."

The horsemen guffawed, but there was an edge to their laughter that told me my point had pricked. Padron flicked the tip of his crop across my breasts. "Gart, what can you offer in exchange for your girl's hide?'"

"The cutter. It's a combat cutter. Nobody can fly it but her!"

"She can." He switched my belly. "But will she?"

"Maybe. Mostly she does as I say. But you won't get anywhere beating her. Unless you're doing it for kicks. Like Axe thrashes his mare for kicks!"

"That's a lie!" Axe jumped at Jan, hitting out.

"You do, you bastard!" lied Jan, rolling away. "I saw you! On the road!"

Padron made a gesture and Axe was pulled back, insisting that he never beat his horse. Jan sat up, working his shoulders where Axe had hit him. "That girl—stubborn as a frozen bearing. Lean on her too hard and she'll break off before she gives. Let me have a try at shifting her."

"At what price? Gart—are you fishing for a deal?"

"Man with his hands tied. Can't make a deal. Has to take what he can get."

Padron nodded. "And what he gives is worthless." He sat down and studied Jan. Then he studied me. Finally he said, "Untie him. And let her go."

I rolled off the table, relieved to find I could still function, though with pain. I picked up my coveralls and put them on. Nobody stopped me.

Jan collapsed into a chair. "My ankle—broken maybe!"

Padron stood over him. "Who sent you?"

"The Governor. That shithead Shapur."

"What did he know about Kahn?"

"Didn't seem to know much. A routine pickup. To save the slem a walk after his pilgrimage."

"Pilgrimage!" There was laughter among the listening horsemen.

"That's what Shapur said Kahn was doing, screwing around out here. But he didn't tell me I'd get bushwacked. Not a warning! He let us walk into your outfit."

"And what do you think he'll do when you don't return with Kahn?"

"Write us off. He doesn't seem to care much for Ecclesiarchs. He was just kissing the ass of the Ulama."

"No search and rescue?"

"Over these mountains? And with no crash beacon to vector 'em in? They wouldn't know where to look. Wouldn't try too hard anyway. Not for the Patrol. Those gutless bastards in the Guard!"

"So you're a write-off. What's the deal you're after?"

"Anything that'll save my neck. And hers. She'll do as I say. You heard how she answered when I told her to. As long as it ain't against her code. And mostly I can snow that. She's conditioned. When she goes on automatic you'd have to kill her to stop her. I can switch her off auto. Nobody else can." He looked at the faces of the listening horsemen and took their measure. "Like, Padron, I guess that nobody but you could ride that stallion of yours?"

"Nobody has ever tried."

"Well—she's like that. Not that she'll let me ride her. She won't let nobody mount her!" He guffawed. The horsemen laughed.

Padron turned to face me. "Answer my question. What is your class?"

I stood silent. He raised his crop. I did not flinch.

"Tell him, girl!" shouted Jan, "Tell him anything he asks."

"I am rated of the First Class."

"You're a Prime?" Padron stared at me, incredulous.

"How—?" He lowered his whip. "You Pilots—you always speak the truth?"

"As we see it. If we speak at all."

A murmur ran among the horsemen. They were all staring at me. Nobody laughed. Their respect was a recognition I have never had from officers. Padron had called me a Prime, an archaic term with a penumbra of myth, of occult powers. A century ago there were wild exaggerations about the abilities of Prime Pilots. Stories the Order had not always contradicted for awe is a useful shield.

But awe easily degenerates into superstition, especially among the followers of the Lie who delight in debasing Truth. They move in darkness and are drawn into their own morass. These horsemen were servants of the Lie. They would be saturated with superstition. And it is lawful to turn the enemy's evil against himself.

"A Prime!" Axe tried to scoff. "She may think she is. But she's been conned. There's no way her Order would waste a Prime on a slob like Gart."

I turned to face him. "Give me a pistol and I'll prove it. Five aimed shots in a second on different targets."

"Here!" said Saz smiling, pretending to reach for his gun.

"No—she'll drop—" Axe jumped back, then cursed at the laughter around him.

"A Prime! Trained to rattle the Gates!" Padron tipped up my chin. "So your Order sent a Prime Pilot to extract Kahn. They knew he'd be there, but not us. Well, Prime, what's your name?"

"Diana."

"Diana!" Axe stepped back. Diana is an ancient name and for some has a special meaning.

"Artemis!" Padron stared at me, then nodded slowly. "It fits!" He let go of my chin and turned away. "We'll talk after we've eaten."

The castrates began to serve a meal. They were now uncertain of Jan's status and served him with the others. He attacked his food like a dog who fears it might be snatched away, but when he had cleared half his plate he pointed his fork at me. "Refuel her and she'll function better."

Padron laughed and signalled for me to be fed. I ate standing, pushing the food into my mouth with my fingers, Singalese style, watching the horsemen. More were returning from the hunt. Kahn was heading into the valley. They had a pack on his trail. It was no country for horses. He could keep ahead of the druj during the night, but the next morning they would run him down before he was halfway to the Rockfish Gap.

They were mannered and formal. They had been riding hard but before they came to dine they had washed and shaved, their hands were clean, their leathers shining. They talked and ate with zest, at intervals glancing toward us. They were hunters, disappointed at having lost their quarry for that day but sure they would take it the next morning. They were young, competent, and evil.

"Diana," said Saz suddenly. "You seem to see something unusual about us. What is it?"

"Many of you are almost purebred."

"Some of us are purebred. All of us are close to it. And you, where do you come from? You don't look like a mongrel."

"I am from a seafaring family, sailors for generations, ever since the chaos. My father was a Master Mariner. My mother was a navigator and diver. My grandfather commanded the ice-breaker which—"

"She's a survival," interrupted Padron, lighting a cigar. "Diana, are you fertile?"

"As far as I know—yes."

"A purebred," said Padron. I felt his eyes as I have never felt a man's eyes on me before. "A purebred with my pattern."

His words sent a unique chill through me. Genetic selection of a partner is an illegal obscenity and the idea excites as does any effective obscenity. I am proud of my inheritance but had never hoped to transmit it intact; the odds against meeting a match are too long. But now I was the captive of a man who seemed stamped with the same genetic profile as my own. Spiritually he was my antithesis. But the profile of a key is the antithesis of the lock. Padron and I watched each other while Saz questioned Jan.

"Gart, where do you think these come from?" Saz slapped the druj who was pouring coffee.

"Crazy savages. Never thought much about where they come from. Heard a doc say it was a virus drove 'em mad."

Saz laughed. "And us? Earlier you called us dragoons. Why?"

"Dunno. Seemed to fit."

"Diana," said Padron. "What do you think?"

"Hold it!" Jan broke in. "Don't ask her what she thinks. She doesn't think. She'll feed you a line of prerecorded crap. She'll repeat every crazy thing they've stuffed into her. Ask her facts and she'll give you straight answers. Ask her thoughts and she'll give you shuck!"

"Gart, let her say what she thinks. I won't flog your performing filly for doing her tricks. Tell her to answer."

Jan scowled at me. He was either acting well or had no understanding of the situation. "Then answer him, girl. But not with a sermon!"

"What do I think of what?" I asked Padron.

"What do you think I am?"

"I do not think." I met his eyes. "I know."

My answer brought absolute silence in the dome. Padron leaned forward. "What do you know, Diana?"

I felt the Light growing, the Light I needed, the Grace I had earned. I saw the gaps in the armor of Evil. Vanity. Pride. I could speak the truth, but in phrases that would puff Padron's pride. "Padron, you are the Master of the Men of the Mountains. A leader in the service of the Lord of the Lie. The head of the spear. The tip of the thrust. The Captain of the Van. A focus in the struggle."

"A focus in what struggle?" His dilating pupils told me that my dart, venomed with hubris, had slipped past his guard. I had slid it in without his awareness. The curse upon the Son of the Morning fell also on his followers.

"The struggle between Light and Darkness, between Truth and the Lie. The universal struggle. The contest that transcends all time and space."

"For Christ's sake," protested Jan. "She spouts the crap because she's preprogrammed. Conditioned. How the hell can she answer sensibly? She's not responsible for what she says."

"She's very responsible," said Padron, vanity spreading through him. "She's been conditioned to give her own version of truth. And to serve with fealty. But she chose before she was conditioned." He turned to me. "Will you ever again be free to choose?"

"I am bound to nothing forever. At the Chinvat Bridge I,

like all of us, will have to answer for my own acts. We are alone when we answer." I looked around at the faces in the dome. None flinched. They were certain the bridge would be stormed. They were condemned. But they believed.

They were a point, probing for weakness. If they could find a fracture line that gave under pressure they would be the leaders of an army, an army that could grow to a host, the exploiters of a breakthrough. Every man among them would be able to claim infinite honor and inestimable rewards. They were testing the firmness of the frontier of one Sector, one sector on one continent on one small and unimportant world. But when a wall is breached one stone must fracture first. The art is to find the stone easiest to split.

"You admit you've been conditioned?"

"I have been trained."

"Is there any way to free you of your—training?"

"I know of none." I paused for effect. "But, if there is a way, those who trained me would not have told me of it. That would be the logic."

"That indeed would be the logic!" Padron leaned back, drew on his cigar, ambition in his eyes. If I could be made to shift allegiance he could crack the frontier. A renegade combat team, flown by a Prime Pilot would spread havoc along its whole length. We had made ourselves the best team on this world, perhaps on any world. There would be many dead Pilots and broken cutters before we were brought down. And our apostasy would destroy more than cutters; it would destroy trust in the Order, finish what was left of the Patrol, wipe out the last vestige of strike capacity that civilization had.

Padron was lusting after a greater prize than a few butcheries. A local victory could convert the present skirmish into an engagement, it could escalate into one of those battles whose outcome decides the future of whole segments of the cosmos. It could move quickly through the present primitive phase of savage physical struggle into the more savage phase when material weapons, such as ourselves, were outmoded, discarded, and intellect grappled with intellect for dominion over space and time.

That was the temptation that Padron was tasting; the bait that I was garnishing. The hope of rising in the hierachy that served his master. If he had not been enfevered by vanity he would have known it was inconceivable that any Pilot of any class could go renegade. He drew again on his cigar. "Diana, are you conditioned to believe that the Soft One will certainly, in the end, prevail?"

There was a murmur along the table. I quenched it. "Nobody still capable of rational thought could be conditioned to believe such nonsense. The future is open-ended. The outcome of the struggle is unknown because it does not yet exist. Victory will go to the victor. Time is the master of all things. In Time of Infinite Duration, in the hands of Zurvan, there is no certainty. Only hope."

"She's a religious maniac!" insisted Jan, as though determined to break the intent silence of my listeners. "They've stuffed her with religious bull. Diana, I told you not to start preaching!"

They ignored him. For the first time in my life I was speaking to a group of men whose belief was as absolute as my own. We shared a common faith in the nature of reality. We had chosen differently, but we had all chosen. Jan was excluded from our dialog because he was without our faith. Moments ago, when he had challenged Padron, he had for an instant opened his mind, then jerked back as from the touch of a hot iron. When he next spoke his voice was icy with hate. "You bastards! You sadistical bastards! Taunting a poor brainwashed girl!"

"Taunting?" said Padron softly. "Gart, have you no understanding? But I think you understand courage. So listen to Diana. She chose before she was programmed. She had the faith to believe and the courage to choose. A courage beyond your comprehension. Do you know why? Because she chose freely, accepting that defeat was possible. And knowing the consequences of defeat."

"My God!" Jan was staring at Padron. "You're taking her seriously!"

"I do. And you'd better." Padron turned to me and, despite what he was, I felt warmed by his understanding. "These creatures—" He poked the nearest druj, "Do you believe they're devils?"

"No. I used to think that. Now I know that they are men reduced to animals."

"By a virus?"

It was my chance to strike back. "How? I do not know.

But there are the arts of the mountains and the forests, the arts of air and darkness. Arts that are not the prerogative of the Lie alone. There are the ancient arts that turn the hunter into the hunted." I swung on Axe. Diana-Artemis turning to look at the shocked Actaeon.

He recoiled, guarding his face, as though I had struck him. He had hit me hard and I was entitled to make him jerk as he had made me, even if my whip was the lash of superstition.

But the other horsemen were also flinching. Padron snapped, "Enough, enough! Gart, call off your girl!"

Jan, armored by his skepticism, had only vaguely sensed the sting of the weird. But he was startled by this second touch of the psychic and tried to exorcise it by playing the bully. "Stow it, Diana! No more of that stuff! You're starting a bad scene. Come here. Sit down!" He cuffed my head as I squatted at his feet and the horsemen, released, began to laugh. His tactic was succeeding and he used carnality to try to drive the last whip of the mystical from the dome. He cuffed me again. "Stand up!"

I stood in front of him. He unzipped my coveralls and tugged them down to my ankles so I was standing naked. Then he turned me around, examining me under the light. "Want to see if she's damaged."

The conversation and laughter died away. I lowered my eyes as I was turned, but watched the faces of the horsemen through my lashes. I knew I was beautiful and the light made me more so. My hair has a natural wave, my breasts are small but firm and well-shaped, my belly is flat, my hips and buttocks have the curves that men like these would prefer, my thighs are long and my legs slender. I look like a virgin though I am far from one. The welts from the whip enhanced the whiteness of my skin; again, for men like these, the marks of the lash on a woman would make her even more attractive.

When I had been naked across the table I had been surrounded by a variety of lusts. Now I was surrounded by awe. An instinctive response to my beauty, but it was the ancient instinct. Jan sensed the resurgent homage and immediately quenched it. "You guys were pretty free with your damned whips. But she's not hurt bad. A bruised behind won't do her any harm. All right, girl. Cover yourself up."

I pulled on my coveralls. He pushed out his leg. "Take a look at my ankle. It's throbbing like hell."

I knelt and took off his boot and sock. His foot was filthy from the mud of the lake. I palpated his ankle. He winced. "Take it easy!"

He had only the slightest of strains, and I could speak the truth. "No bones broken, sir. You've strained your deltoid ligament. It will be some time before you'll be able to put weight on it without pain."

"Are you a doctor, too?" asked Ras.

"No. But I've been taught many useful skills."

"She's been taught just about every damned thing," said Jan, as though proud of a performing pet. "She'd be a useful asset to any organization." A pet he was willing to sell.

I sat on the floor and leaned against his legs. My body was aching but my mind was easy. We were complementing each other. He had disguised his intelligence with a blustering crudeness. These men, even Padron, were beginning to accept him as a skilled and brutal gunman with a combat cutter and a Prime Pilot under his control. Padron was starting to see us as a key. A key that could open the Gates of Hell. Outward.

> Padron was a soldier of a type I know; a man who would torment for sport but spare for profit. At first I had thought he was using words on Diana as he had used his whip—for amusement. Then I realized he was sodden with superstition. An occupational hazard of soldiering and one that has destroyed armies.
>
> Diana had shown herself as she was: the heroic fanatic. I played the captured mercenary, learning and thinking as I listened to the exchange of absurd theodicy between her and Padron. He, like the Ulama, knew of time transits but, like them, he did not know enough. The Ulama's dates had been wrong as a function of two. Padron had been uncertain about the actual transit site. He had spread his packs over many square kilometers, missed Kahn's arrival, and caught us instead. Nor had he realized that all transits must be at an air-water interface.
>
> How did Padron know about transits at all? I

guessed, and I was right. He knew because that was
how he himself had arrived. It was Satan who had
left the shod hoofprints at Sherando. The Ulama's
date for that transit had been wrong by two years. I
had found their error the night before we had gone
to the Settlement, but had not thought it important
for I had written off "pilgrims" as a superstitious
myth, a religious explanation for the occasional
sudden appearance of accidents like myself. I had
even allowed the Ulama a humanitarian motive, arranging that such unfortunates would be rescued
from the wilderness. If they had told Gart what he
was supposed to be doing they would have saved
two lives.

The Ulama's dates had been wrong, but so had
my mass calculations. The energy released had been
enough to move not only Padron, but his damned
horse as well. I knew Padron had come from
Sherando; his brutality had told me his origins. He
had been one of those bastards who had ruled the
Settlement. Ruled by gallows and lash.

I began to construct a scenario which, after-
wards, I found fairly accurate. The Elders must
have known how to turn men into druj. When they
had evacuated the Valley they had left some to
cover their retreat and taken others to herd the
scattered barbarians they captured on their trek.
Taking the women for themselves; turning the men
into druj as needed. Using their captives as serfs
when they established a new tyranny beyond reach
of the Patrol. Padron had come directly: the
Leader whose return had been prophesied to his
people. He had brought with him the ability to revive the druj. And the Devil knows what other
special knowledge.

The dragoons were only a few squadrons, but
they were young, disciplined, and competent. They
had expendable auxiliaries. Cortes had conquered
Mexico with less. The Sector was as ripe to fall as
had been the Aztec Empire of Montezuma.

X

Selene

The dome was quiet. Padron sat talking to his lieutenants, the others split into small groups. The castrates moved silently between them, pouring wine. The horsemen drank moderately and slowly. A druj, guarding us, shivered.

I looked up and saw its eyes roll back, its nostrils flare, an animal scenting danger. Then I smelled it too—leaf-smoke, from somewhere outside the dome. The druj around us began to shift uneasily. I tensed myself for sudden action and my back muscles, against Jan's knees, alerted him. He put his hand on my shoulder, an affectionate pat which told me he understood.

Outside a horse whinnyed; there was a jingle of harness and a stamping of hooves. A horseman picked up his helmet and crop and strolled out. I heard him shouting at the druj. Then there was a sudden uproar; neighing horses, the bray of a mule, the high yelp of a druj. Our guards began to tremble.

The horseman burst back into the dome. "The zombs—they've got the brush on fire!"

Padron led a rush for the door, then checked and swung on me. "By the Bull's balls, if you've harmed the horses—"

"I have used no magic," I said.

He hesitated. A gout of smoke billowed into the dome. He shouted, "Hold them!" at our guards, and was gone through the door.

The druj who had grabbed us were giving little jumps, like tethered animals starting to panic. I began to walk slowly toward the doorway and Jan followed. Our guards moved ahead of us, as though we were stakes they had pulled up but to which they were still tied. We let them lead us out into the

101

night. The cut spoil was ablaze upwind of the dome and the fire was spreading between the piles.

The crackling of burning branches rose to a roar, along with the shouts of the horsemen, the screams of the horses, and the thunder of motors as the gevs were backed down the road. Their movement jerked out the power cables and the dome lights went off, but the whole encampment was lit by the leaping flames and the brilliant moon above.

The horsemen were turning the panicky druj, dividing them into parties to beat at the burning brush, to fetch extinguishers from the gevs, into bucket brigades to bring water from the creek. Padron, calming Satan, shouted to Axe, "Hog-tie those two!"

Axe hit Jan from behind, knocking him forward onto the ground, putting a pistol at his head. "Keep still! Both of you!" He yelled at the guards to tie us up.

Padron slipped the snap from Satan's halter and started to lead the stallion away. A pile of brushwood flared high. The druj cowered, their hands over their faces. A storm of sparks swept over us and against Satan's flanks. The stallion bucked, Padron tried to mount, the loose girth slipped and he fell. The loss of his master's touch sent the horse frantic. He reared, hooves lashing. Then he wheeled and went charging away across the encampment, scattering horsemen and druj.

Padron scrambled to his feet. I said, "Satan will gallop into the forest. He will wait only a short while for you to come."

"You—" Padron raised his hand.

"If you leave him he will be gone—forever!"

Padron struck me across the face, shouted at Axe, "If she moves—debrain Gart!" and ran after his horse.

Freed horses and mules were stampeding around us. Our guards had scattered in the confusion. When a druj came out of the smoke Axe shouted at it to grab me. It stepped toward me, over Jan's prone body, leaning down to hit Axe across the back of his neck, just below his tilted helmet, knocking him senseless. Jan rolled from under him.

The druj caught my arm, dragging me toward the creek. I tried to twist away, then saw it was Kahn. "Into the water," he gasped. "Clothes off—smear mud!"

We plunged through the reeds. There were naked druj all around us, panicking before fire, instinct driving them to water. Kahn also naked, filthy, hair matted, was as lean and wild as any druj. Jan was too fat and I was too female. We crouched together, trying to hide in the muddy water. Horsemen began wading in among us, herding the druj ashore.

Kahn came through the reeds. "Swim!"

We slid under the surface, down through the dark waters of the pond. It was about a hundred meters across, and we swam breathing and diving. We reached the far side and crouched exhausted under the overhanging bushes. Then we dragged ourselves onto the bank, crawled up the ridge, lay naked and filthy just below the crest, looking back.

"Fire's almost out," gasped Jan. "Axe is up. Within minutes—they'll be after us."

"How far to the Settlements?" asked Kahn.

"More'n a hundred kilometers. Rough country all the way."

"What? So far?"

"Frontier's beyond the Blue Ridge. Come on—under the trees!"

We paused again in the darkness of the forest. "Perhaps— perhaps we should hide until daylight?" said Kahn.

"No!" I said. "They'll sniff us out." There was an ululation from the encampment. "We must try for the cutter. There are guns there."

"They'll have a guard on it," said Jan.

"Maybe not. If so, there are dead druj near, with weapons. It's our best chance." I moved to a clearing where I could see the stars. "This way." I started out in the lead.

I could not hold it. Forcing a trail through the undergrowth was now beyond my strength. I gave the men the bearing to intersect with the old road and made them forge ahead. One after the other we stumbled through the gauntlet of the forest, lashed on by its branches. Its brambles tore our bare bodies. Its stones cut our feet. Its snags tripped us. At intervals, through the leaves above us, we caught glimpses of the stars to give us direction and the moon to give me hope. At times when I fell, the two men had to lift me up. "She's almost had it!" muttered Jan.

"We must hide," gasped Kahn.

I collapsed in the middle of an open glade, out in the moonlight. "This fuckin' moon!" cursed Jan.

His blasphemy shocked me back to consciousness. "Go for

the cutter. We must get guns. The gev can't cross the ridge. They'll have to come on foot."

"Or on their damned horses. They'll ride us down."

"The road. Only fifteen hundred meters. Then it'll be smooth." I prayed. My feet were an agony. I left blood at every step. We would be easy to track, once they picked up our trail. "Keep going. The road."

We kept going, and we reached it. From behind us, to the west, I caught my first hint of the pack. I broke from the men who were holding me and staggered into the lead. We were leaving a bloody spoor along the permac. We ran in pain.

I started to weave; the men caught my hands, tugging me between them, half dragged, half running. We reached the turn in the road with only a strip of forest between us and the meadow. We fought our way through the trees to its edge, then halted in their darkness, looking out across the open ground. The moon threw every bush, every clump of reeds, into silhouette. I leaned against an oak and tested the breeze.

"No guard!" I whispered. "The only druj upwind are dead."

"How—?"

"I know. Trust me. Go for the guns!" I lifted my face and caught the signal. "They are coming fast. Axe. Ahead of his pack."

They hesitated. Then they heard the hooves. "Those are the mare. Go! Go! Get the guns!"

They started forward, out onto the meadow. I staggered after them. They turned back. "I'll not leave you again," gasped Kahn.

"With—bare hands—you—can't save me!"

"She's right!" Jan caught his arm and began to run, very slowly, toward the willows, Kahn behind him. They were almost as exhausted as I. Their naked bodies were white under the moon. I hobbled after them. The mare was coming at a gallop. Axe had seen the blood. I felt his spurs in her flanks.

I looked up at Selene and was swept with waves of cleansing light, such clarity as comes after meditation and fasting. Channels were opening. Contacts were making. I needed a brief span of darkness. There was a cloud She could pull across her face. I implored Her that, when I called, She would draw her veil.

The mare was off the road, crashing through the strip of forest. I turned and called. Selene darkened Herself as I marked the mare's position and dropped into the rough grass.

The cloud passed. Selene shone in all the white fire of Her glory. The mare reared as Axe pulled her up to search the open ground ahead. The two men were pale and clear, a quarry faltering and reeling. Run to collapse. Axe gave the cry of the hunter with his prey in sight. They were an arrow-shot behind me, harried to exhaustion, turning for a hopeless stand.

Axe put spurs and whip to the mare. I felt their sting as she gathered herself, leapt forward, thundering across the meadow, spumes of white foam flying back from her mouth, her reins loose, ridden to the charge.

When she was about five spear lengths from me I rose directly in her path, up on my toes, my arms above my head, my open hands and nakedness my shield.

Her eyes rolled back, the whites flashing. She swerved, trying to turn, instinct wrenching her head with a greater authority than any bit had ever dragged her mouth. For a moment Axe's face was evil rampant, etched by the moon. Then evil shocked as he saw me and the mare went down, skidding onto her side, kicking, rolling. His spine snapped with the crack of an arrow broken across the knee. The mare was on her feet, racing wildly away, streaming empty stirrups and handless reins.

Axe lay spread on the grass, face upward. I knelt by his head, turned it toward Selene, saw the terror in his eyes. "Take Her the message of my gratitude. That She veiled Her face. Do you understand?"

He tried to speak, choked in an agony of fear. I had an instant of pity. "When you reach the bridge, tell the Separator you let me drink. That may help you."

Jan was tugging at my arm, pulling me to my feet. "Move your ass, girl! Move it out. His gang's coming!"

I let him hurry me toward the willows, although I knew there was now no haste. We reached the cutter as the first of the druj came out of the forest, and the men lifted me into the Pilot's seat. I started the turbines and eased from under the trees, out over the lake, almost silent with full muffling.

Drenched in moonlight I rose and hovered at the height of a fifty-year oak to watch the end.

The pack poured onto the meadow, milled about their fallen master, then drew back so he lay alone, paralyzed, face up to the moon. They began to circle slowly. His face was the white hub of a black wheel, the center to a rim of moving shadows.

Jan grabbed a rifle, pushed open a gun-port. I caught his arm. "No—they have their work to do!"

The rim fragmented as the parts rushed in. Axe screamed as he was dismembered. I waited until he was silent. Then I cut the muffling, roared the turbines, and went up—up—up through the silver air toward the victorious moon.

XI

Fading Albedo

"For Christ's sake, Di! Let me have her!" Jan was trying to override the controls.

"No! I'm the Pilot." The light was fading as it had to fade; channels were closing as close they must. I was flying a cutter, and my body was bruised. I was reverting to reality. The moon was again a ball of sterile rock shining by reflected light. Only in moments of extreme peril or true revelation can the mind make simultaneous contact with both the spiritual and the physical.

He was pulling a blanket around my bare shoulders, squeezing me so I gasped. "You idiot blonde! If the mare hadn't shied you'd have been pounded to a pulp!"

"And we'd be dead." Kahn leaned forward. "Diana, you risked your life!"

"You also, Kahn." Captain Gart turned, reaching out his hand. "You came back to spring us. You fired the bush."

"It was my safest course." Kahn's Arabian accent became more pronounced. "After I had swum the lake I planned to neutralize their automatics. By the time I was in position you were already captured. There were packs all around me. I took the stench from a dead druj. I looked much like one already."

"Must have been a tough pilgrimage!"

"Pilgrimage? Oh—yes." Kahn peered down into the Valley. "The Settlements? Where are they?"

"There!" I lifted over the Rockfish and the spangle of lights was spread before us. "That is Sector Ten. All the way to the sea."

"Civilization's never got beyond the mountains," said Captain Gart, and I heard Kahn catch his breath.

I dropped toward Ive. The fortress was a stark black star under the moonlight. The Captain muttered, "If we're seen like this we'll be shot on sight!"

"Kate's gone home. We told her we'd be out for days. So there's only the Compradore and he'll be asleep."

Kahn broke in. "But this is Ive—the great Patrol base!"

"We're the Patrol. The only Combat Team in this segment. Diana, let her down easy. My ass is too sore for a bounce."

I landed as gently as I could. The two men had to carry me from the cutter to my room. I groped toward the shower. "First, we must get rid of this filth. Of this stench. Please help me!"

They washed me and themselves, soaping away the dried blood, the dirt, the vomitus of evil, lathering our bodies and hair under the hot water, flushing the feculence away until we were cleansed. Then they laid me on a clean sheet, Captain Gart brought ointments and dressings, and we treated each other's wounds. My body was a network of lacerations from the whips of the forest and the riding crops of Padron and Axe.

"Thank Christ Axe got his!" cursed the Captain as he swabbed.

"Axe is facing the Separator." I warned. "Let him be!"

"There's still Padron to settle with!" His hand hardened. "I'll hunt him to the gates of Hell and skewer him to the bars!"

"You would be justified. He hit me after you had challenged him."

"What? Oh that!" He was already suppressing his moment of insight. "Kahn, Padron knew you were coming."

"Yes." Kahn was spreading ointment on my shoulders. His touch was healing, but I felt his fingers quiver. "Who sent you to meet me?"

"The Governor. The Ulama asked him to arrange the pickup. But nobody warned us we might get jumped."

"Nobody would know." Kahn stood up. "I must call Crete."

"Put some clothes on first. And have some food." Captain Gart pulled the sheet over me. "I'll rig you out. Then I'll fix chow."

I listened to the voices of the two men in the kitchen but was unable to catch their words. Later they came to my room and Kahn helped me to sit while the Captain spooned broth into me, much as I had once spooned it into him. Afterward I lay against the pillows, caught their hands, asked them not to leave me. They sat, one on each side of my bed, talking. I tried to listen, but I fell asleep.

I was awakened by the sound of a ship landing. It was morning. Presently Kahn came to thank me, to say good-bye, and to bind me to silence. As few as possible must know of his return from pilgrimage. I tried to keep him by me for a short while, but he had urgent duties elsewhere, so I asked for his blessing. After I had heard his ship taking off I lay aching in my bed.

Captain Gart was alarmed to find me crying; as though he had imagined I was incapable of tears. He wanted to get a doctor, or at least call Kate. I insisted my injuries be kept secret. So he had to dress them himself, and he was a gentler nurse to me than I had been to him. I tried to talk but he made me take a capsule from our medkit and sat watching me as I fell asleep.

I slept through the rest of that day and through the next night. When I woke my body was aching but my strength had returned. He helped me with my toilet, and afterward I asked him where Kahn had gone.

"First to Maylan, then to Crete. Everybody's been in the act. Shapur's called three times, ordering strict secrecy. I told him about Padron and those goons. He tried to seem surprised. I don't think he was. Those damned autarchs know a lot more about the druj than they've told us."

"Kahn asked for silence."

"He's talked to Shapur. I made him tell Marshal Mitra. So the Guard will know what they're up against."

"Then soon everybody will know." I sighed and looked toward the window. "Kahn—he is a good man!"

"He's a brave man." Captain Gart sat down on my bed. "He could have left us. He came back. That makes him the best man I've met since I—" He paused, then said heavily, "But he doesn't know what the hell he's doing. Kahn's a fake!"

"A fake?"

"Like we're all fakes. All except you!" He smiled and touched my cheek. "And you're crazy!"

"That may be true."

"Di! I was only kidding! I didn't mean—"

"I know my faith may be only a structured delusion. That those moments when I feel the Light—they could be petit mal epilepsy. On Naxos they could have impressed me with a whole set of false convictions. The conditioning Padron suggested. I know the alternative explanations for all religious experience."

"I didn't mean you were crazy-mad!"

"But you did. I accept the possibility that my faith may only be a way of escaping the fatigue of trying to live without it. I have considered all the possibilities. And that is what they remain—possibilities. The probability is what I accept; the evidence of my mind and body. That was what Padron meant when he said I chose knowingly."

"Padron! That sadistical gleet! Fooling you for his fun!"

"Captain Gart." I raised myself onto one elbow. "Believe I'm crazy. Believe Kahn's a paper prophet. Believe we're all fakes. But don't be deceived about Padron. He is no fake. He is evil. When I looked into his eyes I looked into Hell. He knows what he is doing. He knows whom he serves. And his ambition is boundless!"

He took my hand. "That I'll swallow. If evil's real, then Padron's it."

"Also—like Kahn—he is from the past."

He let go of me as though I was electrified. "From the past?"

"Those stories of time transits, they are not all superstition."

"Stories?" He was gaping at me. "I've never read any stories."

"They aren't written. They're narod myths. But I am a Prime Pilot. I can read the Hidden Gospel."

"The Hidden Gospel?"

When Captain Gart is playing for time he has a habit of repeating my last statement back at me as a question. I suppressed my irritation. "You've read the Teacher's Gospel, haven't you?"

He nodded.

"The Hidden Gospel lies within it to be read by the initiated. So what you read as parable I can read as fact. In that Gospel there is a passage instructing his disciples to carry his wisdom into the future, to maintain the purity of his teaching among the generations to come. When read through enlightened eyes it tells how selected disciples will enter stasis, let time sweep past, and then emerge into a future when the wisdom they bear will be needed to aid civilization. The Hidden Gospel tell how such disciples can be recognized. I recognized Kahn as such a one."

"You mean—Kahn gave a secret sign?"

"Not explicitly. The signs were in his speech and acts. And the circumstances of his sudden appearance. He did not come down any road through the forest. He appeared suddenly in the mist without warning. He was astounded to find we were the only team manning this fortress, that the frontiers of civilization were still east of the Blue Ridge mountains."

"Anything else?"

"I could sense something about him. A sense of pastness. A smell is the best way I can describe it. My sense of smell is acute."

"Have you ever sniffed out anybody else?"

"Yes." I paused and his face went rigid. "Padron!"

"Padron! Good God! Your Teacher sent Padron?"

"Never! Padron serves the Darkness. But once he served the Light. I think I know who he is. The Teacher had a disciple renowned for his beauty and strength. That man became the leader of the heretics in the Ulama, as Sherando was the leader in heresy among the Settlements. Defeated in the Great Council he returned to Sherando and plotted secession. When the Order destroyed Sherando he disappeared. The picture fits Padron. He misused his knowledge to escape through time. Now he is spreading his evil in our age."

"Padron from the past. Kahn from the past. Time transits! So that's what pilgrims are!" He was pretending surprise but his basic emotion was relief. "Di, did you ever meet another time traveler?"

"No. Nor have I ever known anybody who has. But I am sure of Padron. Not only his smell but his knowledge. He knew when Kahn was to arrive and where. He called me a Prime—a title we have not used for a century. He comes from the wilderness but is neither barbarian nor bandit. Also—" I hesitated. "Padron is evil, but he is a Leader. Today, there are no men who are Leaders."

"Leader? A Führer! Diana, should we tell Shapur about Padron and Kahn?"

"Kahn would deny it. Ecclesiarchs can lie for the Faith! And the autarchs would laugh. They have cut themselves off from revelation." I gripped his hand. "But you—you still have faith. I can feel it in you!"

"Faith?" He kissed my forehead. "That's your department, Di. But whatever Padron is, we've got to nail the bastard. Thanks for telling me about time transits. Now—drink this!"

I was awakened by the sheet being turned back from my shoulders and Kate's cry of horror. She was staring down at me. "He's—he's started beating you!"

"Katy, it wasn't the Captain. I'll tell you later. Where is he?"

"Gone to see that woman. Said you were wounded. Not to disturb you. But I came—" She sank, sobbing, onto my bed. "Why? Oh why?"

I comforted her and worried about him. He was neither physically nor mentally in any state to fornicate with Rajuna. When, late that night, he arrived back at Ive, it was evident he had not. I was in the kitchen, still comforting Kate, when his cutter landed with an even greater thud than usual, and he came stumbling into the house.

It was the first and only time I have seen him intoxicated. He slumped at the kitchen table, repeating "That bitch!" at intervals, while Kate gave him black coffee. After a while of muttering he sobered somewhat and said, "She's met him!"

"Who's met whom?" My back was aching, and I was in no mood to humor a drunk.

"Rajuna—she's met Padron. So's Shapur." He ignored Kate, listening wide-eyed. "I went to warn her about Padron." He stared into his mug. "Then I find out they've been meeting Padron at some place on the frontier for months. Working up a deal. Those gutless politicos. They make deals and leave us to get killed."

"They're negotiating with Padron? Well, that's their duty."

He stared at me, lost his line of thought, and muttered, "The bitch—she admires him." He took a mouthful of coffee and fumbled with a cheroot.

"Did they know Kahn would be ambushed?"

He shook his head. "They hadn't bargained on that! But Kahn made it sound like an accident. He's trying for some kind of deal with Padron himself. He's gone off to Crete to work it out with his pals." The Captain attempted to light his cheroot and failed. "Tried to get Rajuna to see what Padron is. Started to tell her what he did to you. She laughed!" He broke the unlit cheroot between his fingers. "So I hit her!"

"You what?"

"Slapped her face!"

My alarm swamped my annoyance that he had told Rajuna about my whipping. "She might have killed you!"

"With her toy pistol?"

"They may be ornamented like toys, but they're deadly at ten meters. And she can use one. She may not approve of shooting druj. Or Sila. But insult her—and she'll shoot as fast as any other autarch."

"Well—she didn't. Just sat there sniveling."

Rajuna sniveling! "You're lucky. She must have remembered what she owed us. You've called that debt in! Don't insult an autarch again unless I'm with you. They're experts and you're too slow with a pistol."

He grunted. "No more autarchs for me. No more politics. The Marshal wants me. Staff Major. Told me so himself. He's laundered my record. Back to the Guard." He belched. "After we've nailed Padron!"

The next morning he had a hangover, but went out after Padron with the zeal of a new convert for a jihad. As I was still stiff and he was still shaky I had to remind him that if he got us both killed only Padron would profit. After a day of casting furiously around Padron's burned-out camp he shifted to a more sensible strategy.

We now knew that Padron's column was gev-based and so would have to stay near the old network of permac roads. These were mostly hidden under the trees of the forest, but I had prechaos road maps and Captain Gart extracted an airborne magnetometer from the Quartermaster at Rimon so that we could detect vehicles moving beneath us now we were alerted to their presence.

He also tried to get rockets and cannon; our cutter still had fittings to take them. But they were vestigial, hangovers from more primitive periods of design, like the human appendix, and no such weapons had been available for generations. He did get a supply of thermite grenades which he proposed to use as bombs.

I protested that any bombs, and especially incendiaries used from the air, were banned by the Code as inhumane and indiscriminate.

"Take another look at your damned code," he snapped. "You'll see that what's banned is the chemical fireball. There's nothing there to stop us using tracer. Or shoving a thermite up Padron's ass. If the druj get their paws on another auton I don't want to have to go after the gunners with a rifle for the second time. I plan to burn the bastards out!"

The legality was doubtful, but there was logic to his remark that we were already using tracer which, after all, is an aerial incendiary weapon. And we now both felt pushed for time. As soon as the Council came to terms with Padron we would no longer be free to hunt him. Our part in the struggle would be over, but I detested the idea of leaving him alive to spread his evil by peaceful means. The Captain's drive to destroy him was less ethical; he was goaded by a mixture of jealousy, hatred, and a hunger for revenge.

We couldn't catch Padron but we did frustrate him. During July he tried to move along the foothills, and across the valley toward the Rockfish Gap. At sunset, toward the end of the month, we caught one of his gevs crossing a patch of open marsh, went in low, and plastered it with thermites. It burned, to use the Captain's simile, like a brewed-up tank, and we were able to circle it in the dusk, picking off its crew and outriders.

The loss of that gev apparently convinced Padron that he could not probe across the Valley, at least in our segment, and he pulled his column back into the mountains. He also reduced the number of druj raids along the rest of the frontier, although there were still sufficient to keep the Guard busy and dissuade farmers from returning.

The Guard began to congratulate itself that it had the druj threat under control. The politicians however would know that Padron could start another panic and upset the Sector economy any time he chose. Captain Gart took the idea further. "Padron's easing the pressure because those damned civilians are vacillating while they negotiate. If he doesn't get what he's after he'll hit 'em with all his packs at once. Everywhere except our segment. The Council will lose what nerve it has and meet his terms." He proceeded to quote historical precedents to support his argument.

On this occasion they were not valid. We learned another reason for Padron's hesitancy when we saw the first nonhostile druj. We were flying slowly above the Shenandoah River; it was lying face-down on a rock out in the open, and alone. "What the hell's it up to?" asked Captain Gart, starting to sight.

It reached down into the stream. "Fishing, bear-fashion," I said.

It ignored us and suddenly flipped a fish from the water to the rock. Then it sat up and began to tear at the catch with its fingers. "Unarmed," said the Captain. He lowered his rifle and we hovered, watching it eat. "Put me down. Far bank. Ready for a fast lift."

I let down quietly and he stepped into the shadows. I hung at fifty meters while he walked slowly upstream. The creature winded him when they were about level. It looked up but neither bolted nor attacked. Captain Gart stopped and they stared at each other across the water.

The druj held its half-eaten fish toward the Captain. "Christ!" I heard him breathe on the com. "It's offering me a share!"

"Be careful," I urged. "Evil is full of wiles."

"I don't like raw catfish!" He hefted his rifle. The druj advanced a few steps into the river, still holding out its offering. The Captain lowered his rifle. "Lift me off, Di. Slow and easy."

I picked him up on the skids. The druj watched us rise, then still chewing on its fish it loped away into the forest.

The Captain climbed up into the cabin. "Diana, what do you make of that?"

"It's gone mad."

"Or becoming sane?"

Whatever the reason for its anomalous behavior we reported it to both the Guard and to the civilian government. We got no follow-up or request for further information. Apparently the existence of nonhostile druj suited the plans of neither.

XII

Autumnal Equinox

On the day of deadlock between Light and Darkness we were heading unsteadily westward through the updrafts of the Rockfish Gap when the com pinged. We were far outside com range and Captain Gart, who had insisted on flying the cutter himself, let it lurch. "What the hell?"

"Hello, Douglas!"

Our rotor-wash lashed the treetops before I could wrench control from him and take us soaring back above the pass.

"I see you heard me. Diana, that was spectacular flying!"

"Padron!"

"Sergeant—forgive me—Doctor! I'm offering you a chance to talk. If you're wise, you will."

"Satan," I said, "is somewhere along the western flank, near the ridge."

He was not listening; he had the expression of a man who has just been hit in the stomach. His hand went fumbling to the microphone switch. "Okay, Padron. Talk."

"Face to face, Douglas. Communication is more than words. We must meet."

"We will. And when we do I'll spread your guts on the grass!"

"Not if Diana is moderating."

"Diana!" Captain Gart's voice thickened. "Padron, whatever you're planning for me, don't hurt Diana again!"

"Hurt Diana? Of course not. I need her help. Let me talk to her. You won't believe me. But you will believe her."

The Captain switched off his mike. "Di—can you bear to listen to him?"

"Yes." I saw his face. "It might be best if I did."

116

He chewed his lip, hesitated, then muttered, "Okay, go ahead."

I switched on my mike. "Padron, I hear you."

"Greetings, Diana. If you are a Prime you know the protocol for truce?"

"I do."

"And you know how to moderate a parley?"

"I have never moderated one. But I have been taught how to moderate."

"Diana, when you were my prisoner, did I break the Law?"

"No. But Axe did."

"It was I who removed the halter at your demand. And you have settled your account with Axe."

"His pack settled theirs. Yours is still to be paid."

Padron laughed. "Well, we are all in the paws of Zurvan. But I kept the Law then so I can invoke it now. I want a parley with your master. And I want you to moderate."

Captain Gart knocked off my mike-switch. "What's he up to? What crud! Not breaking the law! He flogged you with a riding-crop!"

"That was legal, although cruel. But he did remove the halter. Which was illegal. He is asking for a brief truce and a face-to-face meeting with you. He wishes me to moderate the meeting. He has the right to ask. You have the right to refuse."

"Moderate? What does that mean?"

"That I cover you both while you are talking. And shoot the first to make a hostile move. Shoot you both if you both do."

"My God! What crazy—?" He stared at me. "You'd do that?"

"If you agree to a parley. Then I will."

"He'll trust you to hold a gun on him and not blow him apart?"

"He will take the word of a Pilot. He will want to make it formal; he will require I take the Oath. But when I am bound he will trust me with his life. And you already have, many times." I watched the conflict on his face; for some reason he was being dragged to a meeting with Padron. I warned him. "The Oath is binding. It would force me to shoot you if you broke the truce. Can you trust yourself?"

He looked away, then spoke on the com. "Padron, what'll you do if I tell you to stick your truce up your ass?"

"Regret it. So will you. So will Diana. All three of us will regret it. But you and Diana will regret it most. For I will publish the truth. And the truth will set you free. Free to wander as an outlaw across the wilderness. A miserable life, Douglas. For Diana even more miserable than for you."

"Diana, she's nothing to do with this."

"She would go with you. Faithful unto death!" Padron chuckled. "You must know her mettle by now. At present she is your creature. But when her briefing fades and she finds herself wandering, starving and disgraced, with a man who has tricked her—then I can't forecast what she'll do!"

"Padron, I'll call that bluff. What have I to gain?"

"Information. Information you need to make wise decisions."

I touched Captain Gart's hand. "Accept the parley. You have nothing to lose. You have just outmaneuvered him. He does not realize that. You will outmaneuver him again for he is blinded by vanity."

"Di, you don't—" He spoke on the com. "Padron, what's all this bull about parleys?"

"Just do as Diana tells you. Follow her instructions very carefully." Padron chuckled. "Diana, will you moderate?"

I glanced at Captain Gart. He hesitated, then nodded, I spoke to Padron. "I will moderate." I began the Oath. Jan listened, chewing his lower lip. "Now, I am bound." I moved the cutter along the ridge to hover over the place I had picked.

It was a grassy plateau with both flanks of the mountain bare for about two hundred meters down to the trees. There was a large rock I could put my back against. I called, "Padron, ride along the western slope until you are level with me. I will know when you are in position. Wait while I land on the eastern slope. Gart will stay with the cutter. I will be lying behind the crest with a rifle. When I call, ride out of the woods up to the foot of the crest. Dismount and stand. Is that clear?"

"Check!"

"I will rise when I am sure it is safe. When I am ready for the parley I will call Gart and you up to face each other. Do you understand?"

"Diana, your operation orders are a model—"

"Do you understand?"

"Yes. I'm moving."

"If there is any sign of treachery before the parley starts I will shoot Satan through the head."

"You posturing little bitch! By the shit of the Bull—" A laugh. "My apologies, Diana. I am not staking my life on your word to commit treachery."

Jan leaned over and touched my hand. "Di, if you'd rather not—"

"Be careful, Jan! I am close to what you call automatic. Best not to touch me nor make a sudden movement."

"Jeez!" He leaned back and wiped his forehead.

I sensed Satan in position and swooped down to land. "Jan, stay by the cutter where I can see you." I went to lie behind the crest and study the forest below. There were no druj and no horse except Satan within range. I called, "Padron, come out."

He rode from under the trees, trotting the great black horse up the slope. He dismounted at the foot of the ridge and stood with open hands. "At your service, Diana."

I drew my pistol, and moved to place my back against the rock. I looked down, first at one man, then at the other. "Gart! Padron! Come up and meet face to face."

They climbed slowly under my orders and reached the ridge together. "Stop!" I said when we formed an isosceles triangle with myself at the apex. "No closer! I cover you both."

"Douglas," Padron was smiling. "Be very careful. Diana is no longer under your command. Do not make a move she might interpret wrongly. She'll drop you as readily as she'll drop me."

"Bullshit!" I said. As I rarely use obscenities mine still have impact. "You have not yet signed the parley. Only the truce is on."

"A stickler for protocol, aren't you, Diana? Where's your recorder?"

"There." I had already thrown it on the grass.

"What the hell?" asked Jan.

"Douglas, there is a whole body of arcane law of which you know nothing. Customs which you cannot be expected to know. But Diana has been steeped in them. We are participating in a ceremony of great age. At the moment we are in truce. The instant it changes to parley she will react only in accordance with the Law. After the parley is over, she will remember nothing about it. I will be saying things you will not wish her to hear. That is why I made sure she has shed her recorder. Diana, please confirm."

"Padron is correct. The Moderator remembers nothing. And acts to support protocol. Gart, I know you are a skeptic. So, for your own safety, think of it this way. Have you heard of hypnotism?"

"Sure! But—"

"Listen, please. There were once stage hypnotists who amused audiences by making their victims act out absurd roles that had been suggested to them while under hypnosis and of which they remembered nothing. Regard me in such a light. Only my role is not absurd. Do you understand?"

"Sure! Sure!"

"Before the parley starts I must warn you both. If either of you attacks the other I will shoot the attacker. I can fire five aimed shots on different targets in a single second."

"Thank you, Diana. You mentioned your skill once before. Now—"

"A moment, Padron. I had not finished. I will shoot the attacker. But you are both fast, even if you are not particularly skilled. So if either of you loses control I am liable to kill both of you with the same burst."

"That—" Padron had lost his smile. "That's not protocol!"

"It is truth. It is a warning that I am capable of error—"

"For Christ's sake, Di! Quit grandstanding. So you're a hypnotized killer and a smart girl with a gun!" Jan's nerves were as taut as Padron's. Both men were now eyeing the muzzle of my pistol with an equal distrust.

I savored the moment. Then I said, "Each of you—make the sign."

"Sign? What sign?" asked Jan.

"The sign you hold sacred. When you are both signed the parley begins."

Padron laughed. He held up his right hand, palm toward me, his middle fingers clenched, his outer fingers spread, the old sign of victory and peace. Then he slowly turned his hand to show me the nails. A far older sign. The Horns of the Goat.

Jan misread both. "Fuck you too!" He hesitated. Then he made the sign of the Cross.

My memory blanked.

The following is the transcription I typed later from Captain Gart's recorder. I include it here to maintain continuity.

The whistle of the wind. "Douglas, I know you."

"Padron—how the hell?"

"How? I too am a traveler. I came by choice, not by chance. I did not fall, I stepped."

The wind moaned. "Padron, what are you after?"

"An understanding. Kahn—you—I. We three are unique. I have already reached an understanding with Kahn. Now I am seeking one with you. But we are different from Kahn. We are of the same stock and lineage. We should be comrades, not rivals."

"Comrades in what?"

"In the rescue of mankind. Down there is Sherando. Once it was rich and powerful, spreading civilization through the Valley, its influence reaching to the sea. The lawful inheritor of our great nation. In it discipline and honor were preserved. One of the few pure settlements in the world. The others— mongrels, scratching their fleas, yelping at their betters." A pause, and the wind sighed. "Look at it now! A habitation laid waste. Despoiled! As our nation was despoiled. The nation for which you fought."

"I never fought—"

"Douglas, I know your past. It was I who helped prepare the Table of Transits which the Ulama is using, using without understanding. Like all mongrels they are consumers, not creators. I was once a member of the Ulama. But I am a purebred; I was not satisfied with tables. I looked behind them and found—a Convolution! That was long ago, but I remembered. After you escaped I had a contact in Maylan check Gart's record. It did not fit the man who faced us in the dome, far less the soldier who has denied us Sherando through the summer. For the Ulama Hudson's Bay was just another unused transit site to be watched. For me—it was the place where Douglas died. The Douglas Convolution. The memorial to a great mathematician. I read his biography. I recognized a man who can help me to save civilization."

"Civilization? Sherando style? That gallows and whipping post? In Virginia—they're obscene!"

"In Virginia? So the old bond still holds? Sherando was all that was left of the real Virginia. We preserved it through the chaos, held it against the mongrels. Until those evil hags on Naxos interfered! Sent their murdering automata—mindless killers like Diana at this moment—against us. We were a Settlement under siege. Yes, we hanged traitors and criminals. We whipped the lazy and immoral. As they did at Jamestown. As the founders of our nation did when their civilization was threatened. Like Jamestown, we survived. Like Jamestown, we had to move."

"And left the druj to cover your retreat!"

"You have more insight than all the mongrels down there!"

"Careful, Padron! No sudden movements! Diana twitched."

"Forgive me! Yes, we have had to use the druj. As our ancestors used the Iroquois and the Sioux against their enemies. As the Order uses poor brainwashed girls like Diana against us."

"Padron—you bloody hypocrite! Poor brainwashed Diana! You bastard—you who tortured her!"

"Torture?" A laugh. "Douglas, which of us is the hypocrite? You must have interrogated female prisoners."

"Never! By God! No!"

"Yet I am sure your comrades in arms questioned villagers. You must have used the information they extracted. Your anger shows your guilt. And what did I do? A few strokes with a riding crop! Hardly the way a serious inquisitor would interrogate a woman. But in one sense you are right to fault me. I should not have called Diana poor and brainwashed. I respected her from the moment I saw her. I respect courage. That essential virtue which makes all the others effective. I respected yours. I had no intention of harming or humiliating either of you. I took off the halter. One does not humiliate an enemy one respects."

"Not humiliate? Putting a girl naked across a table—"

"For Diana a supreme moment in her life. No, I'm not calling her a masochist, unless you call every martyr a masochist. But it gave her the chance to flaunt her courage, her loyalty, her devotion to her cause, her ability to withstand pain. She had the beatific expression of Saint Catherine being broken on the wheel.* She delighted in being forced to display her body. She is a true female. She may not come into heat, but she glories in her beauty, at the hunger in men's eyes. Mine also. She relished the adulation—without guilt. For she was not naked by her own choice. I had her stripped by force. You forced her to strip in submission. To demonstrate your mastery over her. You humiliated her more than I!"

"God—I'm ashamed!"

"But you should not be! You were watching my face as you turned her around. I was watching hers. The seduction on her mouth! A willing slave girl on the auction block. Reveling in her power over men. It was we who were humiliated, not her! The bitch earned her whipping!" A pause. "But I didn't come here to discuss Diana."

"I can see that. What's this understanding you have with Kahn?"

"If I am allowed to return to Sherando, I'll call off the druj. And it's you who's forced me to deal with Kahn! You and Diana! I'd have taken Sherando without trouble if you two hadn't joined the fight. You controlled the approaches to Sherando. You drove my packs from this Gap again and again. But the future has outflanked you. I am gaining Sherando without more bloodshed."

"You're getting Sherando? The Ulama's agreed? Those gutless prigs! So you can bring back the gallows and the whipping post?"

"I doubt I'll need either. Anyway, which is worse, to mark a man's back with the whip or destroy his will with a drug? A man's back heals and he remains free to choose. A drugged man doesn't even know his will is gone."

"You mean—Paxin?"

"Of course. The beastly product of Fort Detrick. The civilian warmonger's dream. The mongrel's weapon. The stuff that steals a man's will to fight—or disobey. The stuff that Shapur and his kind use to keep their narod docile!"

"Why are you telling me all this? What do you want?"

"I want you. As an ally. Down there, to the East, what do you see? A mongrel society in decay. A Guard without guts

---

* *It was the wheel which got broken, not Saint Catherine. She was beheaded! Flawed, like most of Padrons statements.*

or will. The systems failing. The narod fleeing. Autarchs choking from their own greed. No creative scientists, no creative engineers, no creative artists, no creative anything! Those drugged mongrels cannot create. They can only consume! They have been living on the fat of the past for generations. And the fat is turning rancid."

"Because they can't synthesize Paxin?"

"Because they can't synthesize anything they can't copy! They're more like monkeys than men. Douglas, I want you with us. We are a determined brotherhood. We carry in our genes the pure races, each with its separate talents. The races that raised mankind to what it was. Who will raise it to what it will be. We are the future. You saw us, recognized us. In your heart you know you are one of us."

"You want me for more than my genes."

"I want you for your genius. The master of the Convolution. The Master of Time. I want you as a soldier, the ablest I have met. I want you with me because we share race, nation, language, philosophy."

"What you want is an escape hatch into the future!"

"That is true. Time is a strong weapon if one can afford to wait. But we will not have to wait long. The mongrels are starting to yelp, to nip. Soon they will be snarling, biting, savaging each other. You have seen the signs."

"Their Paxin is running out. They can't make more. But the Ulama has reserves."

"Reserves!" Padron's laugh. "Kahn hates me, but is ready to deal. Guess why?"

"Because you have Paxin?"

"Kilograms—kilograms! All safely hidden in cocooned storage deep in the wilderness. I can help Shapur and the rest keep their narod quiet for years—if they restore what their fathers stole from me. That is why Shapur, Kahn, even those old hags in Diana's Order are ready to deal."

"To deal?"

"We are negotiating a Treaty under the Law of Infolding." Padron's laugh. "Shapur will want to use you. You're his only resolute gunman. He'll keep you as his bodyguard for any treaty signing."

"Padron—I'm no traitor!"

"I'm not asking you to be. I would have no use for you if you were. It is because I trust your word, and the word of

Diana, that I have risked my life to parley with you. All I want from you now, while you're still bound to those mongrels, is to make certain they do not attempt trickery when we meet to sign the treaty. All I want is your word that you'll make sure Shapur keeps his."

"Padron, you'd be a fool to take my word. And you're not a fool. It's Diana's oath you're after. I'll go this far. I'll be bound by hers; if she decides to give it. Though, by God, if I was her I'd have blasted your guts out by now."

"Of course! But you are not Diana. I think we both realize there is nobody on Earth like Diana. Perhaps that is just as well! But later, after you have thrown off Gart's shackles you will join us and claim the honor that is your due. One warning! Don't mention this parley to Shapur. He hates you. Because Rajuna found you more virile than she found him. He resents you, as as he resents me, as any mixed breed resents the thoroughbred. He is proud, as only a mulatto can be proud. If he finds you are not his inferior in intellect, or that we have spoken, his jealousy might swamp his self-interest."

"Padron." Silence and the wind. "I need time to think."

"Take it. There is a place waiting for you in our leadership. For you are a Leader. All the cadre admire you. And remember, first Sherando will be ours, then Sector Ten. Shapur and Rajuna have planned well for their private gains, as their fathers did before them. Ten is now critical to the technology of the world. Whoever controls Ten has all the other Sectors by the throat. The world by the scruff of the neck!"

"Easy, Padron, easy! Diana's getting tense."

"By the Bull's balls, she is! We must break off. I don't enjoy being under her gun."

"The parley is finished," I said. They were staring at me, two guilty boys caught in some indecency. "Gart, go back to the cutter. Padron, go back to your horse. The truce ends when you are out of my sight in the woods."

"Diana, one day we will talk theology again. Your steel is worth crossing. You are the first woman I have ever admired. You are—"

"Padron, I said go back to your horse!"

He shrugged, smiled, and went down to where Satan was waiting. He mounted, saluted with his riding crop, and cantered back to the forest. I watched him until he had disappeared among the trees. Then I holstered my pistol, picked up my rifle, and walked down to the cutter.

Captain Gart was standing by it. "Sir," I said, "it is over." I was exhausted.

XIII

Apogee

That night I slept deep and undreaming. I don't think Captain Gart slept at all for in the morning his bed was undisturbed. I found him standing on the wall, staring at the mountains. He did not look at me. "Diana, what do you remember about yesterday?"

"The truce, but not the parley. For the Moderator key phrases alone have meaning. Nothing is stored, not even in my subconscious."

"What'll you report to Naxos?"

"Only that a parley occurred."

He reached into his coveralls, took out his recorder, and weighed it in his hand. Then he gave it to me. "Listen to what we said. Transcribe it. Read it. Then come and tell me what you think."

When I had finished the transcription he was still standing on the wall, so I made a mug of coffee and took it to him with the typescript. He seemed cheered by my gesture, and stood gripping the mug with both hands. "Well, Diana?"

"Padron is the renegade Disciple. Many of his facts are wrong and his quotations inaccurate."

"Yes—yes! What else?"

"Padron's tempting you. Lying with half-truths. He's learned about your past and he's trying blackmail."

"He sure is!" Captain Gart was starting to sweat. "But Douglas—the name?"

"I've heard you call it out."

"What?" He cursed as he spilled hot coffee onto his hands. "When?"

"In your sleep. Perhaps it's an old alias. Maybe somebody heard you and told Padron. He has friends in Maylan."

127

"He has! He has!"

"You outwitted him. As you did before. Padron's blinded by his own vanity. But he said one true thing. He called you a Leader."

"Me? A Leader?" He laughed. "I'm a Sergeant at heart." He seemed extravagantly relieved. "Diana—you see everything the way you want it to be."

"I see in terms of what I know. And I know that Padron is for the Dark. And that you, underneath, are for the Light."

"For the Light! Me?" He sipped his coffee, put the mug on the parapet, and lit a cheroot. "So Padron lied. And I tricked him with the truth. I wish to hell I knew what the truth was. Di, what do we do?"

"Our duty. To defend the Light when Evil uses force."

"Padron's switching to politics. This Treaty's more dangerous than the druj."

"Perhaps. But not our responsibility. The Light sets the ends; we are the means. Ecclesiarchs fight Evil with words. We fight with guns."

"With guns! Diana, you believe that crap? Yes, you do! You're a fanatic. But no hypocrite." He began pacing up and down the wall. "Neither am I. Padron's trying for a deal. The autarchs are running out of Paxin. The Sector's in no shape for mass cold-turkey. I don't like chemical pacifiers, but they're candy compared to Padron's persuaders—if he grabs control."

"He can't. If he tries we can stop him again. As we have already."

He stood and studied me. "Diana, so smart and so naive! If the Sector drifts into chaos we'll be lucky to fight our way out. It's the techs and the narod who do all the work. The techs are mostly timids. If the narod start smashing things the techs will bolt. So will the autarchs after a few of 'em have been lynched. Padron's right. If Paxin runs out he'll walk in. Sooner or later. Us? No techs means no fuel. A grounded cutter—and we're just a pair of sharpshooters."

"That's probably why Shapur wants a Treaty, but it's not our business. If the Ulama have agreed—"

"That bunch! Kahn's the best of 'em. And he's a fake." He chewed his cheroot. "The question is—what do I do?"

"Follow your conscience. The Synod named you a nexus in the reticulum. That means the Light shines on you, even if you're blind to it. But your conscience will turn toward the Light. As a flower turns toward the sun."

"A flower? Me?" He laughed. "Diana, you're the mystic. Point me in the right direction. What the hell does your Light want me to do?"

"To stop Padron if he uses force."

"But let him have the Sector, maybe the world, if he shifts to politics?"

"Neither of us knows anything about politics."

"Maybe not. But I do know right from wrong. Okay, so I've got to play it by ear." And he went off to play with the computer.

Whatever the tune the tempo quickened. Disquiet was spreading through all classes of civilians. The uneasiness was most obvious in Sector Ten for ours was the only Sector being stressed by the druj while short of Paxin. But the reports I got from Naxos suggested that everywhere the social structure was distorting, the strains were showing. Paxin was the mortar which cemented together incongruous social, political, and economic elements. Everywhere the demand for Paxin was rising, the supply falling.

In the dome I had seen Padron's cadre as the point of a spear striking a wall, sounding for a fracture-line. That could have been a true vision, or only the fantasy of a mind made frantic by pain and fatigue. But hallucination or vision, the facts were the same. The druj raids had not only driven farmers back from the frontier, they had alarmed every timid in the Sector, and a timid's reaction is to run. The atmosphere in Ten was becoming as agitated as the air around a hive about to swarm.

Padron's claim that Kahn was involved in the treaty-making was given substance by a signal from Naxos. A Pilot named Vanda, flying an Ulama ship for the Ecclesiarch Kahn was on her way to Ten and would be contacting me on her arrival. Captain Gart read the message and tossed it on the desk. "Kahn's coming for the Ulama's cut. Bunch of Pharisees!"

The next prelude to a treaty was a request from the Council that we refrain from harassing any peaceful barbarians who approached the frontier. It was followed by the arrival at Ive of Mansur to inform us of the Council's pacification policy. The ultimate incongruity—a Director of Security coming to explain the decisions of the Sector Council to a Patrol Captain! He was indeed a nexus in something!

"The Council's aim is to restore peace on the frontier. The Governor has asked me to seek your aid in achieving it," Mansur was saying when I joined them in the parlor.

"So Padron and his goons can run free in the Valley?"

"Padron has invoked the Law of Infolding. Any barbarian band can claim admission to civilization if it agrees to abide by the unifying concepts of the United Settlements. The most important is the freedom of the citizens to move as they wish."

"Which the narod are claiming by the planeload."

"That is why we have to consider Padron's application, despite his barbarous behavior. The liquidation of holdings, the financial burden of the enlarged Guard garrisons, the growing zone of devastation along the frontier. All these are bringing the Sector close to bankruptcy." Mansur hesitated. "Nor do I forget the cost in life and suffering."

Captain Gart studied the tip of his cheroot. "Mansur, why is the Council so keen to make a deal with this butcher? You know his druj are turning non-hostile. We've got him nailed. Why not let him hang?"

I was disgusted. Captain Gart knew perfectly well why the Council was trying to come to terms. His behavior was dishonorable and I tried to attract his attention.

He ignored me and went on, "Last Spring a bunch of your Wardens vamoosed and left Diana and myself to save a gev from Sila. We shot Sila in the process. That gev was loaded with Paxin. The last reserves you had in this Sector. You can't make the stuff. All the other Sectors are short. So where are you going to get more?"

Mansur began to blink. "The shortage of Paxin is not secret. You don't use it. Neither do I. But it's how most people meet problems."

"Is Padron buying the Valley with Paxin?"

Mansur squeezed his hands together. "He is not buying the Valley. He wants to return to that ruined settlement—Sherando. And his band have a claim to the place. They are the descendants of the men and women who were driven from it when it was destroyed. They wish—well, you might say they are asking to return home."

"You might say that. Complete with druj, slaves, and a column of armored gevs. Plus, I suggest, Paxin from some cache in the wilderness?"

Mansur's blink-rate increased. "The Ulama has approved its use. Kahn is taking part in the negotiations. The Survival Axiom. Later, when the situation has stabilized, we will be able to phase it out."

"As you've been doing for the last century." Captain Gart laughed. "When the wolf comes through the door ethics and Ecclesiarchs exit through the window. Bargaining with Padron! Do you know what he is?"

"Indeed I do!" Mansur's eyelids were fluttering. "As Director of Security I have seen more gutted farms and mutilated bodies than even you. To stop that devilry I would deal with the Devil himself."

"You are!" I said.

"Quiet Diana." The Captain waved his cheroot at me. Then he chewed on it. Presently he said, "If Paxin dries up there'll be chaos. So if Padron has the stuff to trade, then for God's sake—trade! But why spill your heart out to me. I'm not involved."

"Captain—" Mansur swallowed. "Your agreement is necessary."

"My agreement? How the hell—?"

"Padron has insisted that you and Diana supervise the security of the meeting when the Articles of Infolding are signed." Mansur fiddled with his glasses. "That is why Shapur sent me to talk to you. Padron has confidence in your honor and Diana's oath. He does not have the same confidence in ours. Shapur, of course, is insulted. I have tried to point out to him that Padron's caution is to be expected. Padron has nothing to gain from treachery, whereas the Sector and the Ulama have much."

"But for Padron to say he trusts me after what he did—"

"Padron was impressed by the courage you showed while you were his captive. He believes, rightly I think, that if you and Diana have sworn to prevent treachery at the signing then there will be no treachery. And he will not enter the Sector until the Treaty has been signed."

"If he won't enter the Sector where's he going to meet Shapur?"

"In Sherando."

"Sherando!" Captain Gart laughed. "He wants to rub your noses in the dirt!"

"Captain Gart, I'm ready to eat dirt to end the carnage." Mansur stopped blinking and faced the Captain. "But I think his reasons are more cogent than a desire to humiliate us. His column is a long way from its base. He needs to take over Sherando as soon as possible. Winter is approaching."

"He needs time. And you need Paxin."

Mansur shrugged. "We both need peace. We distrust each other. But all of us have absolute confidence in the word of a Pilot." He bowed toward me with genuine courtesy.

Captain Gart grunted. "I can't make Diana promise not to shoot the bastard on sight."

"Padron and his dragoons must have women back at their base," I said. "What's going to happen to them?"

Mansur turned to me. "They are why your Order has agreed to a treaty. Padron and his people are returning to orthodoxy. When they are settled in Sherando they will be as free to move as any other citizens of the United Settlements. Diana, it is only through this treaty that Padron's women can ever become free. Your Synod has agreed that Sherando can be rehabilitated. The Ulama consulted your Order as soon as the possibility was raised." He gestured toward the phone. "Call Naxos if you doubt me."

"There's no need. I can see the logic." As Captain Gart had once remarked, the Order had destroyed Sherando but had not rescued the women. Seventy years later we would be doing their descendents a better service by freeing them than by killing their masters. The concept of a restored Sherando disgusted me, as it must have appalled the Synod, but the alternative was to leave the women in slavery, and that we could not accept. "Once Padron's community is back in Sherando the Order will be able to oversee it, and ensure that women who want to leave are free to go."

"There may not be so many," grunted Captain Gart. "Those dragoons looked like a fine bunch of studs!"

For a moment I hated him. Then I said, "Tell Padron I'll give my oath."

Captain Gart stared at me. "So!" He hesitated, then said to

Mansur, "If the Governor's decided on a deal with those goons, and if he wants me to run security, then I will. But with what?"

"I will select a squad of the best Wardens for you."

"Wardens? Good God! Why not a couple of gunships and some armored gevs from the Guard?"

"You forget, Captain. Marshal Mitra would never allow the Guard to cross the frontier. He is restricted by the Expansionist Heresy; the acquisition of new territory by a Sector. The Marshal is very orthodox."

Captain Gart muttered something obscene.

"Doubtless after the treaty has been ratified Sherando will be incorporated into Sector Ten, and then the Guard will be justified in establishing a defense line to the west of the Valley. But until then he won't move over the mountains. It would not be legal."

"So it's up to Diana, myself, and a bunch of limp fuzz to see that Padron doesn't jump the lot of you. Who'll be there?"

"The Treaty will be signed by Shapur as Governor, Kahn on behalf of the Ulama, and Rajuna as Director of Special Systems."

"Her? I thought I smelt that woman in this."

"Captain Gart, you do Rajuna an injustice. She—"

"So Kahn's coming too? He's got a ship. Flown by a Pilot. Tell him I want it. Pilot, ship, crew. I'm like Padron. I trust Pilots, and nobody else."

Mansur hesitated. "I will speak to him—"

"Don't speak to him. Tell him! Either he lets me have his ship until after the Treaty, or there won't be any Treaty for him to sign."

Mansur sighed. "I will give him your message. Captain, I wish—"

"How are your Wardens armed? Rifles? Have your picked squad over here pronto. I'll teach 'em to use thermites. In case some rejuvenated druj get into the act. Those animals fear fire."

"Thank you, Captain. I myself will be there, under your command, of course. As indeed we all will be."

"Under my command? But you're Director of Security."

"I have no legal jurisdiction outside the boundaries of Sector Ten. Neither does Shapur or Rajuna. Officially Padron is the leader of a barbarian band. So this meeting is a military operation under the command of the senior Guard Officer present. Which will be you."

"You mean I'm the fall guy if anything goes wrong."

Mansur sighed. "I do not mean that, Captain. I mean that if an emergency arises I know that you will act wisely and effectively." He took off his glasses and wiped his forehead. "This is a most difficult time for me. We are no longer organized to meet crises." He replaced his glasses, bowed to each of us, and walked slowly out to his ship.

Captain Gart stared after him. "With cops like him we can't afford crooks!"

"He became autarch and rose to Director through his abilities, not from his birth."

"It certainly wasn't because of his looks."

"He's trying to do his duty. And you amused yourself humiliating him. You were not behaving like an Officer. You were acting like an autarch."

"You impudent girl!" We glared at each other. "And you're not acting like a Pilot."

"I'm starting not to feel like one. I'm beginning to find this patrol disgusting. I'm long overdue for debriefing and leave. The sooner they sign the Treaty, end the fighting, and let me return to Naxos, the better."

This for him was evidently a new thought. "You mean—when the fighting stops you'll quit on me?"

"Of course. You'll become a Staff Major and fawn on Marshal Mitra. I'll be free to go skiing."

I left him staring out of the window toward the wilderness.

XIV

Libration

A ship wearing the green of the Ulama landed at Ive the next morning, and I went to greet the Pilot as she jumped down from the flight deck. She was young and small, but she had handled her ship well. We kissed as sisters.

"I am Vanda." Her chestnut hair was bobbed after the custom of Pilots flying for the Ulama. It may remind the Ecclesiarchs of choirboys, but it made Vanda look like a child. "Before I left Naxos I was told to report to Diana, the Pilot in control of this team."

"I'm Diana. The team's usually out of control." Her face showed she was fresh from briefing. For weeks humor would be absent and semantics absolute. "Captain Gart's the officer."

"The Prioress called him unique. I am to tell you he has our protection."

"What?" I had never heard of a Patrol officer being placed under the Shield of the Order.

"The Synod has named Captain Gart as protected."

"Protected! Him! Here he comes. Careful Vanda, he's short-fused."

"He's what?"

"Liable to explode on contact."

The Captain had just emerged from the house, stopped to stare at the ship, and was now striding across the yard. Vanda saluted with the snap typical of Ulama Pilots. It brought Captain Gart up all standing.

"Good God! Another Girl Scout with a gun!"

"No, sir. I am not a Scout. I am a Pilot of the Order, rated of the Third Class, seconded to the Ulama, serving with the

Ecclasiarch Kahn, who has placed my Unit under your command. My name is Vanda."

"Vanda, eh? Mine's Gart. I guess you know Diana?" He glanced around, "Where's your unit?"

"At present I'm alone, sir. A crew will arrive when and if available."

"No crew?"

"Not yet, sir."

"Christ!" He stared up at the ship, looming behind her. "They let a kid like you fly a thing that size? Where've you come from?"

"From Naxos, sir. I spoke to His Grace on the radio and he directed me here."

"His what? Oh—Kahn!" He continued to stare at the ship. "You mean you've just brought that from the Med?"

"I crossed via the Azores and refueled ten times. I was told His Grace needed the ship urgently."

"How long have you been on passage?"

"A week, sir."

"No wonder you're bushed! A kid like you! Halfway around the world. Flying alone for a week. What the hell—" He caught her arm and turned her toward the house. She checked her reaction to knock him flat though he, of course, did not notice. "Come in and get fixed up." When she hesitated, glancing back at her ship, "Forget that damned thing. It won't fly away. Diana'll snug it down. You need food and sleep. Also a bath." He pushed her gently toward the front door where Kate was waiting. "Katy, take this young lady upstairs. Give her a bath. Feed her. And put her to bed!"

Vanda showed her confusion. A recently briefed Pilot is prepared to deal with stereotypes, not eccentrics like Captain Gart. She disappeared with Kate, torn between her duty to her ship and obedience to her titular commander. I followed him into the parlor.

He was puffing furiously on a cheroot. "What the hell do those hags on Naxos think they're doing? Sending a child alone across the Atlantic?"

"Vanda's a Third, so she's at least nineteen. In the old wars there were male aces younger than her. She must be better than competent. Also, as she's assigned to the Ulama, she has special talents. Ecclesiarchs are as hard to handle as Patrol Officers."

"We pinch your bottoms and they tickle your souls, eh?" He laughed at his own joke. "Poor kid! Another icicle! She reminds me of a girl I once knew."

"Who was that?"

"She called herself Diana!" He again enjoyed his humor. "Will Vanda become human as she gets run in?"

"Pilot's aren't machines! But yes, she'll become more sensitive. As I have. You'll be able to hurt her if she stays long enough." He almost dropped his cheroot. "She has brought extraordinary news. The Synod has placed you under the Shield of the Order."

"What the hell does that mean?"

"If you are harmed unjustly you would be revenged."

"Good God! Like I'm some girl who gets herself raped? Revenged? What help is that?"

"Few of your enemies would wish to feud with the Order."

"Bunch of fanatic schoolmarms!" He chewed his cheroot, wondering whether to be flattered or insulted. "Why me?"

"Months ago I told you that the Synod had identified you as a nexus in the reticulum, a critical junction. The omens are justified. Yesterday a Director came seeking your agreement to a treaty both the Ulama and the Sector Government think is essential. And you only a Patrol Captain!"

"Only a Patrol Captain—"

"The omens must have forecast that the current of Time is carrying another divergence toward you. The Synod wish you to be without external threat when you decide."

He said something cynical but I sensed his conceit. Also a paternalism I had not suspected he possessed. Vanda had aroused it. When she appeared at breakfast the next morning looking almost adult he put her through the kind of interrogation I was starting to remember from my own youth.

She answered the Captain's questions concisely when she knew the answers, and added one of the Order's aphorisms when she thought one appropriate. She had been serving with Ecclesiarchs for months and had acquired their speech habits, much as I had acquired some of Captain Gart's antique slang. But the Captain had little taste for either the aphorisms of the Order or ecclesiastical syntax, so he left Vanda to me. I found conversation with her exhausting; rather like talking with an earlier and expurgated edition of myself.

After she had finished eating and had gone out to service

her ship, the Captain stood in the parlor window watching her work and deploring the impropriety of women being under arms. It was becoming one of his commoner themes. "I don't like to see girls getting mixed up in all this violence."

Contact with Vanda had whetted my temper. "It's right for us girls to get violated. But wrong for us to resist?"

"Diana, you know I don't mean that!" He waved his cheroot toward the ship. "Kids like Vanda with guns! Soldiering's no business for women."

"Not for most women. But many have been good at it." I quoted some prechaos heroines.

"Those?" he broke in. "Those women weren't soldiers! They were guerrillas, terrorists, assassins!"

"Is there a difference?" He was beginning to annoy me beyond bearing. "If you want a woman with an official command—try Joan of Arc."

"She was a Saint," he said in a complete non sequitur.

"She was also a first-class general. She raised the siege of Orleans and defeated the Duke of Bedford, the best military commander in Europe."

"Diana, you have an obsession with Joan of Arc. She was an exception. You're an exception. All I'm saying is that it's unnatural for women to fight."

"But natural for us to be murdered, raped, burned, and enslaved! Unnatural for us to defend ourselves and each other! Though you're right about one thing. Brutality is more natural to men. Genetically, they're closer to the brutes. They're also expendable. The druj have proved that! As you once remarked—they're all male!"

"You're starting to chatter line a worn bearing! You need a dose of—what do you call it? Rebriefing?"

"So I'll be like Vanda?"

"No! God forbid! I'll take you as you are. Noise and all." He turned to look back out of the window. "She's as rigid as a wired-in program. A smart kid, Di, but not in your class."

"She will be, one day. Right now she's fresh from briefing. And she hasn't had the benefit of serving for eleven months with you."

He read that as a compliment and went off to welcome the squad of selected Wardens which Mansur had sent him to train. He came to me later, cursing their incompetence. "If they're the best Mansur can do, God help us all if Paxin dries up. Most of that lot don't know if their holes are bored or punched! How the hell are we going to provide security for this treaty-signing with ten grots and one teen-ager?" He stared out of the window. "Who's that helping Vanda fix her ship?"

"Kate."

"Kate? So it is. Didn't recognize her backside in coveralls. How long before Vanda gets her crew?"

"I doubt she'll get one. The Order's short-handed, and officially Vanda's only here to haul a cargo of Paxin from Maylan to Crete."

"Get a signal off to that Prioress of yours telling her that I want a crew for Vanda's ship, and I want it pronto."

I sent the signal, and got an acknowledgment but no promise of a crew. The Captain cursed the Synod's irresponsibility. Vanda was too small and young to use if any serious trouble started. He knew as well as I did that servos replace muscle, that a pistol hits with more punch than a fist, that fast reaction times are more lethal than brute force. He knew all these things rationally, but emotionally he could not surrender his belief that combat and killing were male prerogatives.

A week before the day of the treaty he again started to grumble that Naxos had sent a girl to do a woman's job, forgetting his critique of women warriors now we were nearing the crunch. "Vanda, I know you can fly that ship alone. But what happens in snafu? You can't shoot and handle a ship. It's not like a cutter."

"I agree, sir. A ship handles quite differently from a cutter."

"So if you're alone and have to land you could get jumped."

"Yes, sir. That's why I've arranged for a crew to cover me. Also to operate the radio and drop thermites or smoke if required."

"You've arranged—? Who?"

"Kate, sir. I asked her and she's agreed."

"You've asked Kate?" We were eating our evening meal and Captain Gart put down his fork to stare across the table. "You've done what?"

"I've recruited Kate into my crew, sir."

"Who the hell told you to do anything so absurd?"

"Nobody, sir. I have the authority."

"Have you—hell! Listen, young lady, you haven't got the authority to do anything without my permission. Let alone get Kate involved in this damned mess!" He glared at her. "You're under my command. Remember?"

"I do remember, sir." Vanda stopped eating and stared back at him. She had large brown eyes, soft round cheeks, a full mouth, and a child's chin. At that moment she also had the expression of a sea captain whose authority aboard his own ship has just been called into question. "My unit is under your command, Captain Gart. But I command my own unit. You are not entitled to interfere with its internal operation."

"Your unit? You silly girl! Your unit is you."

"My unit has an establishment of six. So I have five vacancies. I have arranged to fill one of them by local recruitment."

"You impudent brat!" They faced each other across the table.

I had an instant of deja vu from quite another time and place, and I broke in, "Vanda, you must be more respectful! But sir, Vanda is correct. If she is able to recruit locally she has the authority to do so. And if Kate wishes to volunteer—"

"Volunteer! We'll see about that. Kate!" he bellowed. "Come here!"

"She's aboard the ship," said Vanda. "Checking the hydraulic filters."

"Is she, by God? Listen, you two. I don't give a damn whether Kate volunteers or not. I won't see her turned into another gun-toting Amazon. Kate's a decent, kind person."

"She is also intelligent, competent, and can handle a shotgun," said Vanda with all the stubbornness of a Pilot who knows she is in the right. "A repeating shotgun is ideal for close cover. I must have somebody with me."

"If not Kate, sir," I said, "perhaps a pair of Wardens could crew?"

"Wardens? They'd be more danger than use!" He went to the front door and shouted across the square. "Kate—get your ass in here!"

Kate came, wiping oil off her hands. She was in coveralls and in command of the situation. "Of course, I'm crewing for

Vanda. I'm not going to let her fly alone over Padron and those devils. This treaty could be a trap."

"Padron? Treaty? What do you know about it? Who's been talking?"

"You have, Jan. Often and in a loud voice. I speak Anglic and understand quite long words." She eyed him. "You gave my father a spiel about staying to protect his farm. He had the sense to leave for Australia. But you convinced me. I stayed."

"Goddammit—I didn't mean—" He tried to be rational. "Katy, you don't understand. This is a job for professionals."

"Like those Wardens of yours?"

I interposed, soothingly. "Sir, we probably won't need Vanda's ship anyhow. You were going to hold it on standby, up on the Pinnacle. If things go wrong they'll have plenty of time to evacuate."

He stared at our three faces and accepted defeat. "Okay—okay. Kate, your blood's on your own head." He stamped off to abuse the Wardens.

"Kate," I asked. "When did you stop using Paxin?"

"When that woman got her claws into him. Paxin dulled my sorrow. I wanted to feel the pain. So I cut it out."

"Was it hard?"

"Bad headaches at first. Now they're almost gone. And I feel more myself."

I told Captain Gart about Kate's experience, and he had the grace to look ashamed. "Those headaches are a conditioned response," I explained. "Users get headaches when they stop taking Paxin, so they take it again to stop the headaches."

"Like booze in a hangover?"

"More than that. Paxin's a chemical reinforcer of conditioned behavior. That's what makes it an efficient pacifier in an educated population. It reinforces all conditioned responses, including the headache response. It's an elegant example of feedback. Negative feedback because it reduces social instability."

"Negative feedback, my ass! Elegant example! I never realized what beastly stuff it really is. So under this Treaty Padron gets Sherando and Shapur gets to keep his chemically conditioned narod."

"The system is elegant," I insisted. "I'm no longer sure it's ethical. Kate's a different person since she stopped taking Paxin."

"She's become as stubborn as the other two girls I've got to deal with!" We were flying toward the Rockfish Gap for our last reconnaissance along the Valley. "Hell, the whole setup's wrong." He gestured toward the farms and villages below. "All of us are wrong. Guard, autarchs, ecclesiarchs! Flying around, arranging, deciding, shooting, quarreling. Nobody thinking about what the people down there want."

He was overcompensating. "All they want is a quiet life. There are enough farmers and techs on the Council to throw every autarch out of the Sector if they voted that way. They're certainly not conditioned to automatic obedience or they wouldn't be selling out and leaving. Shapur's told them the danger's over. He'd force them to stay if he could. He can't. When things go well they let the autarchs run things and the Guard protect them. When things go badly they move."

"Take the piasters and run! Gutless good sense! Look what they've surrendered already." We were passing over the frontier and the recent expansion of the wilderness stood out like a spreading ulcer. "God—why should I care?"

There was no reason why he should; there was no reason why I should. Our duty was to patrol the frontier. Neither of us should be concerned with political or social problems; those were the responsibility of people trained for such tasks. The treaty would end the fighting with the druj. The fact that Padron would be a threat to the future of Sector Ten, to the whole United Settlements, was no concern of ours unless his threat took physical form. We should not care. Yet we both did. There was nothing we could do, except our duty, so our concern was pointless.

Our immediate duty was to ensure that whatever trickery Padron employed, force was not a part of it. He appeared to be keeping the truce agreement. He had despatched his druj homeward where, he had assured Mansur, they would in due time revert to peaceful farmers. But many of them after starting west would return to tag along behind Padron's column. He insisted that none were armed and all were harmless, and such was certainly true of all the druj we saw on our last patrols.

We flew from the Gap across the valley, circling Padron's

column which was now some ten kilometers from Sherando, and moving cautiously toward it under the trees. After two passes over the column I said, "Satan's down there."

"Di! You and that stallion! Your natural drives may not have surfaced, but some strange ones are sure showing. Did you scent any druj?"

"None with the column. Many trailing behind."

"Poor brutes! Diana, I think I know what Padron's using to breed druj."

"You do?" I looked at him in surprise. "What?"

"Lunaton." He chewed his lip. "Ever heard of a place called Fort Detrick?"

"No. But I saw the name in the parley transcript."

"Well—" He paused. "Maybe I'm wrong. I'll tell you when I've got something more concrete than suspicions."

That night we held a final council of war. The four of us sat in an operations room capable of controlling a small army and Captain Gart muttered something about one fake and three broads. Then he started to outline the evils of Paxin and how it must be phased out when all this was over.

Kate brought him back to reality. "What are we going to try and do tomorrow? Save civilization or see that Padron doesn't jump the Governor?"

He glared at her. "Kate—you're an example of the squeeze Kahn's in. Stop the Paxin because it's unethical. Everybody starts doing their own thing. It could be chaos!" He chewed his cheroot. "Thank God only civilians take it. The Patrol doesn't use Paxin. We use discipline. This is a military operation beyond the frontier. Remember that, girl!"

Kate began to laugh.

"Oh God!" He began to laugh too. "You're right, Katy! It is absurd, isn't it? We four—what a quartet! Well, as Diana would say, we're all in the hands of Zurvan. Whoever he is!"

XV

16th October 2171

At noon on the day of the treaty Vanda took her ship up to the Pinnacle with orders to watch the Valley while we landed at Sherando for a last check. Captain Gart was suspicious, not of the inherent evil in the place, but of the pattern which Padron's search parties had followed. They had been shifting rubble, knocking holes in walls, exploring old storage areas. He stood staring at the concrete platform with its veralloy gallows and whipping-post; the thing I still thought of as an altar.

"Those goons have been looking for something and they haven't found it. What's Padron after?" He climbed into the cutter. "What's his reason for wanting to get this place back?"

"Religious; heretical but religious," I said as I took off.

He grunted and studied the forest below. The cargo gev we had tracked up the Valley was waiting hidden under the trees, but the dragoons were riding around openly, protected by the truce. "Look at the cabron. Acting like they owned the place already!"

"There are still druj tagging along and more coming up," I said. "All unarmed and non-hostile."

"That bastard Padron! Like somebody who moves and leaves his dogs to starve." He radioed Shapur's ship, waiting to take off from Maylan, that Sherando seemed clear, and that Padron was following protocol. "Now I suppose I've got to speak to the slem myself."

Padron had called us at intervals during our flights above him. Captain Gart's replies had been brief and formal, although he had followed each exchange with a string of blasphemies after he had cut his mike. He had only allowed

144

Padron to speak to me once, and that was to give my word that I would not make any hostile act during the period of the truce if Padron observed the terms.

The Captain called now and got an immediate answer. "Greetings, Captain. I have just spoken with your Governor. He has lifted from Maylan and is on his way. And he has agreed that you should ride with me into Sherando for the ceremony."

"He has, has he? Well, Shapur can—"

"Please treat it as my personal invitation. Purely a precaution. Once I am in the open Diana might be swamped by her zeal and remember some prime axiom which would let her start shooting." Padron chuckled. "The Governor has already seen my point. The lady Rajuna is down here, traveling with me."

"You've got Rajuna as hostage? Shapur's given—"

"Please! Not hostage. Honored guest. As Director of Special Services she is especially concerned with the outcome of today's rapprochement. She seems to be enjoying the experience. My officers are already her servants. I have mounted her on the best stallion she's ever been astride. She rides very well. I have a beautiful mare waiting for you."

"Padron, I can't ride."

"Can't you? You must learn. Well, perhaps on this occasion you can travel in the gev."

Captain Gart cut his mike and cursed. "He's got me boxed! Shapur, the fool, doesn't he realize what Padron is? Giving Rajuna as a hostage!"

"She's no hostage. She's an accomplice. She's been pushing this treaty harder than any other autarch."

"Diana, you're acting female!" He called Padron. "I'm landing."

"Sir—you can't—"

"Don't pick now to argue! Let's show the goons a combat drop-off."

The mention of Rajuna had sent him out of control, and I had to obey. I made sure the maneuver was perfect. I felt my rotor-blades flex as I checked with my skids brushing the grass. I was back at fifty meters and going up while the Captain was still on his first roll. Even an auton would have been depressing for the swoop when I was already on the rise. I hung at three hundred, watched Captain Gart pick himself up, dust himself off, straighten his helmet, and walk toward the forest.

"What's happening?" asked Vanda on the com.

"Captain Gart's landed. He's joining Padron for the trip into Sherando."

"You let him do that, Diana?" Vanda's voice, faint at the limit of range, was accusing. "He is under the Shield of the Order."

"Then you come and hold the Shield. He's out of my control!"

Vanda's terse reply snapped through the static. "Lifting off!" Moments later she called again, her signal stronger as she closed. "Governor's ship nearing Rockfish."

"Check. Vanda, you hang high. He'll go ape if he sees you."

"Say again?"

"Captain Gart will be angry if he learns you're not safe on the Pinnacle." I was not even in good control of myself.

Shapur's ship appeared over the Blue Ridge, dropped down to circle Sherando, and landed by the altar. Mansur was first out, directing his Wardens to positions along the edge of the plaza. Shapur came down the gangway, stood looking around him, then began to speak on his com. Kahn emerged last, his worry clear on his face. He had put on weight and his black beard was now neatly barbered.

Padron cantered out of the forest, Saz on his right and Ras on his left. They rode together up the hill to the Settlement, then the two lieutenants dropped back so there was no doubt who was the Leader when they trotted through the ruined gateway. Padron was a victorious commander riding into a conquered town.

He reined Satan in and looked about him. Saz and Ras halted behind their chief and all three sat their horses with an easy pride, relishing their victory. Presently Padron glanced down at the civilians standing by the ship.

He studied them, then saluted. Shapur bowed. Padron dismounted and walked casually across the plaza, leaving Saz and Ras still sitting their horses. Shapur strolled to meet him. The two stood talking. Far apart in blood, build, and outlook, they shared the same kind of arrogance. Presently Padron spoke on his com.

A group of dragoons rode out of the forest, faces I knew.

Next the gev lurched from under the trees with Captain Gart standing in the gunner's hatch, grasping the rim to steady himself. The dragoons formed a screen of outriders and then came Rajuna with three more as her escort.

The gev wallowed across the field alongside the lake. Rajuna kicked her horse into a gallop, and went past the gev, sitting bolt upright, her hands low, with never a glance at Captain Gart being thrown about in the turret. Her escort had to ride hard to stay with her, and when she jumped a section of ancient cedar-rail fence they did not accept the challenge but separated to gallop around it. She drove her horse up the hill, pulling ahead of the rest, then wheeled in a graceful turn before the gateway to allow them to catch up. Nobody must doubt that Rajuna could ride better than any man there.

The gev clambered up the hill, slewed through the gateway, and floated over to Shapur's ship. Captain Gart was climbing out of the turret as Rajuna came trotting through the gateway in an entrance that almost matched Padron's. For her, as for Padron and Shapur, style was essence. She checked her horse beside Ras, swung out of the saddle, and tossed the reins to the nilote with the cool arrogance of the trueborn. She walked across to where Shapur and Padron were standing and all three saluted each other with elegant bows.

Watching the trio through the telescopic sight of my rifle was like watching a comedy of manners. Padron must have known I had him covered but he did not so much as glance up at my cutter. None of them paid any attention to Captain Gart who was helping Mansur arrange the Wardens into something approaching a military attitude.

Padron, Shapur, and Rajuna walked to the altar on which Kahn had been spreading maps and documents; presumably the Articles of Infolding. Padron called to Saz who dismounted and went to join them. The crew of the gev opened the hatches. Rajuna left the group at the altar, vaulted up onto the catwalk, and began to inspect the cargo. Presently she waved to Mansur and the ship's ramp was lowered. Some of the Wardens put down their rifles and went to start transferring the Paxin. A few goons dismounted to help.

Vanda called from high above us. "There are figures on foot moving around the margin of the forest. They come a little way out into the open, then dart back to the trees. The largest group is two-three-five from the entrance. There are others spread along the northern and eastern perimeter."

I acknowledged and drifted over to look for myself. They were all unarmed nonhostile druj, the scattered wanderers who had been trailing their masters and had seen them disappear into Sherando. They stood, staring toward the ruined Settlement, as though gathering the courage to approach. I flew low over them, hoping to frighten them back into the forest, but they ignored me, so I circled and called Captain Gart. "Better warn Padron that his creatures are starting to crowd in."

Padron was deep in negotiations and Shapur waved the Captain away. He walked across to Ras, who was still sitting his horse in the middle of the plaza. The nilote listened, saluted politely, called to three other dragoons, and all four cantered out through the entrance.

Their appearance brought druj surging out of the forest, jumping up and down, and waving their arms. The groups coalesced and went bounding up the hill toward Ras, clustering around him in a paroxysm of affection. Moments later all four dragoons were enveloped in bounding druj as more came rushing toward them. After several minutes of shouting and slashing the four wheeled their horses, rode down the druj in their way, and galloped back up the hill.

The packs wailed their disappointment and started after their masters. To the north, where the forest was closest to the earthworks, more druj were creeping out from under the trees. One, more daring than the rest, scrambled to the top of the ramparts and stared across the roofless buildings toward the plaza. It saw Padron, let out a howl of recognition, and began to race along the walls. Its yell brought more druj chasing after it, each shouting its pleasure as it saw its master among the horsemen. There was suddenly a stream of druj scurrying along the ramparts.

I dropped low, ready to shoot if any became dangerous. The sight of their fellows on the walls excited the druj loping up the hill and they went pouring through the entrance after Ras. Both groups erupted onto the plaza at the same time, and although they were nonhostile their appearance was terrifying. Their effect on the Wardens was dramatic. They dropped the aluminum cases they were loading and ran for their rifles. Mansur and Captain Gart started shouting at them to stand firm and not to shoot.

Shapur, Rajuna, and Kahn, pistols drawn, were backing toward the edge of the plaza. Padron was shouting at his dragoons to herd their druj out of the entrance, but they kept evading the whips and dodging back, each crowding around its own master.

Ras was moving to cover the ship when his pack charged toward him. The Warden flier, seeing the horrors bounding in his direction, tried to take off with his loading ramp still down. The ship lifted, swung, caught the scaffold rising from the altar, and crashed onto the gev, spilling cases of Paxin across the plaza. Wardens, dragoons, druj and autarchs had surged back as the ship rose, tilted, and crashed. The flier, crawling from the wreck, found himself faced with three leaping druj. He threw a thermite grenade at them.

The grenade flared, the druj shrieked, and the white-hot thermite rolled among the spilled Paxin. It began to smolder with a brown smoke. Captain Gart, running toward the wreck, stopped to stare at the altar. The veralloy scaffold, unbending, had split the plinth as a struck wedge splits a rock. And from the cavity within came a tumble of ammunition carriers, checkered red and yellow.

"Lunaton!" Captain Gart shouted on the com, turning, reaching for his gun. "Padron!" He was engulfed in a wave of brown smoke. Somebody, I think one of the Wardens, started to shoot.

The plaza became a maelstrom of people running for cover. More thermites, flung wildly by panicking Wardens, skidded across the plaza. Spilled fuel flooding from the wrecked ship was raised to flash-point by the thermites and began to burn sullenly, lapping around the carriers from the broken plinth. A yellow-green mist came seeping out to mix with the brown smoke from the Paxin.

Vanda was calling on the com. "Situation report, please."

"General confusion. Come low prepared to rescue."

"Diving!"

The smoke from the burning Paxin and the stuff the Captain had called Lunaton was now welling out from the area around the altar. The druj, howling their fear of fire, were escaping in all directions and the whole plaza was a swirling mass of men, druj, and horses. I could not distinguish Captain Gart among them but I heard him coughing and shouting on the com, "Padron—where are you? I'll rip out your guts!"

I was calling to remind him that the truce was still in effect when Vanda arrived, her rotors screaming as she checked after her long swoop, their wash sending colored clouds billowing across the Settlement.

"Vanda! You silly bitch!" Captain Gart was choking as he tried to shout. "Get your ass out of here! Back up to the Pinnacle!" He gagged and gasped, "Diana!"

"Yes, sir."

"Keep out of this stuff!"

The breeze was from the east. I called, "I'm landing on the eastern rampart. It's clear. To lift you out."

He coughed an acknowledgment. The plaza was a basin filled with a multicolored mist, the shapes of men and horses moving through it like ghosts across marshland. I touched down on the rampart and walked to the edge of the wall. There was thunder over the mountains.

"Diana, you there? Listen, girl. This smoke—it's mad smoke! You keep out of it. D'you hear? I'm trying to keep under it. Wrap a wet cloth over your mouth. Don't ask why! Do as I say!"

An eddy sent a wave of the mist over the rampart, and I got a whiff. It was a strange mixture of smells, aromatic rather than sweet, but with a cadence of chords. I soaked my field dressing in a puddle of rainwater and tied it over my mouth, as Jan had told me. I could not understand why, but I wanted to please him. It forced me to breath through my nose.

Below me, on the plaza, some of the shadows had started to ride toward the entrance but none reached it. They slowed, checked, turned, moved aimlessly like men following a secret dream. I sensed Satan, alone, somewhere in the fog, confused and lost. He must have recognized a friend, for he moved closer to where I was standing.

"Diana, darling," said Jan on the com. "Stay where you are. I'm coming."

"Jan—I'm waiting!"

XVI

Lunar Transit

The events of the next few hours are ridiculous in fact but eidetic in image. I can describe my thoughts and emotions; I can recall brilliant hues, bright sounds, intricate details. But my thoughts, feelings, images, and actions are, in retrospect, so bizarre that I cannot comment, only recount.

The world was strange, but beautiful. The forest was a sea of autumnal colors, flashing under the angry sunshine of the gathering storm, great waves of vivid scarlets and shimmering greens surging up the sides of the mountains. I lay in the grass on the edge of the rampart, gazing down at the plaza, waiting for Jan to come to me. Colored mists swirled around men, horses, and machines.

Satan appeared, standing below me, uneasy and riderless. His coat glistened heraldic sable. To the west the sun was hot gold above the Shenandoah Mountains, to the east the white moon of the day was rising over the Blue Ridge, to the south black clouds were crawling north along the crests.

Jan came from under the layering smoke, creeping on hands and knees, his wet undershirt wound about his head to hide his scarred face. He crawled past Satan, *statant gardant*, saw me wave, and scrambled up the steps from the plaza to the rampart where I lay. He took off my mask so we could kiss, mouth to mouth. Then he lay beside me, hip to hip, not talking, not doing anything except enjoying the beauty of the fall colors and the nearness of each other.

Our peace was too perfect to last. Presently he roused himself and asked, "Where's Raji?"

"Out there somewhere. Shapur'll look after her."

But Jan feels responsible for everybody. He pulled his undershirt back up over his face. He looked loveable and ridicu-

151

lous. I giggled. He patted me. "Time to go. Got to collect the others." He walked carefully down the steps and groped his way into the smoke.

I dozed while I waited, my cheek on the grass. I heard somebody singing, a sweet childrens' song. It was Rajuna. Jan was leading her by the hand. Her other hand was holding Shapur and he was leading Kahn. Mansur stumbled along last, clutching Kahn by the belt.

They snaked around Satan and came up the steps. I stood to greet them. We grouped around Jan, who counted us. "All here! Di, where did you park the car?"

I pointed to the cutter.

Padron came weaving out of the smoke, reaching for Satan. The stallion was tethered by his loyalty but his longing was for the mares at the edge of the forest. Their scent came on the breeze. With a twist of my mind I set him free.

He tossed his head, gave the shout of the war horse, reared like a unicorn, charged across the plaza. His hooves thundered, echoing through the ruined Settlement. The pillars of the entrance rang as he went between them. His shout came back from the hill. Padron lay face down on the ground. Jan said, "That'll teach the kid not to fool around with strange horses."

Rajuna ran down the steps crying out, "He's hurt! Oh, he's hurt!" She knelt beside him and called, "He's unconscious. Help me save him from the fire!"

Shapur and Mansur went down into the smoke and carried him up the steps with Rajuna keening behind them. "Put him in the back of the station wagon," said Jan. "We'd better take him to the hospital."

I interpreted "back of the station wagon" to mean the cargo compartment of the cutter. Folded properly Padron filled it nicely. When we had him stowed Jan lined the rest of us up and loaded us aboard. He put Rajuna in the back, between Shapur and Kahn. She stopped wailing and started kissing both men. He put Mansur in front and stopped me when I tried to get into the Pilot's seat. "No, love, I'll drive. You look after Mansur. He's asleep already."

"He's lost his glasses," I said as I was crammed between Mansur and Jan. "Maybe we should go back and look for them."

"Best get away before it rains. We'll buy him another

pair." Jan scraped the edge of the ramparts with the skids as he took off, and we lurched across Sherando at an absurd angle, climbing above the smoke which was drifting away. Dragoons and Wardens were wandering about on the plaza. Some looked up toward us and waved.

Jan picked up the microphone of the loud-hailer and his voice boomed down onto the Settlement. "Peace and love! The Light shineth in the darkness! Praise the Lord my God who giveth my hands to war and my fingers to fight! I will overcome! I will return!"

We slewed over the forest and I sensed the passion of Satan, mating in the trees beneath. I reached for Jan, but he caught my hand. "Later, honey. Gotta drive now. Where did Vanda park the truck?"

"The Pinnacle. They're on the Pinnacle." I called on the com. "Vanda, sweetheart, we're going to the Pinnacle. To watch the sunset!" I switched off the mike, giggling, "And to make love!"

Mansur was asleep with his mouth open, his head on my shoulder. Rajuna had started to play with the pair in the back, but they dozed off, and after complaining a while so did she. Presently I dozed myself.

I woke to the crunch of metal. We had arrived. I crawled over the still sleeping Mansur and out of the canted cutter. Jan had landed hard and the port strut had collapsed. We were high above the Valley, on our old eyrie, washed by the mana of the mountains. The storm sun was setting scarlet to the west. To the south the storm clouds were rolling up the Valley. To the east Selene was white, rising into gold.

The ship swooped down. Vanda and Kate jumped from the flight deck and came running toward us. Jan, clambering from the cutter, tried to throw his arms around Vanda, who tripped him and ran on to the wreck. He climbed to his feet, laughing and tried to kiss Katy. She slapped his face and he stood rubbing his cheek, protesting, "Drunk, darling? Not a drop. I swear it!"

I went to comfort him while Vanda and Kate were unfolding Padron, extracting our somnolent passengers from the canted cutter, and confiscating their toy guns. He led me away to a sheltered place among the rocks, private and out of the wind. He had my coveralls unzipped and his own mostly off when Vanda found us. She had an autoinject in her hand.

Jan was starting to climb on top of me and she rammed the needle into his behind. Then she knocked him sideways with a light chop across his neck and called to Kate to get him dressed while she rezipped my coveralls and propelled me toward the ship. As she pushed me aboard I felt it shivering under the rising wind. Rain was sprinkling the Pinnacle. Selene had grown huge, rising to power, the Hunter's Moon. Soon She would be gone behind the storm clouds.

Kate guided Jan toward the ship. He stumbled aft to the cabin and checked our passengers who were asleep on the fold-down bunks. "Kids all here? Good. Best get moving before the rain starts. Roads are going to flood. Weekend traffic." He saw me sitting in the jump-seat. "Di—you need a lie-down. Go and flake out on the floor."

I made myself a pad on the deck of the cabin as he had told me and lay relaxed, happy, and comfortable. I thought about Jan and all the people I loved, sleeping around me. I listened to Jan teasing Vanda. "I'll drive the cutter. You snug down the kids."

We were in a ship, not a cutter, and Jan is not good at flying either. If he was going to fly this one somebody should tell him the difference, particularly in the buffeting wind. But Vanda would not let him into the Pilot's seat, and I heard him grumbling as we took off.

Instantly we were seized by the updrafts over the peaks, tossed around by the turbulence. Mansur was thrown out of his bunk on top of me. Kate came aft to help hoist him back and Rajuna fell out of hers. "We'd better tie them in," said Kate and ran to fetch lashings.

The ship steadied as we wrenched free of the mountains, but we must secure our passengers against more turbulence ahead. Kate pushed me away and called for help. "We're on autopilot," said Vanda, scrambling back to the cabin and loosening the lashing I had just put round Rajuna's throat.

I was able to stretch out again on the deck and I watched them making our passengers comfortable. I was drifting off to sleep when the ship lurched and Vanda trod on me as she ran for'rd, calling, "No, sir! No! Leave the autopilot alone." I fell asleep with the three of them arguing on the flight deck.

Jan was fumbling with my coveralls and I had to help him. As he pulled down my underpants I slid my arm round his neck and drew his mouth toward mine. He jerked his head free. "Darling!" I protested, shivering from the touch of his hands on my body. I reached out for his.

"For God's sake, Diana! Take it easy! Hold still!" He rolled me over onto my stomach and I lay expectant, my behind bared. He started patting my left buttock with something wet and cold. Then the sharp jab of a needle. I squealed from frustration rather than pain. When he pulled up my underpants I began to cry. I was still crying when I fell asleep.

I awoke with a twanging headache. The ship stank of every human smell. Mansur was vomiting, splattering the cabin and everyone in it. Other people had vomited earlier, while I was asleep. I staggered to the toilet to clean myself. Jan had charts spread all over the navigation table and was saying to Vanda, "I tell you I don't know where we are! So how can I give you a course to fly?" He saw me disappear into the toilet and came to pound on the door. "Get your ass out of there, Diana! Come and navigate!"

I saw my face in the mirror and was shocked. Fortunately the cabinet contained a set of basic cosmetics for the convenience of passengers and I was able to make myself look presentable before I went to find what he wanted. His own face was a greenish-white and he hadn't shaved.

He stared at me. "Lipstick, for Chrissake! Lipstick! We're lost over the mountains and the girl takes time out to make up her mouth!" He seized me by the shoulders and pushed me to the chart-table. I leaned across it, nauseated. "Sober up, Di," he shouted. "Or I'll give you another shot in the backside!"

I didn't want that so I concentrated. We were dodging thunderheads and were hundreds of kilometers outside navigator range. They were lost all right, but it was none of my business. This was Vanda's ship, and if she had been so irresponsible as to allow Jan to interfere with the operation of her command that was her problem. Nevertheless I tried to help them. I managed to identify three distant radiobeacons and plotted an intersection. The cocked-hat error was large but the best I could do and it showed how they had gone wrong. "You're around here, Jan," I said, and started toward the toilet.

He dragged me back to the chart table. "How the hell can we?"

I sniggered. "You've had the autopilot on reciprocal! You've been heading for the Pacific coast. This ship hasn't the range to make it." He was so damned smart, but he hadn't been able to read a compass. And as for Vanda! Ulama Pilots might be strong on theology but their navigation evidently wasn't much.

He called, "How much fuel left?"

"Three hours forty-six minutes, sir."

"Oh God!" He drew circles on the chart. "We can't get back, that's for sure. We'd crash in the mountains." He laid off bearings, then called to Vanda, "Fly two-seven-five. We might make the Mississippi. At least we'll be able to land."

That was his problem. I put my head down on the chart table and started to drift off to sleep. He slapped me. "Wake up, Di—I need you!"

It was nice to be needed, even if it involved being slapped. I giggled. Jan groaned. "Oh God! She's going again!" He put his face in front of mine. His breath was foul. "Get a grip on yourself. We can't raise anybody on the radio. We're lost over the mountains. We're running out of fuel. And we've five zonked passengers."

That suggested one obvious step. I stood up and started aft. He followed me. "What the hell are you going to do?"

"Jettison Rajuna and Padron. Reduce load. Give us extra range. You can toss out Shapur."

"Christ!" He caught my arm, dragged me to the jump seat, and pushed me into it. "Sit there! And don't move till I tell you!" He surveyed the stinking mess in the cabin, muttered another invocation, and returned to the flight deck.

I sat sullenly, aching for a lost happiness, feeling it slip away from me. I dozed, then woke to cry softly to myself. All the bright colors had gone, all the sweet scents. I was surrounded by gray shadows, and small yellow lights, and stench. I went to sleep, sitting up, still crying.

XVII

Hunter's Moon

It was daylight when I woke. I was free from happiness, madness, and misery. I was rational. We were dropping through cloud and came into the clear above a great bend in a broad river.

"That's it!" Jan's voice was brutal. "Fuel status?"

"Twenty-two minutes, sir."

He studied the forest and river below. "That cove on the east bank. Sandy beach. Patch of grass. Only clear space. Land fifty meters back from the river."

We touched down among the long grass and the fall flowers. Vanda stopped the turbines. I watched the sun rise. Kate ran aft to free our passengers. Jan snapped off his harness and stood up. He straightened his helmet, jerked at his coveralls, and tightened his belt, as though about to go on parade. He checked his pistol. Then he walked aft to the cabin. He did not glance at me as he passed.

I heard Kate cry, "Jan! Be careful! They're not themselves yet."

The cabin door slid open and Shapur fell out. Mansur followed. Rajuna spun through the doorway, hands and hair flying, sprawling onto the grass. Kahn faced into the cabin, protesting, then dropped to the ground. Padron jumped after him and the whole group clustered together. They were filthy, their hair disordered, their clothes streaked with dirt and vomit. They stared back at the ship.

Jan appeared in the doorway, Kate's shotgun in his hand, swinging the muzzle to check their forward surge. He shouted, "Diana! Vanda! Bring the rifles! All of them!"

We could not have refused even had we wished. We followed him as he drove our passengers toward the river. They

157

stumbled along under the menace of his shotgun, uncertain of his intent but frightened by his madness. Padron called, "Diana! Your oath! The Truce!" Jan ignored him and, as yet, I saw no reason to interfere.

He herded them to where the bank dropped steeply to the water. Then he faced them. "Remember this!" He hefted the shotgun and tossed it, end over end, out into the river. Its splash was a fountain, the drops cascading golden in the young sunlight.

"Diana—Vanda—the rifles!" He took them from us and threw them one by one after the shotgun. Shapur, protesting, lurched forward. Jan drew and fired into the ground at his feet. Shapur jerked back.

Jan reholstered his pistol and reached behind him. "Vanda—your gun!"

She surrendered her sidearm and watched it arc out into the river.

"Now yours, Diana."

"Please—" I said. "Please—"

"Your pistol! At once!" His voice was a blow. I flinched. I drew the heavy combat pistol I had worn for so long. I held it by the butt. I changed my grip to the muzzle. I handed it to him, butt first. A band tightened around my chest as it splashed down, far out in the current, beyond hope of recovery.

He drew his own weapon, his muscles tensing as though his hand was fighting to disobey his brain. For him, as for me, it was like detaching a part of oneself. He held his pistol up. "Our last firearm!" He tossed it after the others, but carelessly. "Now there are no more guns."

Shapur again staggered forward. "Gart—are you mad?"

"Some. Like we all are. I'm getting saner." He touched the hilt of his knife. "Crowd me—and I'm still mad enough to use this."

"Why have you thrown away our weapons?"

"Because we can't be trusted with them. I couldn't trust myself not to shoot the lot of you. By God, I nearly did!" He turned his back on them and walked away toward the river.

Padron stood asking, "Where are we?" The rest, released from fear, subsided into the long grass.

"That's the Mississippi," said Vanda.

"The Mississippi!" Padron stared at the river, shook his

head as though to clear water from his ears, then stared at me. "The Truce lasts till the Treaty's signed."

"Or until you break it."

"Break it? When I'm alone and unarmed among eight enemies?"

"Not enemies!" Rajuna reached up her hand and caught his. "Not any more." He sank down onto the grass beside her, and I watched him trying to think. She pushed her tangled hair back from her eyes. "Shapur, radio for a ship to come and pick us up."

"Pick us up!" Mansur raised his head from his hands. "We are a thousand kilometers from any frontier. No ship has that range!"

"Nor has the radio," I said. "It's frequencies are all above twenty megahertz. Its range is only quasioptical."

Rajuna struggled to her feet and stared about her. "What has that pandour done to us?" She saw Jan by the river. "I'll kill that killer!"

Kate came running from the ship. "You're not yourselves yet!" She caught Rajuna's arm.

Rajuna shook her off. "I'll kill him! I'll kill him!" The others were standing, their eyes taking on the empty stare of the druj and I knew that Jan had been right. He had shouted "Lunaton!" when the red-yellow carriers had tumbled from the broken plinth. They had inhaled its smoke. Traces were still flooding them, raising surges of inchoate anger. They started toward Jan. I moved to head them off. They ignored me.

Vanda was in their path, her hand on her knife. "Captain Gart is under the Shield of the Order!"

They paused, drew back from her, their madness fading. She stood with her hair dishevelled, her eyes ringed with fatigue, a weary child. But stood balanced, like a poised javelin. Small and deadly, like the Egyptian asp. I saw myself as I had once been. They feared her now as they would never fear me again.

"Come back to your bunks! You're not yourselves yet!" Kate caught Mansur's arm and guided him toward the ship. "Don't talk till you've rested."

Their surge of animal fury died. Like animals they followed her, Rajuna clinging to Padron. The antihallucin injected into Jan by Vanda and into me by Jan had restored the two of us to sanity but the others were still half mad. Now was the time to eliminate them all. But when I went to suggest this to Jan he waved me away and continued to stand brooding, gazing across the river.

I at least was still capable of decisive action. I took Vanda to help me strip the shocks from the landing gear. We would use the spring permasteel to back our bows. The rifles need be no great loss.

Archery was a sport I enjoyed even before I joined the Order. Perhaps that is why the Synod named me Diana. By midmorning I had made a longbow from unorthodox materials but effective for my purpose. I had no time to search for osage orange, the prime wood for bows in these forests, but I backed a straight length of hickory with permasteel to give a draw-pull of some fifteen kilos. I hand-ground five lengths of veralloy rod to needle sharpness and fletched them with goose feathers I found by the river. Then I checked the map on the flight deck and fixed it in my memory.

At noon Jan returned from contemplating the river and called us together. Padron and the civilians were still asleep and I hoped that Jan's brooding had brought him to see the obvious solution.

"Diana—does our oath allow me to kill Padron?"

"No, sir. Not Padron. We swore not to harm Padron or his followers. But we didn't swear not to harm the others. We are free to dispose of everybody except Padron."

"For God's sake, Diana! The others are not to be harmed. Am I still your boss?"

"Of course, sir."

"Then nobody is to be harmed. That's an order. Do you understand?"

"I understand," I said. "It is the most foolish order I have ever received in my service as a Pilot. But I have obeyed orders almost as foolish."

"Oh God! She's still zonked! Vanda, keep Diana from doing anything crazy until she's back to normal!"

"I'll try, sir."

"Diana, does that damned Oath force us to take Padron back to the frontier?"

"No, sir," I said, relieved to see his plan.

"So we don't have to return the bastard to civilization. Is that clear? To all of you?"

Vanda and I nodded. Kate began to protest. "That's not honorable! If you leave him—"

"To hell with honor! Would it be honorable to release that devil Padron back on your people?"

"I'm for leaving them all," I said. "Especially Raji! Though maybe we should take Kahn. And Mansur. He tried to do his duty."

"Jan!" Kate broke in. "Leave Padron perhaps. But the others—you're responsible for the others."

"They can look after themselves."

"But they can't—they can't! They don't know how to survive out here!"

"Kahn does," I said. "He lived in the wilderness. Let him lead them out."

"Kahn couldn't lead three sailors to a whorehouse!" Jan chewed his lip. "They chose to deal with Padron. They tried to fix the deck. Now let them play the hand!"

"Jan, you're not yourself yet. Diana's not herself yet. You agreed to the treaty. You said this was a military operation. So you're still responsible."

"Oh God!" Jan rubbed his forehead. "You're right, Katy. Brains scrambled again." He gestured at the ship. "Are they still zonked?"

"They're all asleep."

"Then let's break out the lifeboat and get it rigged." He saw my face. "Diana, don't you dare scowl at me!"

"I think—"

"To hell with what you think!" He stepped toward me. "You insolent bitch." He raised his hand.

For the first time in my adult life I feared a man's anger. I flinched. He checked his blow. He stood, rubbing his head. "Christ! This stuff comes back in waves. Di, get away from here. Before you kill somebody. Or goad somebody into killing you!"

"May I go hunting? We need fresh meat."

"Go where the hell you like!" He swung on Vanda and Kate. "Get the gear out quietly. I want the lifeboat rigged and inflated before that bunch recovers."

Delighting in my release I went downstream round the cove until I found the railroad I had seen on the map. The

sterile railbed was still clear of trees and gave me a pathway
into the forest. It was my first chance to hunt with a bow,
and my zest was increased by a legacy from the smokes
which raised my perceptions to new highs. I was surrounded
by the brilliance of the fall colors and the beauty of the day;
by the songs of insects and birds, by the swish of the underbrush as I moved through it. The woods were rich with the
scents of game.

I hunted through the afternoon, stalked a group of white-
tailed deer, selected a yearling buck, and started back to
camp with a haunch and a shoulder. By the time I reached
the river the sun was low and as crimson as my hands.
Across the cove Jan was loading stores into the inflated lifeboat, so I hid my bow in the forest and started round the
bend to show him my prize. When I reached the bank above
the beach I found Shapur had come from the ship and was
demanding to know what Jan was doing.

"Getting ready to go down the river, Governor. It's our
only way out."

"You've tried to call on the radio?"

"Couldn't raise anybody when we were at three thousand
meters so there's not much chance now that we're on the
ground. They took out the long-range radio after Vanda'd
crossed—"

"How long will it take, going down the river?"

"Maybe the best part of six months to reach the Delta. Or
get where they'll hear our crash beacon."

"Six months! Good God, man, I can't be away that long!"

"We'll move as fast as we can, sir. But mostly we'll have to
depend on the current. And the river may not be clear. Nobody's bothered to find out what's happened to the Mississippi during the last century. We'll have portages. And we'll
have to gather food. We've only got the emergency rations.
Six people for five days. And we're eight people—"

"Eight? You mean nine." Shapur stared at Jan. "If you're
thinking of leaving Padron—we cannot. He's no longer an
enemy. The treaty—"

"You never signed the treaty. You were saved from that
disgrace!"

"Gart—you insolent—" Shapur checked himself. "The
treaty was signed in spirit. It would be dishonorable for me to
betray Padron now."

The two men eyed each other across the boat. Then Jan shrugged, "If Raji wants him—I guess we're stuck with him!"

"Rajuna! What has she to do with this?"

"She's away in the bushes screwing with him now."

Shapur's hand went to his thigh, to where his pistol should have been. "Gart, you blackguard—"

"Just as well I tossed the guns away, wasn't it, Governor? For God's sake! That woman's insulted both of us. If you give a damn about Rajuna warn her what Padron is. She's infatuated by him. And he's the devil incarnate. He'll use her and destroy her!"

"Nevertheless, Captain Gart, my orders are we take Padron with us." Shapur swung on his heel, walked across the beach, climbed the bank, and started toward the ship. His face was black with anger and pain.

"Cram your orders!" Jan was muttering, but his face too was so dark that I did not go down onto the beach but followed Shapur toward the camp.

Kate was building a fire to cook a meager supper and was delighted to get my fresh meat. She put the haunch on a spit and the smell of the roasting venison attracted everybody, for none of us had eaten for over twenty-four hours and now that the effects of the smoke were fading all of us were ravenous. I took the shoulder away toward the river and knelt to extract the arrow.

Padron and Rajuna had emerged from the forest at the first scent of the meat. Padron walked over and stood watching me. Presently he said, "A fine kill, Diana! You are indeed well named. But where is your bow?"

"Where it is." I worked the arrow free, stood up, and showed it to him. "This went right through the buck."

He felt the point. "As sharp as a brain-probe! But why no barbs?"

"My arrows kill. They do not hang and fester."

He laughed. "And the other Pilot—Vanda—she also has a bow?"

"A crossbow. A small one, but as deadly as an autarch's pistol."

He smiled at me. "Diana! The chaste Archer of the Moon."

"The chaste Huntress of the Moon," I corrected him.

"Padron, your quotations are usually inaccurate. And there the error is important."

"Why so?" His smile was edged.

"Do you remember the calendar?"

"This is October the seventeenth, is it not? No, I cannot remember anything notable about the date."

"There is nothing notable about the date. There is about the Moon. It is the full moon of October. They called it the Hunter's Moon." I walked past him down to the river to wash the blood off my hands.

My venison turned an otherwise Spartan supper into a feast. We ate in a measure of companionship, and afterward we crowded closer to the fire to shut out the chill darkness. Kate distributed the last of the coffee, pouring it like a sacrament, and we drank it slowly as if indeed we were sipping a common libation in the temporary truce of a sacred ceremony.

Jan gripped his mug and stared into the flames. "I've checked the maps. That's the Mississippi all right. Beyond it—forest, the Bad Lands, the Black Hills, the Rockies. Behind us—wilderness, Lake Michigan, the Appalachians. To the north—wilderness, marshes, snow, the Great Lakes. To the south—cliffs, wilderness, forest, swamp. The only way out is down the river. And winter's close." He rubbed his forehead. "I've got an idea navigation used to stay open until November. If it starts to freeze early we'll be trapped. So we move off tomorrow." Before anybody had time to speak he pulled out his cigar case, looked at his remaining cheroots, took one, and then gave the case to Kate. "Hand these around, Katy. They're all we've got and Shapur's dying for a smoke. He won't take one from me. Maybe you can persuade him."

Kahn waved the case away. Mansur took the cheroot offered. Shapur hesitated, pride competing with desire. Desire won. Kate started toward Padron, then glanced inquiringly at Jan. He nodded.

"Thank you, Captain Gart. Thank you indeed. A generous gesture." Padron took the remaining cheroot. "I interpret this as a cigar of peace."

"Interpret it as our last smoke," said Jan.

Padron looked at Shapur. "Governor, I presume you are planning to maroon me when you leave on your voyage?"

"Maroon you?" Rajuna, sitting beside him, gripped his hand. "Never—"

"Of course not!" snapped Shapur. "I have already told Captain Gart that morally the treaty has been signed. You are coming with us. Gart, be standing watches down by the boat. Diana, come with me."

I followed him away from the fireside to the darkness of the beach. He stood looking out across the river, his face lit intermittently by the glow of his cheroot. I asked, "What is Lunaton?"

"Lunaton? A prechaos chemical warfare agent. Made for generals to use on their own men. Designed to turn on a soldier. It did too good a job. One dose lasted months. Turned decent fighting men into brutal killers. The kind of troops civilians despise and demand. Obedient, competent, expendable professionals. An extra dose—and they had druj!"

"It was the chemical in those red-yellow cases hidden in the altar?"

"That was the cache Padron was after. He didn't know where it was. Well, he found it. We all found it! We also all found the mindbending effects of a Lunaton-Paxin mix! God, if ever a gang deserved what they got, we did!" He tossed the butt of his cheroot out onto the river. "Wondering how I know all this?"

"If it's a CBW agent I expect it was in the prechaos manuals you were always reading."

He laughed. "It never reached the manuals. But it's in the literature. Cross-indexed and filed but unread. There for anybody who got an idea and went to look. I had the idea and I looked. They never made much of it. Stuff's too beastly for even armchair warriors to stomach. But Sherando must have got what there was. Sherando had friends in Washington. And in Fort Detrick. Sherando had friends everywhere. It had fertile women to trade! The place was as bad as everything you said, Di."

"So that's how the druj appeared in the Valley! They used Lunaton to turn some of the farmers into druj to cover their retreat and get killed. They'd only need a few with them to herd their captives and bring in more men to turn into more druj when needed. Lunaton allowed a fast military buildup! Typical of a system with positive feedback."

"Diana—must you still force fit everything into terms of your damned systems?" He stared, brooding, out across the dark river. "But you're right. As they went they'd have scooped up survivors of the Chaos to take along. The southwest's probably full of supply dumps cached away by the Affluence. They set up an oligarchy somewhere out there. Screwing every woman they caught. Selecting the 'purest' boys to join the Cadre. But when Padron arrived to take over, why did he bring a war party east?"

"They must have been running out of Lunaton," I said. "Padron knew there was a reserve hidden somewhere in Sherando. He must have used what Lunaton they had left to build up the biggest war party he could to recapture Sherando. He expected it to be a quick job. And it would have been—if it hadn't been for us!"

"He got it anyway. Bought it with Paxin. He got his Lunaton too. All at once!" Jan laughed. "But he'd already run out and his druj were reverting en masse. There's what the books call a 'paradoxical rebound' as the effect wears off. From obedient killers to docile ever-loving slaves before they became poor bloody peasants again. He had over a thousand on his hands. Padron and his goons were swamped by over-affectionate druj. God sure moves in a mysterious way!"

"That rebound effect is quite common. It occurs with many drugs. But there is something else interesting about this Lunaton. It is a superlente drug."

"Superlente? What's that?"

"Very long-acting. You said one dose lasted for months. We got only minute amounts in the smoke, but we can expect to observe its effects for quite a while."

"Never thought of that." He hesitated. "Di, do you realize that at times today you've been acting crazy? Really crazy?"

"I've noticed periods of heightened sensory perception in myself. And moments of madness in you and the others."

He sighed. "Well, try to watch yourself when you feel that way. The stuff gives recurrences. Return trips they used to call 'em." When he stood with his back to the river the moonlight lit his face and showed me the shadows of worry upon it. "Where's that bow of yours?"

"Across the cove. I hid it with my other arrows."

"Fetch it at dawn." He went to the lifeboat, took out one of the sleeping bags, and gave it to me. "Go and lie down up there in the shadow of the bank. We've got to see that Padron doesn't jump us, but you need sleep. I'll call you when I want you to take over the watch."

XVIII

Sagittarius Victrix

He did not wake me until it was light and smoke was rising from Kate's fire as she started to prepare breakfast. I went around the cove to fetch my bow and, looking back, I saw that Shapur had come from the ship and was standing by the lifeboat, talking to Jan.

I was too far away to hear what they were saying but I could see they were wrangling. They walked across the beach and climbed up the bank to the meadow at the moment that Rajuna and Padron emerged together from the woods. Both men stopped as though struck; then Jan strode across the meadow to join Mansur and Kahn who were watching Kate cook. Shapur swung around and stared across the river. The scene was peaceful enough so I ran into the forest to fetch my bow.

When I returned Shapur was still standing on the bank with his back to Rajuna and Padron who were loitering along the beach, two lovers strolling together in the early morning. Padron had his arm around Rajuna's waist. When she called to Shapur he glanced at her over his shoulder then deliberately turned his back and walked away. She did not call again.

She did not call again because Padron had clamped his hand over her mouth. And she was walking beside him because he had her arm twisted up the small of her back. I shouted a warning but the wind was against me and my cry did not carry across the cove.

They reached the lifeboat. Padron bent to push it afloat. Rajuna, with a sudden lunge, broke free. He jumped after her, caught her flying hair, and jerked her backwards onto the sand. Her scream echoed across the water and the

168

meadow. He knocked her out, picked her up, and tossed her into the boat.

Shapur had spun around at her scream and was racing back across the grass, down the bank, and along the beach. Padron waited in the easy stance of the skilled fighter and when Shapur arrived hit him once. Shapur dropped at the edge of the water.

I was too far away to interfere and had to watch the outcome of Jan's blindness and Shapur's distorted honor. Padron was about to take both Rajuna and the lifeboat. We would be well rid of her but to lose the boat would be disaster.

Rajuna might lack morals but she had quality. While in Padron's grip she had gone limp. When he had tossed her into the boat she had feigned unconsciousness. The moment he bent to push it off she grabbed him. Padron attempted to subdue her and launch the boat simultaneously. It was like trying to string an eel and gaff a trout at the same time. When Jan, Kahn, and Mansur came over the bank and this time he let her lie, for the three men had fanned out in a pattern that showed even Mansur knew something of combat tactics. I relaxed. The three of them had the strength, time, and anger to pulp Padron. I waited to watch them do it.

The crack of a pistol came across the water. They all froze. The autarchs were astounded that Padron had been carrying a concealed weapon, though why they should think an apostate would observe their absurd proprieties, I don't know. As for Jan and myself, we had seen Kate leave his combat pistol on the Pinnacle and neither of us had imagined a soldier carrying a toy inside his tunic.

A toy, but deadly at ten meters. Padron's warning shot stopped his attackers' charge. Vanda, arriving on the bank, raised her crossbow, then lowered it as Padron pointed his pistol at Jan. Still facing the petrified group, he eased the lifeboat out into the river. The muzzle of his pistol dropped as he got it afloat and the tableau broke into a flurry of simultaneous movement.

Shapur, who had staggered to his feet, threw himself at Padron. Padron fired. Shapur fell. Padron gave the boat a heave and Vanda's dart struck the water centimeters from his legs. A close shot at an extreme distance but a near miss is only good with grenades, and before Vanda could reload he

had jumped aboard and the current had swept him beyond
her range. The major defect of a crossbow is its slow rate of
fire. I notched an arrow on the chance that the river would
bring him within my reach.

Padron started the motor and circled back upstream. He
hung offshore, picked up the powered megaphone, and his
amplified voice drowned Jan's curses. "I apologize for having
to use violence. But I must resume command of my cadre as
soon as possible. I will travel faster if I travel alone. I had
hoped Raji would come with me. Now she must wait with
you. Stay at this camp so my men will be able to find you."
He studied them through the lifeboat's binoculars. "I am glad
to see that the Governor is alive and I trust not seriously
hurt. I regret having to shoot you, Shapur. Violence is not
your metier. Please say *au revoir* to Diana for me. I look forward to seeing her, and all of you, when my men bring you
in!" Then, with a wave, he sent the boat speeding out into
midstream before stopping the motor.

Vanda was already padding Shapur's wound with her field
dressing. There was nothing I could do that Vanda could not.
Padron had some fifteen hundred kilometers to go and fuel
for only fifteen hours. The current was about three knots and
he was letting it carry him as he would have to let it carry
him for most of his journey.

I reviewed the map in my mind. In about eight hours he
would reach the last point where I could hope to intercept
him. Although the railbed was rough it could still give me a
path across the great bend in the river. I went back into the
woods, found the track, and started along it. I would not
have commenced such a forlorn chase had not the map shown
the railroad led to a bridge, and after a hundred and fifty
years that bridge should be down. I pictured a barrier of
fallen spans and broken piers, a place of snags and torrents. I
set that hope before my eyes to block off fatigue and settled
down to run.

I ran as the sun climbed, rested briefly when it reached
zenith, ran again as it started to slide westwards. When I had
fled from Axe I had been the hunted and I had run in pain.
Now I ran as the huntress and I ran in joy. Padron had broken the Truce and exposed himself to my vengeance. As my
exhaustion grew, channels to the eternal began to open,
strengthening my resolve.

At mid-afternoon I reached the bridge and before I collapsed I saw it was as I had imagined. When I recovered I crawled out along the wreckage, looking upstream. Padron would have to navigate carefully through the broken spans and the crumbling piers. I hid at the edge of the widest passage I could reach, hoping it was the one he would choose. There I waited, looking upriver, praying that the Mississippi would bring him to me.

Late in the afternoon a black dot appeared, distant on the calm waters, turning into the lifeboat as it drifted closer. Padron studied the bridge through his binoculars, and then started the motor. He came to within three hundred meters of me, then turned the boat and made a sweep across the river. He did not try to run the rapids but steered to a long narrow island about a bowshot from the east bank. He fastened the painter to the branch of an overhanging tree and began to unload the camp kit onto the rocky beach.

That was wisdom. He had picked a safe campsite, and the next day he would be rested and better able to maneuver through the snags and torrents. The island was thickly wooded with a swift current cutting it off from the shore and an open beach facing the milder flow of the river. I watched him collect kindling and scout the island. He would not expect I could have run through such rugged country in time to intercept him, nor cross the swift channel to catch him if I had.

I would not dare it after dark. It might be beyond me even in daylight. Already it was shadowed by the trees as the sun fell across the river. I went through the underbrush until I was upstream of the island, stripped naked, fastened my arrows in my hair, put my bow across my back, and gave brief thanks to the Mother of Waters that She had brought Padron within my reach. Then I slid into the current, praying for strength to take the prize.

By Her mercy and my own extreme effort I reached the downstream tip of the island before I was swept onto the broken piers of the bridge. I caught a root and slowly worked my way upriver, hidden by the bank and the trees. The sound of my exertions was drowned by the noise of the torrent and I pulled myself ashore when I judged I was level with the boat. One virtue of the materials I had used for my bow was that the water would not degrade them.

I eased through the underbrush until I was within a spear-length of the lifeboat, bobbing at the end of its painter. Padron was standing on a rock, a little way upstream, out in the shallows, fishing. More wisdom. Even early in his voyage he was fishing for food while he had the chance.

He was about ninety meters away, the "prince's range," and had his back toward me. I could certainly have shafted him without his knowing he had been struck down. That would have been both lawful and wise, but every execution leaves a stain upon the executioner. So I untied the painter from the branch, looped it round my ankle in such a way that if I fell it would be tugged free by the current, and stepped out of the shadows. He continued with his fishing.

I notched an arrow, bent my bow, and called, "Padron!"

He swung around. I saw his face and for a moment my resolve faltered. He stared, hitched his fishing line to the rock, and then stood with his open hands away from his body. "Welcome, Diana! I knew you would join me."

I raised my bow and aimed at his heart.

He did not flinch, but walked slowly through the shallows toward me, saying, "Diana, do you know what you'll be doing if you kill me?"

"Sending a dishonored servant of the Lie back to his Master. Padron, you broke the treaty."

"Would that I had your faith!" He stopped at the threat of my point. "Diana, if you kill me you annihilate our future. You strangle the line of women who are to spring from you and me. Women who should carry the burden of our conjoined genius down the ages. Women destined to lead and succour our race."

The setting sun made his hair a golden halo. He was as beautiful as Lucifer. And he was my complement. The key and the lock.

"Diana, come with me. I am the only man on earth who is your match. The only man who need not fear you. As you are the only woman who need not fear me. We could not overthrow each other, even if we wished. We need never pity nor patronize each other. We know each other's mettle. You and I—together—can leave our daughter a legacy such as no woman's daughter has ever had before."

I could not allow the thought to crystallize in my mind. If I savored his bait I would swallow it and be lost for ever. I shook the painter from my foot and pushed the lifeboat out into the river. The current carried it away from the beach.

His expression altered on the instant. He swung around, ignoring my drawn bow, and splashed through the shallows after the boat. The current on this side of the island was not as fierce as on the other but was strong enough to have already taken the boat far beyond his reach. It gained speed as the river gripped it, sweeping it down toward the races and sluicing torrents between the shattered piers. He stopped, waist deep in water, staring after it, watching it dip and plunge as it was drawn into the foam of a cataract.

He lifted his hands to the sun and gave a howl of agonized fury as it disappeared. Then he came wading toward me until the water was again at his knees. He had the expression of a devil. I braced myself to withstand a devil's curse. His trite phrase stung more sharply. "You silly little bitch! Why the hell did you do that?"

"Because tonight, on this island, one of us will die. Without the lifeboat, even if I fall, you are still destroyed."

"You Valkyre—"

"Valkyrie," I corrected him. Then I said, "Draw your gun, Padron. At fifteen paces it rivals my bow. I will not loose until the odds are even."

The formalities restored him. He drew his pistol and stood facing me, his face calm, his eyes intent. The lists were set.

"You may advance, firing at will."

He walked slowly toward me, his pistol raised as my bow was raised, aiming at my heart as I was aiming at his. He advanced until the water was down to his ankles. Then he fired.

Too soon. His slug buzzed past me, into the trees. He had lost. I loosed.

I had aimed at his heart but hit him low, just under the sternum. My arrow missed the aorta but sliced the great vein, for he took three steps up onto the beach before he collapsed. I ran to kneel beside him.

He looked up at me, his blue eyes already clouding. "Diana—is there any message?"

"My gratitude to your master for sending an enemy of such worth." I kissed his forehead and he died.

My arrow had impaled him and I had trouble extracting it. Then I hauled logs to pile on the kindling he had already gathered until his pyre would flame up, a red whirlwind, consume him utterly, so that nothing of him would be left for the buzzards. I dragged his body to the top of the pyre, an effort that exhausted me, so I had to rest before I drew his knife and cut off his head.

A barbarous custom but ancient and sensible. A head on a spear is absolute proof to an enemy that their leader is dead. And proof to any others who doubted his death. Those in the camp might think me hallucinating if I only told them I had killed Padron. His head must serve for his body.

I packed it with vines in the fishing satchel, slung it across my back under my bow, then lit the pyre with his lighter. I told the River that now She could take me if She needed a sacrifice to atone for spilling a life into Her waters. But She was satisfied with less. She washed Padron's blood from me, then dragged me across the rough concrete of the fallen piers, smearing my body with my own before She released me to struggle ashore. I forced my way back through the brambles and branches until I reached my clothes. The pyre blazed high and his pistol cracked as the heat discharged the remaining rounds.

Dressed and armed I stood looking across the black waters, keeping the vigil. Padron had been an evil warrior. All along the frontier were scattered the remains of men and women and children who had died horribly for his ambition. I had no forgiveness for him. He had chosen the Darkness as against the Light. He had been defeated by the Light. He was now in double jeopardy; the Light would punish him for his crimes and the Darkness would punish him for his failure. But he was dead, and I could allow myself to mourn for him.

XIX

Vernal Equinox

It is five months since I started this report, and I am not what I was. It is March and still cold, but the ice is floating free on the river and spring is coming closer. And I am changing with the seasons; as we are all changing.

Last November, when he told me to write this, he said he wanted you to be convinced by the "logic of events." I still don't know what he meant, but I have tried to include everything that might help us to understand why we are stranded in what used to be Wisconsin. I spent many cold evenings working in the ship; sorting, transcribing, and editing my notes and recordings. Living again through the past year, reviewing the changes in my attitude and style, has cleared my mind of much rubbish.

My account of Padron's death completes my report; you know the rest for we have lived through it together. But to break off abruptly at a point where both my acts and my descriptions give the impression of a deranged fanatic would be unfair to me and to the report itself. Unity is the claim every written work makes on its writer. I left Padron without a head; I cannot leave this in the same state.

You all saw the lingering effects of the Lunaton-Paxin smoke; in retrospect our words and acts seem bizarre. I was as crazy as anyone. I should have shafted Padron when I stepped from under the trees. It would have been more useful to have returned with the lifeboat than with his head. It was barbarous when I staggered into camp to demand a spear on which to mount it.

None of us were sane, not even Vanda and Kate. It was Jan who guided us through the despair and madness of those terrible days. It was Jan who recognized that Shapur's chest wound was a flap valve so that with every breath he pumped himself up and took himself nearer death. Jan must have seen a tension pneumothorax from a combat wound before. He needled it and saved Shapur's life. It was Jan who preserved Raji's sanity and helped me to recover mine. It was Jan who drove us to build the cabin and gather supplies to meet the winter. The fact that we have survived is due to Jan. For months he was detested by us all.

Raji and I reached an understanding two days after my return while she was dripping guilt and I was weak from my exertions and feverish from my injuries. She blamed herself, rightly, for our predicament and for Shapur's wound. She came to me as I lay in the shelter of the ship watching the men dig postholes for the cabin. I had asked that Padron's head be buried under its foundations after the ancient custom, but Jan had taken it away into the forest and, so Kate had informed me, given it a Christian burial.

Raji had been irritating everybody with her self-flagellation and demands for forgiveness. She came to unload her guilt and seek absolution from me as she had from the others. And also to hear the details of Padron's death.

My fever and my grief made me sympathetic and I comforted her by confessing that my own hunger for Padron had also tempted me to the verge of treason. I had longed for his daughter rather than his body, but to Raji that was a distinction without a difference. I pointed out that it was his arrogance which had caused his downfall. He had never believed that any woman could reject him; even with my arrow through his guts he had not believed it. He had been confident he could debauch a Prime Pilot and a Director; women who had both been classified in the upper tenth top percentile.

We finished that delirious discussion in each other's arms, lamenting our common loss, and sealing our alliance with our mingled tears. However absurd the circumstances, however emotionally unbalanced we both were, our rapprochement, though often battered, has survived the winter.

Since December we have been crammed together in a six by five cabin for nights of up to sixteen hours, snow up to the roof, temperatures dipping to negative twenty outside and rising to positive thirty inside. A place without privacy where we have been forced to expose ourselves to each other. Months when we could do nothing alone or in pairs except in the frigid ship or in the deep snow. Weeks when conversation was our only entertainment and whatever was said by one was heard and discussed by all. A time when we learned the cost of lacerating arguments and the nature of our obsessions.

Because of Jan none of us have killed each other. Instead we have grown to understand, even to like each other. With the exception of Jan whom nobody understands now and everybody disliked then. We still resent him, but the rest either admire or want him.

I had always known him to be introspective; I was surprised to find him unselfish. He had always avoided responsibility; when it was forced upon him he became an incisive leader. I had seen him flinch before authority; now he is arrogant in enforcing his own. He has astounded all of us by his competence in areas for which he was never trained and his knowledge of things far outside his education. Raji has reconciled the anomaly of a Patrol Officer with brains by deciding he must be a lapsed autarch. Kahn argues that his interest in theology shows he once studied in an Ulama seminary.

Jan's "faith" is turning out to be a kind of metaphysical mathematics. Ludicrous for a soldier educated in neither metaphysics nor mathematics. He has started with the naïve thesis that a group with our peculiar talents could never have been snowbound together by chance alone. He ignores the obvious causal antecedent—Vanda's navigational incompetence. He has got himself tied up in Markov Chains of conditional probabilities. His theology is even more primitive than the morass of superstition from which I am at last extricating myself. Jan's deity is a cosmic pawn-master who has dumped us for a winter in the middle of the American continent either to do something together or to learn something from each other. Jan, ignorant of the statistical laws governing improbable events, treats this as obvious and is agonizing over what we are supposed to be doing or learning.

Kahn encourages his speculations. I would have hoped that even such an overtolerant Ecclesiarch would have influenced Jan toward orthodoxy. Instead Jan is edging Kahn toward heresy. Though I now realize those are empty terms, the percussion grenades of debate, all noise and no punch! I watch the absurd spectacle of an Ecclesiarch, trained in theology, listening to a Patrol Captain expounding on the nature of God, the purpose of the universe, and the Arrow of Time.

I suspect that Jan has challenged Kahn with my guess about his origin, but neither has said anything to the rest of us. We listen to Jan's nightly sermonizing because we have no alternative if we want to keep warm.

Raji and Shapur are impressed despite themselves. Mansur argues with Jan, but more for the pleasure of argument than from any concern about the identification of truth. Mansur is the man who has been the most improved physically and personally by our winter of isolation but is still a bureaucrat at heart. Kate is falling in love with him. Jan rejected her as he has rejected everything female. He seems to be identifying sex with sin.

As Raji says, "God help us all! Jan's got religion! He's growing a beard. Soon he'll be waving a staff and reading us some document dictated directly to him by the Almighty."

I've managed to dissuade him from the beard but not from his other nonsense.

Shapur's pneumothorax healed without sequelae, thanks to Jan's initial actions and my later care. He not only forgave Raji, he took her back with open arms. I almost fell over them last December, lying together in the snow between two of my half-cured pelts.

We had to use my furs to cover the walls and floor of the cabin during the winter. They stank, but so did we once the river had frozen. I would have expected that I, with my acute sense of smell, would have suffered the most. Instead I am beginning to understand the pleasure a dog takes in the scent of familiar human beings.

My last "briefing" has almost worn off. Vanda's is wearing thin and she is showing more than a dutiful interest in Kahn's welfare. We are watching an outpouring of delayed adolescent love! Kahn is basking in it. Vanda is the only one of us who still treats him with the respectful admiration to which an Ecclesiarch is accustomed. He now looks more like the lean ascetic we rescued from Padron than the plump prelate who came to Sherando.

Jan is obsessed by the meaning of the world; the autarchs are arguing about how to change it. What Jan calls the "Government in Exile" of Shapur and Rajuna has decided to start by phasing out Paxin, now that they have learned what it feels like to be a drugged idiot. They talk like naïve idiots! My new sensitivity to the feelings of others has prevented me from telling them they are living in cloud-cuckoo land. I know something of what is going on back in Sector Ten. I have heard snatches of conversation on the radio.

Last November I reserved the remaining fuel to keep the ship's batteries charged so I would have power for the word-processors I needed to prepare this report. When I checked the electronics I found that the radio could pick up the occasional ionosphere-reflected signal, and from such scattered interceptions I have been able to piece together an outline of what has gone on since we left. I did not tell the autarchs because it would have driven them frantic with impatience to get back. Nor will I tell Jan until I know enough to give an accurate picture. At present I am rigging a tuner to shift the receiver frequencies to the lower long-range radio band.

Raji is pregnant. By Shapur, thank God! I could not have trusted myself had I learned she was carrying Padron's child. But her pregnancy will make the trip down-river more difficult. And I am starting to realize it is important that Jan returns to the Sector as soon as possible.

Because I am beginning to suspect he too comes from the past, by the same route as Padron and Kahn but from quite a different origin. Now that I am free to think I remember the parley with Padron, and there is only one explanation which makes sense of their exchange. When I broached the subject to Jan he ordered me to silence in a voice he rarely uses but which we all heed when he does.

Jan in the past was sometimes brutal but I had never seen him intentionally cruel. Until now. And only to me. He respects everybody's feelings except mine. As though I were still the desensitized automation of a year ago. He used to

smile at me. Now, when I catch his glances, they are angry
or sad. He used to come to me for advice; now he avoids me.
He used to tease me; now he never jokes with me. Perhaps
that is because I am no longer an easy butt for his wit.

Last week I caught him unawares and so had him briefly
to myself. I was returning from my trap-lines and he was
marking trees to be felled for the raft which will take us
down the river. The drifts in the woods are still deep and I
was on snowshoes so he could not evade me. When he saw
me there was a flash of pain and pleasure on his face. I was
pleased and hurt. I stood and studied him.

"You don't seem to like me now that I'm not a zomb!"

"Di, you never were a zomb. You were—" He shrugged
and turned back to blazing a young pine with his machete.

I moved around the tree so he had to face me. "I was
what?"

He stuck the machete into the trunk. "The best comrade I
ever had!"

"But I'm not now?"

"You're in the middle of some kind of metamorphosis.
When the change is over—"

"The others are starting to like me. Even Raji!"

"You never used to give a damn about being liked! Now
you're as touchy as the rest of that bunch!"

Anger surged up in me. "You don't want me to become
myself, do you? You want me to go on being your brainwashed stooge! Do you know what Owen Hassen once called
me? A charioteer to a thug! A docile charioteer—"

He laughed at me for the first time in months. "Docile? Di,
you may have been a charioteer, but you were never docile!"
Then his face went sad. "Diana, you're the finest person I've
ever known. The only unselfish, dedicated, brave—"

"That's your definition of 'finest.' It's not mine any more!
We used to talk. Now you just issue orders!"

"Di, how can we talk?" He made a weak gesture with his
hands. "Later on, when you're yourself again, as Kate would
say—"

"I'm myself now!"

"Christ, I hope not!"

"Don't worry! You're still the boss. We all think you're a
prize bastard. The civilians are afraid of you. But Vanda and

I, we're not afraid of you. Neither is Kate. We go on support-
ing you—" I began to flounder in words as he floundered
toward me through the wet snow.

I shook his hand off my arm and mushed back toward the
camp.

Rereading the parley transcript. As my vision clears I see
more and more. Hudson's Bay. Where Karen died. Where
Douglas died. Where Gart died? The Douglas Convolution.
The memorial to a great mathematician. Jan a great mathematician? Too incongruous even to consider.

But the Order's computers named him a nexus. They
remember everything. They know about time transits. They
would know Douglas died up there.

A Gart-Douglas switch? Gart's sudden competence. But
Douglas was a mathematician, not a soldier. It doesn't make
sense, not to me. It had made sense to the Order's computers.
They had identified Gart as something. But what?

If the comps had known it was Douglas who was rescued
from the wreck, why didn't they identify him? And why post
me, a Prime Pilot, to take over this team?

Only one reason: the Order thinks we need a good soldier
more than a genius mathematician.

"I have again rechecked my transcription of the parley. I
must have had blind spots conditioned into me. Things I
could not see before now jump out at me.

Padron: I want you for your genius. The Master of the
Convolution. The Master of Time. I want you as a soldier—
the ablest I have met.

Jan: What you want is an escape hatch into the future!

The Master of Time! Perhaps Jan indeed knows the way
that a team with our talents could first lay the foundations of
things to come and then move to supervise their completion,
to make sure our plans are not distorted by inept successors.

I am no longer brainwashed, but I still have the qualities
and skills of a Prime Pilot. I prefer that title to "Pilot of the
First Class." I will revive the honorific "Prime Pilot" when I
return to Naxos.

Jan—or whoever he is—has been nagging me to finish my report. I had intended to round it off with this chapter. Now that I have read the last few pages through clear eyes I can see it would be counterproductive to show them to anybody out here. So I will terminate my report with the death of Padron, truncated though it will be. This, and whatever else I write, will be epilogue, composed for my own satisfaction and so that its changing style and content will serve as a reminder to me in the future of my evolution into a free woman.

XX

Crescent Astarte

At last I know what Jan was, what he is, and what he should become. Yesterday he brought me his Introduction, and issued the same order as when he gave me the recording of his parley with Padron. "Transcribe it. Read it. Then come and tell me what you think."

I typed it last night and at dawn I went hunting. This is the first hot day of spring so when I returned to the camp at noon I bathed in the river and washed my hair. It now cascades golden to my shoulders. Afterward I stood on the bank drying in the sun and watching the others working on the raft. Jan left them and came toward me, my report in his hand. Nudity annoys him so I slipped on the chiton I had made from the panel of a parachute and started to braid my hair.

He said, "I was waiting!"

"Waiting for me to bring you a mug of coffee? There isn't any! We finished it—"

"Waiting for you to come and tell me what you think." When I only continued to arrange my hair he barked, "Well, what *do* you think?"

"What do I think? That's the question Padron was fond of asking me!" I looked at him. "I think you're even more devious than Padron. You fooled him. You fooled us all."

He flushed. "Di—I'm sorry. Perhaps I should have told you the truth at the start."

"Thank God you didn't. I'd have reacted as programmed and turned you over to the Order. And that bunch of hags would have screwed things up for sure. The Order's comps must have known who you were. I don't think the Synod ever caught on."

183

"Diana, I've come to respect your Order—"

"Cram my Order! I've read your Introduction. Have you read my report?"

"This?" He weighed the typescript in his hands. "Most of it isn't a report. I told you to give the relevant facts—"

"And what relevant facts have I left out?"

"You haven't left out a damned thing. But you've added pages of irrelevancies. Plus your own interpretations. That's not the way you used to write."

"How I used to write is irrelevant! I've reported what happened as I saw it. That's what you asked for. And if I hadn't given some idea of motives the whole thing would read like the diary of a pair of crazies. Of course, I was crazy for most of the time. And you were certainly crazy when you got us lost out here."

"Diana, you knew I wanted this so the others could read—damnation, girl—the way you describe Raji and me—"

"I described your relations with Raji as delicately as I could. They are certainly relevant to our debacle. And it is certainly a fact that you screwed her hard and often! You had your fun! I warned you—and look where it's got all of us! Now you're angry because your image develops out grubbier than you like!"

"Never had any illusions about my image. The point is how the hell can I show this to them?"

"There's no need. You've brought us through the winter with your bullying. You don't have to make excuses to them. You've saved their lives! They're not grateful, but they know it. Forget about that bunch. You're a soldier. Back east there's work for soldiers."

"A Marine—not a soldier! And I got out of the killing game when I was twenty-seven. I was dumped back into it because I miscalculated a constant."

"If you hadn't miscalculated you'd have been dead long ago. Have you considered that?"

"Skip the metaphysics. I'm a mathematician."

"Then why didn't you go back to being one after you found the real situation here? You didn't have to go druj-hunting with enthusiasm! You didn't have to make us the best combat team there is!"

"We had to stop Padron and the druj."

"So you saw where your real duty lay then! That's where

your duty lies now. You're a talented fighter. You always were. I read your biography. Wounds and medals. What was the job that got you that medal? I'll bet it wasn't forced on you! You like fighting and you know it."

"Di, I'm a throwback—"

"A throw-forward!"

"We're both atavisms. But we don't have to act like primitives. Anyway, how the hell can you know what's happening back east!"

"Radio!" I said.

'Radio? How—?"

I interrupted. "One of those fumblers is about to kill himself."

He swung around. "Oh God! Look at the fools!" The men had a log teetering on the lip of the bank. Raji, her hands clasped across her swelling belly was giving them advice. Jan started toward them shouting, "Hold it! Do you want to smash your legs?"

They stopped work to wait his arrival. They were always ready to let Jan take over any practical problem. I watched as he ran a skid-rope to a holdfast and then arranged the three men along the length of the log. The sweat glistened on their bare backs as they bent to their task. They had been eating well for five months and working hard for weeks. They were full of the fresh meat which Vanda and I had provided, the vegetables, nuts, honey and roots which Kate had collected and stored, the fish which Raji had caught. Shapur had put on weight and the others had taken it off. They are not at all a bad-looking trio.

Shapur, I can see now, has the qualities of a leader but has never learned the skills. He has been surreptitiously studying Jan's techniques. His reactions will be interesting if he ever learns he has been taking a course in practical man-management from a sometime Sergeant in the United States Marine Corps.

As will Kahn's reaction if he discovers he has been arguing theological philosophy with a student of the Jesuits. The Society of Jesus survived the Chaos in an attenuated form and, I suspect, is one of the power groups behind the Ulama. I can see the effects of their education in Jan. The priests who taught him two centuries ago planted a weed which is flourishing in this wilderness. Now I understand his mixture of crudeness and erudition, his fear of women and authority, his brooding concern for the state of his soul. The introspection which could destroy our future if I do not rescue him.

"Heave! Together!" Jan shouted. They strained in unison. The log shifted, then slid safely down into the river. Vanda and Kate splashed through the icy water to float it into position. The men strolled back toward the clump of trees they were felling, arguing as they went. Jan came toward me. I walked upstream to a strip of forest fringing the river.

"Diana, come back here!" he shouted.

I ignored him and slipped away among the trees, down to a private place of soft green turf on the edge of the water, sheltered from the wind and open to the noon sun. I took off my chiton and lay sunbathing, listening to Jan floundering around in the undergrowth. Presently he broke out of the bushes, breathing heavily.

His first words typified his attitude. "Diana, put on your dress!"

He used what I now know to be his sergeant-voice, so I pulled it over my head, gathered it at the waist with my snakeskin girdle, and shook out my hair. Then I sat on a fallen tree and looked up at him.

He hesitated, then sat down beside me. "Radio? What do you mean radio? We spent nights trying to make contact. All our bands are quasioptical."

I told him how I had wired-up a tuner. "I didn't freeze all those evenings in the ship just to prepare your damned report! The brains we're supposed to have out here, and two hundred years ago a fifteen-year-old would have known—"

"Knock it off, Di! What have you heard?"

"The autarch's are chattering on their channels like frightened squirrels. Paxin's running out fast. The narod are restless. Grabbing for things. Tossing out autarchs. In every Sector. The Councils are alarmed. They're turning to the Guard, to the Patrol even! The Marshals are starting to think like heretics now that they're scared themselves. Soon the power's going to shift. Toward the soldiers."

"Oh God, if the Guard try to run the show—"

"They will. You're fond of quoting history. That's the pattern of the past. The druj have disappeared. No more Lunaton. The goons, they're joining the Patrol. Just the type to make good Patrol Officers. Worse still, they'll be efficient.

The Synod's so scared they're allowing 'em in. Think the Pilots will be able to control them. Sterile old hags! I couldn't even control you!"

"Di, you did a good job of nursemaid! What's going to happen?"

"You know what's going to happen. Back to squabbling sector-states. Back to chaos. Unless somebody does something about it. And there isn't anybody, except you!"

"Me? A Patrol Captain with a scarred face, a sordid past, and a scrambled memory! Your own description, Di."

"That described Gart. I'm calling on the Douglas!" And repeating Padron's words.

"Douglas—the faker! Anyway, I've been forgotten already."

"Forgotten, you, Jan?" I laughed. "You're instant legend. A myth in six months!"

"What the hell do you mean?"

"They've hoisted you to Hero. The strong Captain raised to defend the Right. The Sword of the Light who flung back the enemy at the Battle of Sherando."

"The battle of what?"

"The Battle of Sherando!" I laughed again. "The SR ships found riderless horses, swarms of nonhostile druj, and mixed Wardens and Dragoons gibbering about how you had stood toe to toe with the Vicar of Evil, Satan himself, the Old Dragon, Ahriman, etcetera etcetera. Those SR crews got a whiff of that Lunaton-Paxin mix and saw all sorts of things. People all over Sector Ten were seeing visions for days. That smoke must have drifted to the sea. Remember the nonsense you shouted over the loud-hailer when you were trying to fly the cutter?"

"I was lunatic! We all were."

"The mob down below reported that you had told them you were pursuing the Evil One into the wilderness, driving him back to Hell, that you'd gone to slam the gates and shoot the bolts. And—" I paused to give emphasis, "That you'd sworn you would return."

"Nobody'll believe that shuck. Not when they're normal."

"Intelligent men have believed crazier stories than that. The Jesuits who taught you were reputed as pretty bright. Yet they believed they could turn bread into God!"

"That—that's different."

"Why?" He did not answer so I went on. "The myth was starting before we left. You created more of an impression on the Council, on the local farmers, on the Wardens, on Raji's friends, than either of us realized. Marshal Mitra reported to Malta that you were the first soldier he had met in a generation. My Order had already called you a nexus in the reticulum! You proved the comps were right. And when Kahn reached Crete he told the Ulama how you'd rescued him. So—guess what? Last month they named you Ghazi! That means Warrior of the Faith," I explained.

"I know what it means!" he said irritably. "It's also a pile of crap."

"Sure. But reinforced when the goons who surrendered gave a romanticized account of our interrogation by Padron. They're now devout converts. I'm their patron saint!"

"You're what? A saint? Those people back east—are they fools or hypocrites?"

"A bit of both. But mostly they're scared shitless. Your story has spread. The Ulama and the Synod, they've applied the usual religious techniques for explaining events they can't understand. Turn it into myth or miracle. They probably half believe it themselves. Everybody's floundering in freedom to think. Most prefer to emote! The first strong man who appears will be made into a leader, whatever he wants. That's what Padron was after. He's dead, so you're the only possibility in sight. The people who've been ruining civilization haven't been encouraging heroic leadership. But you and Padron are from a time when there were still heroes. You're the only man alive who can see, can know, can act!"

"And I'm marooned out here! Just as well." He stood up. "Or I might believe your nonsense, Di. I'm a—"

"Raji sensed it." I jumped to my feet, looked into his face. And saw something that brought obsolete phrases tumbling from me. "The Light shines on you. You are its chosen instrument! Yet you have free will. You can reject. You can sin. What will you say at the Bridge of the Separator? At the Chinvat Bridge? How will you answer the Question?"

"I'll let you do the talking!" He laughed and gripped my shoulders. "Di, we're still a team. We'll cross the bridge together!"

I regained control of myself. For an instant I had been dazzled by a burst of brilliance. That pseudoillumination which is really the aura of petit mal epilepsy. I had to remind myself what it was. "Jan, the winter is over. We can travel fast, you and I alone. If we start now we can reach the frontier before midsummer. You can come out of the wilderness. Back from your victory beyond the mountains. Just as all of them, the superstitious and the intelligent, see the chaos ahead. You know how even the most skeptical, the most cynical, the most sophisticated, grab myths in such times. And everybody who could contradict you will be out here."

For a moment I saw his visions in his eyes. Then he looked down into my face, and asked gently, "What is in you, Diana? Who is speaking to me now? Light or Darkness? Good or Evil?"

I could only answer, "Let us go—tomorrow." And I felt the aura expanding. I told myself it must be the aura of epilepsy. I dreaded the Aura of Grace. I must stay free!

There was a burst of shouting from downriver, Raji's protests soaring above the other voices. Some new crisis was developing.

Jan said, "And desert them? We could have done that any time. We chose not to. But who is speaking now, Diana? The Truth or the Lie?"

I prayed for strength to retain my skepticism. "They'll survive. When you're in control, you'll be able to send a rescue team." Then the chill came over my body, the still, cold, enveloping wind. The rigor of numinous contact. Or a focus of damaged neurones firing somewhere deep in my temporal lobe. I shivered.

He put his arms around me, "Diana—they might survive. But you know the odds. Would you leave Raji to have her baby without you to help her? Vanda, confused about her duty? Katy, lost and wandering? You and I are responsible for them. They come first. Whatever's happening in the Sector will have to go on happening without us until all of them are safe. They're our comrades!"

It was true. We were all part of each other. Jan had achieved his goal and shackled us to them. To desert them now would be dishonor beyond bearing.

The cold wind passed. I did not know whether I had lost or won. I put my face against his chest and whispered, "Jan—who am I?"

He pressed me to him.

I spoke again. "What am I now? I am no longer your Pilot." I slipped my hand inside his shirt and felt him beginning to tremble, as he had trembled when I had dressed him on that gloomy morning, in his hospital room, on the first day we met.

I looked up into his face, seeking my answer. "What am I? Who am I? To whom do I belong? What is my function and duty on Earth?" The questions from the Catechism I must answer anew.

"Diana!" He was teasing me, avoiding the Sacred Question. "You're as nutty as ever!"

"I am sure of everything, except myself."

His eyes changed. He put his mouth to mine. It was like the old novels I have read. In some details the bad ones are better than the good. I pulled him down on top of me, onto the grassy bank beside the river.

Afterward I lay content, his weight heavy upon me, feeling his quiet breathing, lying easy after all our frenzy. I felt the damp earth under me, smelt the scent of sweat and crushed grasses. I lay in a sleepy, satisfied calm. I listened to the birds, the murmur of the river, the voices of our inept comrades, distant, across the water.

Perhaps, as he had jested, I am still mad. Perhaps only while I am mad can I see the vision of possible realities. Perhaps I am mad to feel this irrational certainty that I have a daughter new within me. A daughter to go with us on our journey; silent and unknown. The secret child among us.

She may drown with me in the river or die with me in the fighting, so that it will never matter whether she is flesh in my womb or image in my mind. But image or reality she is already in being. Through her, if I live, we will triumph over Time and Darkness. I will name her "Astarte." She is the rising daughter of the ancient moon.

DAW PRESENTS MARION ZIMMER BRADLEY

"A writer of absolute competency . . ."—Theodore Sturgeon

☐ **THE FORBIDDEN TOWER**
"Blood feuds, medieval pageantry, treachery, tyranny, and true love combine to make another colorful swatch in the compelling continuing tapestry of Darkover."—**Publishers Weekly.**   (#UJ1323—$1.95)

☐ **THE HERITAGE OF HASTUR**
"A rich and highly colorful tale of politics and magic, courage and pressure . . . Topflight adventure in every way." —**Analog.** "May well be Bradley's masterpiece."—**Newsday.** "It is a triumph."—**Science Fiction Review.** (#UJ1307—$1.95)

☐ **DARKOVER LANDFALL**
"Both literate and exciting, with much of that searching fable quality that made **Lord of the Flies** so provocative." —**New York Times.** The novel of Darkover's origin.
                                                             (#UW1447—$1.50)

☐ **THE SHATTERED CHAIN**
"Primarily concerned with the role of women in the Darkover society . . . Bradey's gift is provocative, a top-notch blend of sword-and-sorcery and the finest speculative fiction."— **Wilson Library Bulletin.**   (#UJ1327—$1.95)

☐ **THE SPELL SWORD**
Goes deeper into the problem of the matrix and the conflict with one of Darkover's non-human races gifted with similar powers. A first-class adventure.   (#UW1440—$1.50)

☐ **STORMQUEEN!**
"A novel of the planet Darkover set in the Ages of Chaos . . . this is richly textured, well-thought-out and involving." —**Publishers Weekly.**   (#UJ1381—$1.95)

☐ **HUNTERS OF THE RED MOON**
"May be even more a treat for devoted MZB fans than her excellent Darkover series . . . sf adventure in the grand tradition."—**Luna.**   (#UW1407—$1.50)

If you wish to order these titles,

please see the coupon in

the back of this book.

Presenting MICHAEL MOORCOCK
in DAW editions